Chasing Tail Lights

ALSO BY PATRICK JONES

Things Change

Nailed

Chasing Tail Lights

PATRICK JONES

Walker & Company New York

To Jacqueline Ross, this one's for you.

First published in the United States of America in 2007 by
Walker Publishing Company, Inc.
Distributed to the trade by Holtzbrinck Publishers

For information about permission to reproduce selections from this book, write to Permissions, Walker & Company,
104 Fifth Avenue, New York, New York 10011

Library of Congress Cataloging-in-Publication Data
Jones, Patrick.
Chasing tail lights / by Patrick Jones.
p. cm.
Summary: Seventeen-year-old Christy wants only to finish high school and escape her Flint, Michigan, home, where she cooks, cleans, cares for her niece, and tries to fend off her half-brother, a drug dealer who has been abusing her since she was eleven.
ISBN-13: 978-0-8027-9628-8 • ISBN-10: 0-8027-9628-1
[1. Family problems—Fiction. 2. Self-esteem—Fiction. 3. High schools—Fiction. 4. Schools—Fiction. 5. Drug traffic—Fiction. 6. Incest—Fiction. 7. Sexual abuse victims—Fiction. 8. Flint (Mich.)—Fiction.] I. Title.
PZ7.J7242Cha 2007 [Fic]—dc22 2006027657

Visit Walker & Company's Web site at www.walkeryoungreaders.com

Book design by Amy Manzo Toth
Typeset by Westchester Book Composition
Printed in the U.S.A. by Quebecor World Fairfield
2 4 6 8 10 9 7 5 3 1

All papers used by Walker & Company are natural, recyclable products made from wood grown in well-managed forests. The manufacturing processes conform to the environmental regulations of the country of origin.

ACKNOWLEDGMENTS

This was a tough book with some difficult themes, so thanks to Amy Alessio, Zandra Blake, Sarah Cornish, Jessica Mize, Vanessa Morris, Patricia Taylor, and Tricia Suellentrop, who read and made suggestions on early versions of *Chasing Tail Lights*. Shout out to fellow Flintoid Jon Scieszka for his important contribution, and to Jacqueline Woodson for steering me in the right direction. I got lots of teen input on this book, so special thanks to Sibongile Sithe, Lauren Houston, Kaitlin Flynn, and Stephanie "non-box" Goralski for great guidance. Also thanks to groups of teachers and students: Daria Plumb and her students at Dundee (MI) Alternative High School, Hilary Lewis and her book discussion group at the Carnegie Library of Pittsburgh (PA), and Laura Gajdostik and her students from Hudson (WI) High School. Thanks to other students and teachers I've met on the road doing school visits, which inspire me that I'm on the right path. As always, thanks to Erica Klein for giving me the time and confidence to write fiction.

Chasing Tail Lights

1

september 28, senior year

"Christy, is that a siren?"

"It's Flint, Cuz, 'course it's a siren," I shout to Anne. She laughs, then passes the joint back to me. The sirens are from a police car speeding down I-69 beneath us. Those officers below have no time to check out two seventeen-year-old girls getting high up on the bridge as the yellow sun drops low in the sky. My best friend, Anne, wears the world's thickest black-rimmed glasses and the mall's tightest black T-shirt, while I'm bogged down in my brother Robert's baggy hand-me-downs set off by my short, spiky dyed-red hair. We're stashed behind a big-ass green sign telling drivers how to get the hell out of Flint. It's a direction I plan to follow when this senior year ends. I take the last sip from a can of Coke, take a deep hit from the joint, then press my forehead against the silver wire mesh to stare at the flashing red lights.

"You wanna roll someplace your last free Friday night?" I ask. Even though her parents could hand her the easy life, Anne's doctor father insists she get a job. Rather than hanging out with me doing nothing, she starts next weekend working for one of her dad's friends at some country club. With her new job, it means I won't have as many sleepover nights at Anne's, to my disappointment and her dad's delight. He'd prefer if I were Anne's imaginary best friend.

"I'll be there," Anne says with a confidence in her voice I dream of having. Even if we do nothing but drive, chasing tail lights for real in her red PT Cruiser rather than pretending up here on this bridge, that'll be fine. We'll make our usual drive-bys of "the unattainable" Glen Thompson's house, but I wish we could make laps and chase tail lights all weekend. I'm not looking forward to Sunday morning after church, when my family jams itself into Mama's cramped, crappy old Cavalier to visit my brother Robert and celebrate his daughter Bree's tenth birthday. Trapped in that tiny space with my family, I imagine, is like life in a prison cell.

I nod, then shout. "Usual spot." The spot's the curb in front of my house on Stone Street. It's hard enough, even after two years of Anne's friendship, letting her into my life, let alone my home. Or rather, the place I stay with my family. It's a home in name and address only.

Anne motions for the joint back. "Christy, tell me, how long you've been doing this?"

"What do you mean?" I respond slowly; I'd always rather ask than answer questions. I take a hit to kill time, brain cells, and the cold, hard concrete facts all around me.

"Standing up here, chasing tail lights," she asks in a stoned giggle. It is kind of a silly thing for an almost honor student high school senior like me to do: staring at cars wondering where they've been and where they're going. Since I don't drive, I can only dream.

"I don't know," I say, but that's a lie. There's no need to tell the truth, best friend or not. Everybody's got their secrets; I carry mine like a jagged stone in my shoe. But when I'm up here, I let go of my life, recall my past, and ignore my future. I've been coming here since fifth grade, just after my daddy died. Daddy was a truck driver for a while and "chasing tail lights" was an expression he used. When he felt lost, he'd follow the tail lights of the truck in front of him, until they took him somewhere safe. Daddy had lots of expressions, just like he had lots of jobs. He's been dead over half my life, and sometimes when I allow myself to feel, I feel he took half of me with him. I don't want to turn eighteen in December; I need to be eight again.

"It don't cost nothin'," Anne adds, eagerly waiting for me to pass the joint back. She readjusts her funky Day-Glo green Flint Country Club hat. She's got beautiful long straight jet-black hair, but she covers it up like she's ashamed of it. But then, she's not ashamed of her body, wearing a tight, tiny black DKNY tank top, which I'd never do. Anne's a puzzle and a friend; she's the center of attention while I'm her audience. This seems to work out best for both of us.

"Nothing but time," I say after a long pause. Time is what we're both trying to fill, dateless and mateless on homecoming eve, a ritual that matters nothing at all to either of us. Neither of us ever plan to come home to Flint Southwestern High once we graduate in May.

"Time I got, money I don't," Anne says as I finally hand the joint over. Her parents give her a fancy car to drive, nice clothes, all stuff that I don't have, and I try so hard not even to want. Wanting things you'll never have is the worst feeling in the world.

"I could do this for hours." My body's starting to tingle with warmth. The loud roar of the vehicles racing under us is soothing, not distracting. I stand on this ribbon of gray built for bikes and people, and watch the cars and trucks zip down the highway. The bridge is totally covered in a fence. It's like a big cage, but it sets my mind free to plan, but mostly dream.

Anne points to an exiting SUV. "What kind of ride is that black one over there?"

"That's an Escalade, like Ryan drives," I reply, but this SUV isn't as tricked out as my brother Ryan's ride. I have three brothers. Robert's twenty-four. While he doesn't live with us, his daughter, Bree, does. Mitchell's at home; he turned sixteen this summer. He looks so young in some ways, but acts much older in how responsible he is. Then there's Ryan, three-plus years older than me at twenty-one. He lives in the basement and comes, goes, and does as he pleases. Both Robert and Ryan are my half-brothers, different fathers from each other, and from me and Mitchell. Robert never knew his dad, but Ryan's dad must have been something. While there's not a single photo of my daddy around the house, Mama's room is loaded with pictures of Ryan's dad. He wasn't around long: just enough to pose for photos and beat the crap out of Ryan.

"I need me an SUV," Anne says, and I stifle a laugh, since people like Anne don't seem to know the difference between want and need. The people on her side of the freeway, the area dubbed the Miller Road mansions, can't really know anything about those of us who live on the other side. We live less than two miles from each other with this bridge as the connection, but our worlds are far apart. Our neighborhood was where factory workers lived during the good times; but there are no good times anymore, few factories and fewer workers. Flint's a ghost town full of living people, although day by day, shooting by shooting, the ghosts are taking over.

"You'll get one, Dr. Williams," I say. Anne loves when I rib her about becoming a doctor, like her father wants. Anne wants it too, but she hates agreeing with her dad.

"You too, Speedy," she says back. My tenth-grade English teacher, Ms. Chapman, thinks I should run track, but calling me speedy is like calling Mama tiny or calling me beautiful.

"Gotta go!" Anne says, after checking the time on her thin silver cell, since her watch is always set to 4:20. She takes gum, perfume, and eye drops from her small glossy black purse.

"Later, Doctor," I say sadly, knowing no one except my niece, Bree, even cares if I come home. I drop the empty Coke can, and kick it off the bridge through a hole in the wire mesh. It lands in the back of a white Ford-150 pickup, off for an exciting adventure, while I haul my skinny ass home for some everyday drama.

sophomore year, september

"Miss Mallory, we're awfully sorry to wake you."

My ugly, home-dyed red head snaps up when I hear my name. Seconds later, I wish to bury it into the ground as the ugly sound of laughter fills my first-period sophomore English class.

"Christy, I asked what book you are going to read for your fall project?" Ms. Chapman, tough-as-nails English teacher, stands before me, hands on her hips, disgust on her lips, and my glazed sleepy eyes under her stare. Standing over me, she looks not six, but sixty feet tall.

I rub my eyes with my huge hands, but she doesn't disappear. I look over at Anne Williams, a new girl nobody knows, who sits next to me. We don't have much to say to each other, since we don't have anything in common except our silence. Like me, I sense Anne knows the answers; also like me, she knows better than to advertise that fact. She'd rather show off her body than her brain. I show off nothing.

"The deadline was today to tell me which book you were reading for this assignment," Ms. Chapman continues. "That's five points off. If you don't have it tomorrow, that's ten."

"But I haven't decided yet," I say softly, so unaccustomed to speaking in class. I want to run to the bathroom, but Ms. Chapman would surely catch me. One book on the list is The Invisible Man *by H. G. Wells, which is funny, since my plan for high school is to be*

the invisible woman. I plan to slip under the radar by avoiding any attention.

"See me after class," she says, then turns her attention away from me. She's got this pissed-off look that doesn't suit her. She's beautiful: with that perfect smooth, unfreckled skin, long blond hair, and bright blue eyes, like every model in every magazine, not to mention her athletic body, which shows through the baggy maroon warm-up suits she wears every day. I envy and hate her.

I put my head back on my desk, banging it ever so slightly against the hard grain, wondering why my favorite class—English—had to be first period. Mornings can be the worst, especially Mondays after a weekend when Bree is away. I hate the nights she spends with my aunt Dee and her son Tommy. Most people want their own room, but not me. I wish Bree could always be sleeping safely in our small shared space.

I try to tune out the voices around me as people rattle off books they'll read. Ms. Chapman wants us to choose a book from this list she prepared, read it, and then do an oral report. I'm terrified; I hate public speaking. Just because Ms. Chapman's a show-off, it's not fair for her to expect us to be too. Even if I looked like her, I still wouldn't want to be standing in front of the room for all to see.

"I'm reading The Odyssey,*" I hear Anne tell Ms. Chapman. Anne, the big brain I suspect she is, could probably read it in the original Greek if she wanted. I get a sense she's ready for college as a tenth grader. I know that last year Anne went to the Summit School, this private school that is just over the expressway bridge. I overheard her tell someone she'd rather go to Southwestern, which I don't understand at all. If I had the choice, I'd be out of here like a sprinter hearing the starting pistol.*

"Great choice! Does anyone else know that book?" Ms. Chapman asks. That's typical of her: she's always asking us stuff. I never answer.

"It's the story about a man trying to return home, and in doing so, finding himself," Glen Thompson speaks up, and I take notice. When he says something smart, nobody laughs; instead, he soaks up attention and adoration. I can sense some girls in the room hanging on his every word, just like I do. Just like I have since seventh grade. Any day that he acknowledges I exist is a great one. Right now, we're just friends but I'm always dreaming for that to change.

"Sounds boring," Seth Lewis chimes in. Seth speaks like he's king and we're subjects to his wisecracks. He's also the only boy ever to kiss me, but that was eighth grade. We've had a hate-hate relationship ever since.

"That's your opinion, Mr. Lewis," Ms. Chapman says. "What book will you be reading?"

"Lonesome Dove, *since you won't let me do* Kiss the Girls *or any books I wanted."*

Ms. Chapman just looks at him. I dream of her saying, "Who the hell do you think you are," but she can't. She just sighs and ignores him, which is maybe an example I should follow.

"What's it about?" somebody asks Seth. Like Glen, he has his toadies.

"It's a story about the American West," Seth replies. He spits when he talks.

Glen laughs. "Seth, you live in Flint, Michigan. What do you know about the West?"

Seth stands up, turns on his heel, then points first at Anne, then draws a bead on me. "Right there, you got everything you need to know," Seth says almost in a shout.

"Mr. Lewis!" Ms. Chapman tries to head him off, but he's a runaway train.

"You got the Rocky Mountains," he says, cupping his hands on his chubby chest. He points at Anne's tight black tank molded to her ample breasts. As the laughter builds, he points at my flat white baggy T-shirt. "And you got the Great Plains."

I do then what I do best: I run. I leap from my chair, knocking my books over, like anything in them even mattered. I run out of the classroom, through the dirty halls, and right out the front door of the school. The fresh fall air enters my lungs but just tastes stale.

After a quick trip to chase some tail lights and smoke a joint, I return to school after lunch to take my punishment. I couldn't care less. Like middle school, I'll probably wear out the carpet in the school attendance office between being late and not showing up at all. I often dream about running away. While I have plenty to run from, I have nothing and nowhere to run to. As I'm walking back to my locker, I stop by Ms. Chapman's room. I stand outside the door, afraid to go in and afraid not to. She's sitting at her desk talking to some girl. Behind her is a shelf overstuffed with books, track trophies, and a maroon-and-yellow Central Michigan banner.

She whispers to the girl, some "look at me" blond I don't know, which isn't a surprise, since I don't know, or want to know, my classmates. The girl laughs, no doubt at me, and walks past. She's wearing too much perfume and too smug a look on her store-bought fake-tanned face.

"I'm sorry about what happened," Ms. Chapman says as she motions for me to sit down. "Mr. Lewis will be punished for what he said." I just nod, knowing how easily hurt vanishes.

"Since you didn't choose a book or take my earlier suggestion, I've chosen one for you," she says, turning to the bookcase behind her.

She looks for a second, then hands me a beat-up paperback book called Speak *by Laurie Halse Anderson. "I think you'll enjoy this."*

"Thanks," I mutter, taking the book from her, but all the while averting my eyes. I'm a little disappointed; it's a thin book. Every page in a book is a minute outside of my own life.

"You ever think about running cross-country or track?" she asks, then smiles. "I have to tell you that I was impressed with your acceleration. You could letter with some coaching."

I wish I could smile back, but smiling isn't my style. Instead, I just shake my head no.

"If you change your mind, come see me, okay?" she says, but I just nod and walk away. "One more thing, this book Speak *is pretty good. It shouldn't put you to sleep."*

I frown, a guilty upside-down smile. "Sorry about that."

"Christy, do you want to talk about why you're always so tired in my class?" she asks.

I bite my too-fat bottom lip, filling in a familiar groove, and the pain reassures me. I mumble a nonresponse, then slink away from both her question and my inability to answer it.

2

september 30, senior year

"You look so pretty, Bree."

My niece beams at my remark; her smile so beautiful, despite her crooked teeth. She smiles, not knowing how self-serving my comment was. I wait for a member of my family, all of us piling into Mom's rusted and busted Cavalier, to tell me I look pretty too. But the comment never comes, as usual. They're all dressed in their Sunday finest, Mama decked out in red brighter than any store-Santa would wear, even if there's nothing jolly about this day.

"Get in the car, little girl!" Ryan says sharply to me, after nicely opening the front door for my mother and complimenting her on her dress. It's the first in his long line of false flattery. I don't reply. Instead I look over enviously at my brother Mitchell as he slumps in the backseat, headphones on, music turned up, and already tuning out the world. I hate that Ryan calls me "little girl," but there's nothing I can do about it. He's got Mama's ear, while for me, she's deaf.

Bree squeezes in next to Mitchell, then I sit down next. The springs in the backseat are broken, so no matter how I position myself, I'm not comfortable. Sometimes I think my soul is too big for my skin. Mama's in the seat in front of me, her hacking cough shaking the car. She's so large that she needs the seat pushed back all the way, so my long legs are compacted. It's going to be a painful two-hour trek to visit Robert and celebrate his daughter's birthday.

By the time we get south of Flint, what little conversation we had managed has ended. Mama's napping, which means that Ryan is without someone to flatter, so he stays silent. Bree is deep into one of the books in the American Girl series. My birthday gift to her was an American Girl paper doll cut-out book. She spent the whole morning happily alone cutting out the dolls. I worry sometimes that Bree spends too much time in our room alone, instead of outside playing with friends. She's yet to have a friend over to the house, but then again, neither have I since Daddy died. Anne stays my best friend by staying away from my house and family.

Mitchell's moving his head to the music. If the headphones aren't on, that doesn't stop him, since he sings all the time. It'd be pretty distracting, except he's never home much. He's a year behind me and smarter, but he studies a lot. He's goes to Northern, the science magnet school, works long hours at the Miller Road KFC, and sings in the church choir. When he's home, he's by himself listening to music, singing, and writing in a blue notebook that's almost always in his hand. Mitch and I don't share a lot. Neither one of us like talking about ourselves.

"Breezy, switch places with me, okay?" I ask.

I pick Bree up, sit her on my lap, and then move over. My strength is in my legs, not my arms, and she's getting heavier. She's still a little girl now, but soon she's gonna be a young woman. All I want for Bree is everything I never had growing up, and that's up to me because Mama doesn't have the time. My daddy's sister, Aunt Dee, likes to watch Bree, but she's a flight attendant and is away a lot. Even if Aunt Dee was around more, she's got her hands full. Her son Tommy's fresh from a stint at Genesee County Juvenile Hall and living back at home.

I tap Mitchell on the leg to get his attention. The bass booms from under the headphones and rattles the window he's staring out of. "Mitch, you gonna get me a job at KFC?" I shout.

"You don't want to do that," he says, taking the headphones off. His voice is deep, but always soft. Anne landed a job in a few days, while I've yet to find anything I can do. Selling weed for Ryan at school to the theater and honor society crowds is too risky, even if slinging brought Glen and Anne into my orbit. Anyway, now that I've started, Ryan won't let me stop.

I tap my finger against my head, then say, "Think about it."

"You'd hate it," he replies. "You should do something important, be famous, not work at KFC."

"But I need a job," I say, though without much force. I hate the idea of stinking of fried chicken, like Mitchell does in the few hours we actually see him. I wouldn't mind wearing those fugly brown uniforms, but I'd hate a job where I'd have to interact with strangers all day.

"I know you need money, but I don't think it's a good idea," Mitchell says. He's clueless to my dealing. "You should get a job doing something you'd enjoy, like at a library."

"Thanks anyway, Mitch," I say, taking his rejection as my family's usual reaction to me.

"One day, Christy, I'll manage that store. One day, I'm going to own that store, and all the KFCs in Flint," he says with conviction. I believe that he's not dreaming, he's planning.

"Pucker up, fat boy!" Ryan shouts, which seems his normal volume, since he's used to yelling over his boom car racket. "You don't see me playing that game, know what I'm saying?"

Mama coughs, but she doesn't wake up to stop Ryan's attack. Mitchell and Ryan have never gotten along, which is yet another reason I should try to get closer to Mitchell. Not like that's an easy task. He's always been like me, a lonely person who'd really prefer to be left alone.

"Screw you, Ryan," Mitchell says, taking off his glasses, then putting his headphones back on. There's no use in arguing with Ryan, since Mama always sides with him. He's been her favorite since Daddy died, kind of like I was Daddy's favorite. You can't say anything against Ryan to Mama, no matter what he says or does, so both Mitch and I stopped trying long ago.

"What you looking at, little girl?" Ryan says, his almost black eyes piercing me through the rearview mirror. I bite my bottom lip hard, then melt back in the seat.

"Nothing," I whisper, while my voice silently screams at him. There are one million things I want to say, but I can't bring myself to fight back. Trapped in the car, there's no place to run except back into my own head. I'm safe there: I'd rather live in my head than in my own life.

"Good," Ryan says, then laughs this nasty snicker that chills me down to my spine. The laugh comes with a smirk, and the scent memory of cigar smoke, cheap cologne, and vodka.

"Are Aunt Dee and Cousin Tommy meeting us?" I shout at Mitchell, who nods. He and Tommy used to be friends, but things cooled between them when Tommy got sent away. Mama doesn't want Mitchell hanging with Tommy. It's not so much that she doesn't like Tommy, but she can't stand his mother, Aunt Dee. Mama calls her a Bible-thumper and worse.

"So that wannabe is out, huh?" Ryan says, not that I was talking to him, but he's not a big one on boundaries. "I'm surprised that big mouth snitch isn't dead like he deserves."

I bite my bottom lip until it bleeds and try to ignore Ryan's voice by closing my eyes.

"How you doing, Bree?" Ryan asks, but I know he couldn't care less. Bree is a reminder of Robert, and despite his thug friends and ways, Ryan still fears Robert and I don't blame him.

"Are we there yet?" Bree says, all restless. She's wanting me to braid her thick brown hair. I do my best, but to make the braids tight, I need to pull gently on her hair. I can't bring myself to do that, since I know that feeling too well. It's another reason I keep my hair short. I know my short hair, coupled with my lack of curves hidden under baggy clothes, makes me look ugly. Still, I manage a smile at Bree, who looks as beautiful outside as she is inside.

I finish, then put my head against the back of the hard seat, but just before I close my eyes, I notice us driving under a bridge. I wonder if there's someone on that bridge chasing tail lights. I wonder if there's somebody who understands where I've been; somebody as confused about where they're going. I'm just about to doze off to dream when Bree shakes my arm. "There's Daddy's sign!" Bree shouts, then points out the window at the big square yellow road sign that lets us know we're almost there: "Do not pick up hitchhikers. Prison Area."

ninth grade, september

"Robert Lawrence Mallory."

My brother won't look up at the judge, but that's typical. Robert was never one for looking up to anyone, or looking out for anyone but himself. I would think Mama would be crying, but Bree is doing enough of that for all of us. She's seven, so she understands just enough to know to be scared and sad. Seeing her daddy like that, handcuffs on his wrists and chains around his ankles, is probably an image she won't ever forget. I know that I won't.

"Life without parole." Robert doesn't seem fazed at all, and I can't say that I blame him. He'd dropped out of school at fourteen, got into drugs well before then, and was running the streets paved with bad intentions. Mama knew, but pretended like she didn't. She let him go his own way. Now, he's going away for the rest of his life. But thinking about his life and crimes, it seems Robert was living life without parole long before the judge spoke. No job, no skills other than slinging, and no real friends. His daughter could have saved him. He loves her to death, but that didn't stop him from killing a man at a motel in a drug deal gone bad. Her mom, Roxanne, couldn't care for herself, let alone a child, so Breezy's with us. With Mama too busy, Mitchell too young, and Ryan too Ryan, raising Bree will fall on me. I guess I got sentenced today too.

Robert doesn't say anything to the judge, like I see people do on

TV shows. He doesn't seem scared at all. He told me during our last visit together that you can't punish a person with life in prison if that person is already dead inside. He's not going to repent or show remorse. As they take Robert away, he never turns around, he never looks back. Mama's still not crying, but she's starting to shake, like she's holding it in. Ryan's right there next to her, attached to her right arm, although his dark eyes stare me down. With Daddy dead, and Robert going away, that makes Ryan the man of the family, except we're no family, and Ryan isn't any kind of man.

3

october 8, senior year

"Isn't he gorgeous? He can student teach me anytime he wants."

"Shut up, Anne!" I say, but I don't mean it. Shut up really means go on.

"Christy, just look at that ass," she adds. We're sitting outside of the school theater eating greasy school lunch, less hungry than usual, since we didn't get high in Anne's car before school or at lunch. We've got a big chemistry exam fifth hour, so we're both staying chemical free. We're sitting waiting for Glen to walk by and make my day. Our eyeballing spot has been interrupted by Mr. McDonald facing away from us and Ms. Chapman walking toward us.

"Don't be so gross," I tell her, but I, too, can't stop staring at Chris McDonald, a bearded twenty-something student teacher in theater who is talking in the hall with a few students.

"He's got an honor-student ass," she says softly. "I mean it is like A plus, you think?"

I ignore her comment, which is difficult. Anne's desperate for affection and attention, but she insists that every boy at

Southwestern is too immature, so she's mostly interested in older Romeos like Mr. McDonald. Whenever Anne talks about sex like this, it's mostly a monologue because sex is a subject that leaves me mute.

"Hi, Christy," Ms. Chapman says, stopping in front of me. She's wearing her usual warm-up suit and a small gold chain around her neck. I'd like to ask her about it, but that might lead to her asking me questions. The only question I ask her is "Know anything good to read?" She's never let me down since tenth grade. I notice she's got a book in her hand now.

"Here you go, Christy," Ms. Chapman says, then nods at Anne. In our duo, Anne's used to the spotlight; its weird for the light to shine on me. I take the book from her hand: Lucy Greeley's *Autobiography of a Face*. "I think you'll like it, even though it's nonfiction," she says.

"Thanks," I say, avoiding meeting her eyes. I wonder why she's stalking me. I don't think it's yesterday's weed making me paranoid, but Ms. Chapman is always tracking me down.

"This is your last chance," Ms. Chapman says, then crosses her arms in front of her.

"For what?" I respond. I see from the corner of my eye that Anne is totally gawking at Mr. McDonald. I'm trying to look serious to Ms. Chapman, while Anne's trying to crack me up.

"Join the cross-country team," Ms. Chapman says. "Don't you want to earn your letter?"

I think, but don't say out loud, how I earn good letters every day, mostly As and Bs. I know that's a lot harder work than running through the woods, although just as solitary. Those grades are the only way I'll get out of my house and Flint. I don't study to succeed or read for pleasure; I study to survive and read to escape. "I'm sorry, I just don't have time," I tell her.

"Really?" She's raising a skeptical eyebrow, which is odd because normally I'm a very good liar. I'd earn an A+ if they gave letters for dishonesty. "Do you have a job after school?"

I want to say, "Yes, I'm working by selling weed to actors and honor-society scholars," but that won't get me anywhere but juvy jail. I want to say, "Yes, I'm doing most of the cooking, cleaning, and child caring in my family," but that's none of her business. I can't tell her the truth, so I just say, "I don't have a job, but I just don't have time."

She points to the book in my hand. "If you want a job, you should work at the library."

"That would be nice," I say, but I know I'm dreaming.

"I have a sister who works for the library. Let me give her a call," Ms. Chapman says. But I just shake my head no, not that I wouldn't want a job like that. But if I let her do me this favor, she'll want something from me. "Well, if you change your mind, let me know," she says.

I nod again, and that sends her on her way. I'll apply at the library, if only so she doesn't bother me about it anymore. Ms. Chapman's getting too close, and I'm so nervous around her. I envy-hate her for her beauty and confidence, but am so grateful for her interest in me. Even without weed, I see clearly why I click with her: she's everything I'm not and dream of being.

"I'm all summa come often," Anne says, the second Ms. Chapman heads toward her room. She lowers her large black frames to show off her big made-up eyes if Mr. McDonald should return her stare. She's mock-fanning herself, acting as if she's about to stroke out.

"Just shut up!" I say, but I'm laughing as I speak. I'm laughing at Anne and at the obvious flirting of theater diva Rani Patel, who is talking to Mr. McDonald. Rani's another member of the perfect body-skin-face-hair-life club and sits near the top of my envy-hate list.

"I think I'm going to try out for theater!" Anne says. "Here's your excuse to do it too."

"No way," I tell her yet again. She keeps encouraging me to try out for a play just to get closer to Glen, but I have no thirst for the spotlight. I don't think I'd get a part, except behind the scenes. I'm more like the scenery in theater: tall, flat, thin, and belonging in the background.

"I bet he'd make the bed shake," Anne says, more fanning and mock-hyperventilating. "At least he won't be as immature as the rest of these guys. If you don't want him, then—"

"Enough," I say, but this time it's not meant to encourage. I'm serious, but she's not.

"Come on, you wouldn't want to taste Mr. McDonald's Big Mac?" Anne says, to no reaction from me. "Wouldn't you want to let him slip his sausage into—"

"No," I cut her off. Anne thinks my face is getting tight trying not to laugh, but that's not it. I race toward the bathroom. If Ms. Chapman saw this sprint, she'd force me onto her team.

I race to the bathroom, rush past the girls there who are fixing their hair or makeup or getting their fix. I find the one vacant stall and drop to my knees. I taste the salty spit in my mouth, feel the sweat trickle down my brow mixing with the faintest of tears from my eyes, but manage not to vomit—this time. In this locked yet stinky bathroom stall, I feel strangely safe.

I sometimes think I've spent more time in Southwestern's bathrooms than classrooms. It's here that I learned I am not really alone in living two lives. From this stall, I peek through the crack and see my fellow students' transformations. I see the girls, like Anne, who come to school so nice-girl-normal, then change their look, mostly by undressing and showing skin. I hear the girls who act all righteous in class, but drop f-bombs once they're away from teachers' ears. I smell the girls who wear antidrug red ribbons, but get toasted on green on a regular basis, not that they're my customers. I'm not a dealer, I tell myself, I'm just providing a service to a few friends. It's from the bathroom I taste the bitter jealousy, duplicity, and shallowness of girls at my school. The bathroom is a microcosm of Southwestern's two-faced society.

"You okay?" I hear Anne's voice after a while, her concern coming through the heavily graffitied stall door. "I'm sorry if it was something I said."

"I'm fine," I say just as the bell rings. She's my best friend. Forgiving her is easy and essential. I wish I could be alone in the world, but my soul demands at least one connected life.

"Christy, I know that kind of talk upsets you. Listen, Speedy, I'm really sorry," she says, but I don't respond. Anne talks a lot about sex, but not from any experience. She always says lots of boys are interested, but none of them are interesting. "You know I like to tease."

Teasing, me with her mouth and boys with her body, is one of her main things. "It's just that," I start, then swallow it back. "Never mind."

"Did I embarrass you or what?" she asks, the regret deep in her voice.

"No, you know me," I say through the barrier.

"I try, but you never make that easy, Speedy," Anne says, then laughs.

"Is it safe?" I ask, before coming from behind the green door.

"All clear," Anne says. I take a deep breath, clean up, and emerge. "You okay?"

I walk over to the sink and run cold water over my face. I look into the mirror and that cold vision is more sobering, yet satisfying. I know the primary purpose I serve at Southwestern. I allow other girls, like Anne, to feel good about themselves, since they're all prettier than I am. I know that somewhere behind my wide green eyes, my short, dyed-red hair, and my makeup-free face is some beauty, but the ugliness of my life rots me from inside.

"I'm sorry," Anne repeats, then lightly pats my shoulder, but even her soft touch stings.

She smiles, her perfectly corrected white teeth shine, while I hide my crooked ones with a closed-mouth grin of my own. "You can have Mr. McDonald if you want," I tell her.

"I don't think so," Anne says, pulling out her makeup kit and taking off her black rims. She offers makeup to me. I decline, since that's like putting pretty windows on an ugly house.

"So, you were kidding," I say, still trying to catch my breath.

"Totally," she says, then adds some mascara. She's trying to make her natural eyes look bigger, doing to the ovals on her face what her Wonderbra does to the ones on her chest. "It's creepy to imagine guys Mr. McDonald's age doing it with teenage girls, don't you think?"

"I guess," I say, wishing my eyes were smaller like Anne's beautiful browns. I wish my eyes had less capacity for crying, which I know I do far too much. Anne's words trigger tears, and I'm powerless to hold them back any longer.

"What's wrong with you today, Christy?" Anne says, looking at me via the mirror.

"I don't want to talk about it," I say, and Anne knows when I say "it" I mean sex.

"Is it because you're still a virgin?" Anne whispers even though the bathroom is empty.

It's a conversation we always start, but never finish. "Are you?" I shoot back as straight as the truth is crooked. I hear the second bell ring. It is a much louder and sadder sound than that of Anne's footsteps walking away. Sometimes I wonder why she's friends with me at all.

sophomore year, october

"Can I sit here?"

I look up from the cafeteria table to tiny Anne Williams standing over me, although I'm almost as tall sitting down as she is standing. "What?" I reply, stunned to attention.

"You want some fries?" she says, sitting her tray, then herself, down across from me.

"No," I say, looking at my tray, the table, anything but Anne's moving mouth. The incident in Ms. Chapman's class last week drew attention to me, so I'm trying to blend back into the background, where I belong.

"You're not missing anything." She holds one of the fries up, smells it, and then tosses it back on the plate. "It's a ten-ton salt-and-fat bomb."

Looking closely at Anne, it looks like she speaks from experience. While she's not obese like my mom or even overweight like Mitchell, she's not going to get an offer from Ms. Chapman to run track. With her penchant for tight clothes and revealing tops, however, she will have three years' experience running hall gauntlets of probing fingers, filthy mouths, and leering eyes.

"How's your book?" I ask, knowing nothing else to ask, other than "Why are you sitting with me?" Still, I let her sit with me, hoping not to relive middle school, where I was a black hole of loneliness.

"It's okay," she says, then shrugs her shoulders before starting to eat her green salad. I guess that's my cue to say something, but unlike Glen, I don't know how to do dialogue.

She takes a couple of bites, while I try, and fail, to think of something to say to her. "So, what's the deal with Seth Lewis?" she finally asks, once again offering me her fries.

"He's an asshole," I say in between bites.

"Maybe we need to perform rectumectomy surgery and get him removed from our class."

"A what?" I'm trying not to stare at her big black glasses or tight gray T-shirt with the word ARMY *written across the front. I've noticed she usually wears T-shirts with writing across the front.*

"Nothing, just joking," she says, then shrugs before forcing out a smile.

"Sounds like a painful operation," I finally say, after more embarrassed silence.

Anne reaches into her purse, then looks around the crowded cafeteria, but everyone is indifferent to us. She flashes some cash, then palms it back. "You got any painkillers?"

I hide my eyes, shake my head, and then speak softly. "What do you mean?"

"I heard you can hook me up with weed, is that right?" Anne says in a whisper, which I can barely hear as the noise grows louder as the lunch period draws to a close.

"You heard wrong," I say, knowing now that she didn't come to be my friend, but to use me.

She puts the money back in her purse, then frowns. "That's not what Glen said."

Hearing his name causes a chemical reaction to race through my half-dead body.

"After school on the bridge," I finally tell her as I start to rise from the table.

"What bridge?" she says, looking stupid and lost despite her overstuffed backpack.

"North of the school, the one that goes over the expressway." I tell her the location of my home away from home, wondering if I've made a mistake trusting her even this much.

"Hey, Christy, I'm cool," she says, sensing my stress. "Maybe we could hang out too."

"Maybe," I say, staring at the table and nervously picking at the edge of my food tray.

"If Glen doesn't have play practice, maybe he'll join us," she says. I know I'm not totally invisible, since one of my deepest secrets—my Glen crush—is painfully evident to Anne. If she has Glen's attention, then I'll let her into my life. Or at least the parts of it that I'm willing to share.

4

october 24, senior year

"I got a job shelving books at the public library."

"That's nice," Bree says. It's kind of sad that the only person in the house to tell the news to is just ten years old. Sadder, she's probably the only one who cares. Mitchell's pulling his six-hour after-school KFC shifts, while Mama is working one of her jobs. They've got enough problems of their own, and no reason to think another family member working for minimum wage is cause for celebration. Ryan is out doing whatever he does, but his money never comes back into the house. I guess it all goes into his ride or he blows it partying with his low-life get-high friends.

"But it means I'll be late getting home from school," I almost whisper, trying to break the news to her gently. We're sitting on the floor between our beds. The carpet is mildewed, but anything's better than sitting on my hard bed. "I won't be here when you get home every day."

"You're never here!" She's crying now, a totally justified reaction to my growing selfishness. Ever since Robert went to Jackson, I've been Bree's stand-in parent, but it's so hard. It's too much to ask me to cook, clean, study, work, and try to protect her.

"Don't worry, Breezy," I say, reaching across to wipe away her tears. Even when she cries, she looks cute. Sadly, that doesn't work for me. "We'll still have lots of time together."

"Really?" She pushes the paper-doll book over to me, then scissors. I guess I should be studying, or doing something grown-up, but spending time with Bree lets me feel like I'm eight again. I've tried to tell Aunt Dee not to take her from me even for one night, but that's selfish. I know she can give Bree things that I can't. Bree deserves a much better role model than me.

"Sure, Breezy, I'll be here as much as I can," I say, hating to lie to the child. Truth is, I can't stand being at home, but I have no choice. With her father in prison, and her mother in no condition to care for Bree, it's up to me to do the best that I can. I'll do my best to make her feel safe and loved, two more things I've not felt for almost ten years.

I cut out a few dolls, pass the scissors back over to her, and then open up my chemistry book to try to study for a little while. Anne's working tonight, so I'm trapped in this house. I'll be alone once Breezy heads off to church. I never know when Ryan will crawl up from his cave.

The light in our room isn't good, with just one lone exposed bulb overhead. The fixture fell off last time I replaced the bulb, and we haven't bought a new one. Better there's little light, since this room, like most of the house, isn't much to see. There's a small desk, but it's better suited for Breezy than me. It used to be in Robert's room, so it's all scratched up. He used to sit at that desk for hours, drawing pictures of guns, cars, and, what I realize now were gang signs. He didn't get his real education sitting at a desk but, like lots of Flint kids, on the street.

Our room is the smallest in the house, and it's right next to the bathroom. Mama's room is at the end of the hallway. It smells like smoke even with the door closed, which it almost always is. The wood on the door to her room is splintered. One time, right after Daddy died, she slapped Robert. He chased her into her room, screaming at her the entire time. Mama might be the head of the family, but she's never been in charge. She must have locked the door, but he tried to kick it in: I wonder if he wanted in to kill her or apologize. I wonder if he even knew.

Mitchell's room is next to Mama's. He shared a room with Ryan before Robert moved out. Ryan then took over Robert's room in the basement. Unlike our room and Ryan's sty, Mitchell's room is always neat. He's got his clothes in a beat-up dresser, but at least his threads aren't in cardboard boxes like mine. There's a desk in his room, which he uses all the time, I guess. Whenever Mitch isn't working, he's in his room with the door closed. Sometimes you can hear him loudly singing; other times there's nothing but the soft sound of a pencil working out a math problem.

Mitchell's good with math and science; he could probably be a doctor like Anne will be, but for poor kids in Flint like him, I think that's another dream. Fact is, while lots of poor folks in Flint get into hospitals, it's usually as victims, not as doctors. The walls of Mitchell's room are covered with taped-up posters of Eminem that he's ripped out of magazines. He probably sits at the desk every afternoon, doing his homework, planning to be better than he is. He probably lies in his bed every night, looking at those posters, dreaming of a life and a better place than this.

Ryan's room is down in the damp basement, in what used to be a storage room. The walls are cracked, and it still stinks from when it flooded a few years ago, even though we ripped up all of the carpet. That stinky carpet is in a pile in the backyard, along with the other junk from our lives we can't get rid of for some reason. Ryan throws his dirty clothes for me to wash in a basket in front of his door because I can't bring myself to go in there without gagging. He doesn't spend much time at home anymore, although even one second is too much by my clock.

I hear the front door open, and even from the distance, there's a distinctive sour smell attacking my senses. His big always-new shoes are loud on the creaky, warped wood floors.

"Where's some dinner?" I hear Ryan shout, and I feel the acid in my stomach churn.

I motion to Bree to be quiet, but I know he'll find us. Our closed door is always open to him. Even a chair leaned against the knob can't keep him out.

"I need some food or shit!" Ryan shouts, banging loudly on the door. There's no lock, and the door swings open. His odor overwhelms me; I don't know how he expects me to cook when I'm feeling sick to my stomach. He's standing over me, blocking out the light.

"Hello, Uncle Ryan!" Bree squeals in delight, but he ignores her.

"Fix me something to eat!" Ryan shouts back at me, slams the door, then walks away.

"I don't like it when Uncle Ryan yells," Bree says, then sounds like she's going to cry. I remember how I hated when Mama and Daddy would yell at each other. I can't imagine the hell Bree went through when she lived in that drug den trailer with her mom before we took her in. Anything I can do to protect Bree, I will. I think Aunt Dee feels the same: both of us have written off my generation, except maybe Mitchell, and realize Bree is the only possible hope.

"I don't like it either," I tell Bree with the most gentle expression I can manage.

"I'm gonna tell Grammy on him," Bree says, now in a full-blown pout.

"Don't bother Grammy. She's got enough to worry about." I tell her a lie, wanting to protect her from the true facts of her own life. For there is no telling Mama anything bad about Ryan. It's not that she doesn't believe it; she doesn't even hear it. Instead, she just hears how Ryan is when she's around. Then, he's kind, loving, caring, and does anything for her she asks. But mostly what Mama does best is close her eyes, ears, and soul to the truth. We've taken a vow of silence and wish it away, like all this was happening to some TV family rather than to us.

"Maybe your rich friend could give us some caviar or some shit," Ryan slurs, sticking his body back in the door. He's barely able to stand, let alone censor himself in front of Bree. I get up to leave the room, but he blocks the door with his massive frame.

"I need to go," I mutter to Bree, then head toward the door. He steps back, but makes sure to brush up against me as I escape toward the kitchen.

"She's rich and hot," Ryan says, then laughs. "She's not an ugly poor bitch, like you."

As I race toward the kitchen, I'm upset about so many things that it's like twenty radios are playing in my head at the same time. Once I'm in the kitchen, I pick up a knife and like the dead weight of it in my hand. Even as Ryan's voice chills the air, my fingers feel warm against the cold steel. I start chopping carrots, and the force of the blade helps take my mind off my mind.

Next, I open the fridge to see if there's any meat. Mostly there's leftovers from Mama's job at Harvest Crest Retirement Community or whatever Mitchell brings home from KFC. I find a pack of chicken, which I've got to use today before it goes bad. As the knife slices through the chicken, I'm thinking about the motion, the sound and the texture of flesh and blood. I'm thinking how easy it would be to shut off the noise in my head by slitting my skinny wrists.

"You got some cash for me," Ryan says, staggering behind me, his scent burning the membranes in my nose. I grip the knife tighter, driving my teeth into my bottom lip.

"It's in my room," I say, as he wafts by me. Even with the other smells in our rank old rented house, his scent stands out among them all. I can smell him even in my sleep.

"I'll get it later tonight," Ryan says, then takes a carrot from me. He chews it loudly, swallows, and speaks through his smirk. "It's Wednesday night, you know what I'm saying."

I don't say anything, so finally he walks away. Aunt Dee comes over most Wednesday nights to take Bree to services at the Bristol Road Church of Christ, then Bree stays overnight at her Grand Blanc condo.

"Church night," Ryan shouts from across the room. "Everybody gets down on their knees!"

I don't say anything; instead, I watch the blood from the chicken ooze onto the cutting board. I can't go to church anymore;

every time I'm in church it reminds me of Daddy's funeral. Like so many of my memories, it won't leave me and I can't seem to let it go. Yet, even if I could go, I know better than to believe the words any minister speaks. In church, I would hear about how Jesus teaches us to forgive each other, but Jesus never met Ryan.

fifth grade, october

"Let us pray."

I bow my head to pray. I do it to hide my tears, and so for one second I can stop looking at Daddy. Or what used to be Daddy. That lifeless person lying in the coffin isn't my father.

I'm trying to act tough and older than my years, but the tears and the way I'm clutching onto Hershey Bear, a small teddy bear that Daddy got me one Christmas, reveals the true me.

The only other funeral I've attended was four years ago: my grandmother on my mom's side. It was down in Ohio, where her people are from and most still are. Grandmother Weathers died of cancer; I don't even know what kind, but it was enough to take about half her weight and all of her hair. Grandmother Weathers never had much money, like most folks in my family. Husbands and boyfriends were all introduced as uncle, but none ever stayed too long. About the only thing that ever mattered to her was herself. Mama said when she was growing up, there wasn't enough money for school supplies, for new clothes, or sometimes even for the rent, but Grandmother Weathers always found money for the beauty parlor to get her hair done and talk with friends about the next uncle-to-be. Her clothes might be old and out of style, but her hair never was. Mama left home at sixteen, and she said Grandmother barely noticed.

It was so odd to see Grandmother Weathers in her open casket without any hair. Nobody put on a scarf or a wig, or covered her bald head in any way. The cancer took her life, but then her family took what little dignity she had, even in death. I think Mama and her sisters finally paid her back for her neglect, for her selfishness, and for her vanity. But I wonder if you can really pay anybody back for what they've done to you, because it's done. Can you close a wound by pouring salt into it? If you don't forgive, then how can you ever forget and move forward?

5

october 26, senior year

"Chase him!"

"Got him!" Anne shouts, smoothes out her pink bandanna, then puts her foot to the floor as we take off down I-75, following the tail lights of a black Ford Explorer with California plates.

"Why would anyone from California be visiting Flint?" I ask, which is part of the chasing tail lights game: asking the question, then writing the story to figure out the answer. Now that I'm not doing it alone, and have wheels—Anne's father finally gave her the keys to the car—rather than just words, the adventures are just beginning. Anne loves to drive too fast, do whatever she wants, and act out of impulse. She doesn't plan or dream, she just does.

"You ever been to California?" Anne asks quickly; we've got two hours before she's due at a job she already hates with a passion, while I really liked my first day at the library.

I redirect the question back to her, since I've never been anywhere. "Have you?"

"We used to go to visit family in Los Angeles," Anne says. "It was pretty boring."

"Not like Flint!" I counter, and our laughter fills up the car.

"Cuz, Flint's okay, it's just some of the people who live here, like those immature jerks at school." Anne starts in with one of her constant complaints. "You know who I hate worst of all?"

"Seth Lewis?" I reply out of instinct. We don't have classes together, and it's a big school, so I've mostly avoided Seth's put-downs so far this year, but then, it is only October. It's avoiding Seth as much as stalking Glen that drives me outside the theater every lunch period.

"No, he's too pathetic to hate," Anne says, and I let it go.

"I guess," I add gently, thinking of the things I could say about Seth Lewis.

"Rani Patel, I so hate her," Anne says, knowing I'll agree, since everyone assumes that the great actors Glen and Rani are backstage lovers. "She thinks she walks on water, you know?"

"I don't stand a chance with Glen," I say, then let the car seat swallow me whole.

"Yes, you do Christy, you just have to get some confidence," Anne reassures me.

"Easy for you to say. In case you haven't noticed, I'm not winning homecoming queen."

"That's because you think that way," Anne says. "Come on, you've read enough books to know that beauty, real beauty is on the inside, and not on the outside. Maybe Glen is like other guys at Southwestern, just too immature to know that. We need to hook up with men, not boys."

"Maybe," I whisper. Anne always sounds and looks so smart; she's just gotta be right.

"Glen is all man in bed, I bet," Anne says, fiddling again with the radio and following her sex obsession. Anne dreams of real men, not the boys at Southwestern or the dates arranged by her dad with bright, young boys, sons of his doctor or family friends, each duller than the last.

I fall back on my best ploy: question redirection. "Did your CD player get boosted?"

Anne's pushing buttons frantically, trying to find something of interest in the wasteland that is Flint radio. "No, Dad took it away. Yet another punishment from his highness."

"For what?" Curious, but mostly jealous of the trouble Anne gets into.

"I told him I wanted to quit my job. We had a fight. I lost, per usual," she replies, then shakes her head and gets all serious looking. "He's just jerking back on the chain a little."

"What do you mean? I ask, then shift in my seat as we zip down I-75 north toward Saginaw, or wherever the California plate steers us. I've heard Anne's hard-luck story a hundred times, so I'm thinking about her remark about jerking back on the chain more than listening. We used to have a dog named Brutus that my dad chained up in the backyard. He'd see something, start barking, run after it, and then yelp in pain when he reached the end of his chain. I could see how the fur was all pressed down where the blood matted. I was only seven, but I knew it was wrong to keep an animal chained up, so one day I figured out how to unchain him. Set free, Brutus promptly ran out in the street and got hit by a car. That day, I learned a sad and hard lesson: you can't get set free all at once, you gotta take small steps into the world.

"You listening?" Anne says. "He's ruining and running my life. I should be used to it."

"How's that?" I respond, throwing myself back into present drama not past trauma.

"He still wants to control everything: how I dress, who I date, what clubs I join at school. Everything!" When Anne gets angry, she drives even faster. We've passed our California leader, so Anne must be in search of another set of tail lights as she exits off the freeway.

"That's not fair," I finally respond, lost in my own thoughts of wishing someone would even care about those things in my life or teach me how to dress or how to date or how to talk with people so I could feel normal, if only for just one day.

"I'll show him," she says, a glint returning to her heavily made-up eyes.

"How's that?"

"We're going to get tattoos," she announces at the top of the exit ramp.

"I don't want any stranger touching me, you know?" I tell her; it's only my first line of defense, but probably the rawest emotion races fastest to the surface.

"I know that's right," Anne says. "I know all about that!"

"What do you mean?" I ask as we turn on Clio Road, headed back to Flint. Along the way, we pass dumpy motels, junkyards, boarded-up stores, and many bars with full parking lots.

"My boss at work, you know my father's buddy Mr. Wallace," she says.

I nod, trying to pay attention to her words, as much as to the urban badlands around us.

"The other day, I'm busing tables and he comes up behind me, to tell me he needs my help in the kitchen, but he was just too close," Anne says sounding so fearless.

"What did you do?" I ask.

"He's my dad's best friend, so what am I going to say: 'Daddy dearest, your pal is a perve,'" Anne says, then laughs. "But the way he looks at me sometimes, pretty damn creepy."

"What's so funny?" I ask.

"I'm just thinking how my dad is always telling me to stand up for myself," Anne continues, laughter quickly replaced with an angry tone. "Except when it comes to talking to him."

"You should say something," I suggest, like my advice mattered. Anne and I are like sisters, even though we're so different. Anne refuses to conform to the "intelligent doctor's daughter" stereotype that her father wants her to act out. While I'm a non-box—this great phrase I found on an online quiz—someone who won't fit in anyplace. We're triangles in a world of circles and squares.

"I guess," Anne says, then we're silent for a while until we pull into the parking lot littered with cigarette butts and Halo Burger bags. "This is going to change your life!"

"Maybe getting a tattoo will get Glen to think of me other than as his friend," I suggest.

"You could get his name tattooed on your . . ." Anne says, pointing at my chest.

"Good thing, his is a short name," I joke. With Anne's sexy self around, no boy, man, perve, or lesbian will lay eyes or hands on me. Her attention-stealing looks, along with her fast car, grass cash, and occasional weekend hotel service, top the list of why she's my best friend.

"How about a fire-breathing dragon here," she says, tapping her fingers against her tight black sweater. "How about you?"

"I don't think so," I reply.

Anne parks the car next to a Harley near the front door. "Why not?" she asks.

"For one, who is ever going to see it?" I shoot back. "And don't say Glen because—"

"Because you won't approach him," she reminds me for the hundredth time.

"I'm waiting for the right moment," I say. But it's not the right moment I'm waiting for: it's the right me, instead of this person with so many things wrong with them that he could never love.

"Listen, Speedy, if not now, then when?" Anne says, another constant refrain.

"Still, I don't want to get—"

"Don't worry, I'll pay for it," Anne says, clumsily reminding me of the economic basis of our friendship. She pays and I play along with whatever she wants to do.

"It's not that."

"You scared of your mom saying something?"

"No, she won't even notice," I respond, as the truth of Mama's indifference stings.

"Then what?" Anne mumbles as she presses on more lipstick.

"I don't think my brother Robert would like it, that's all," I say, telling her a half truth.

"Why not?" Anne offers me her dark red lipstick, but I wave her off.

"Robert's loaded with tats," I confess, trying to avoid the subject. "It's a gang thing."

She cuts me off with a wave of her hand. "Okay, then, you just be different."

"Like that is so hard," I say, and then we both kind of laugh at the absurdity of my statement and our situation. Anne and I are probably not that unlike other girls at Flint Southwestern or anywhere in the world. We like to think we're different: a little smarter, a little wiser, a lot better read, and, in just a few minutes, with more decorated bodies than most.

"Let's do this thing," she shouts. "I don't want to go it alone, Cuz, come on!"

I shrug my shoulders, and as always, give in to what Anne wants. "Let's smoke a joint first, okay?" I start to open up her purse to retrieve her recently purchased product.

"Can't do it," Anne says taking the purse away from me.

"Why not?"

"How do you think we're going to pay for this?" Anne says, then laughs. "I'm sure whatever fine and upstanding gentleman is working here might be glad to overlook our underage status in exchange for certain cannabis products, don't you think?"

We walk inside, and it's even worse than I imagined. There's thumping, bone-shaking rap music turned up too loud, no doubt to drown everyone's other senses with sound. There's a burly bald-headed white guy sitting on a stool. His arms, and skull, are mostly covered in tats. He's smoking a cigarette and talking on a cell phone. He makes eye contact with Anne, which pulls her closer to him, while I'm looking for a bathroom and a quick exit. Tatman points toward a notebook on the filth-covered counter, mumbles something to Anne, then continues his loud conversation. Anne starts looking through the notebooks for her dragon design, although I doubt she'll really let this guy take her sweater off. Anne's usually lots of talk and little action. But about this, she seems serious. She pushes one of the notebooks over to me, and I start glancing through it, not really caring or concentrating. The last thing I want or need is something to attract attention, like a tattoo. But, if I need to do this to follow Anne, then I'll get one of those small ankle tattoos that no one but me will ever see.

"What do you want?" Tatman growls, like a hungry bear that just woke up, as he taps the notebook in front of me. The question of what I want overwhelms me, and my strength to resist escapes me. I'm just like our old dog Brutus, shackled around the neck.

"This one." I'm pointing at the book, as I look down at my virgin left ankle for the last time and almost smile.

"Nice choice," he says, as we both stare at the design of a link of chain.

sophomore year, november

"So when are your parents coming back home?"

"Not until after ten," Anne replies, taking the pipe from me. She's locked the door to her room, and we're sitting on a small bench in her big bedroom by an open window, letting the frosty fall night bite us. Anne's moved from customer to best friend quickly to both our surprise.

"They go out often?" I ask. It's getting too cold to chase tail lights from the bridge. I'm looking for some other place to call home. Anne's Miller Road mansion will do nicely.

"Not much, so carpe diem," she says, inhaling deeply.

"Carp what?" I reply. The only carp I know about are those that swim in the Flint River, but it's a river more known for catching fire many years ago than containing fish.

"It's Latin; it means 'seize the day,' " Anne says, looking somewhat embarrassed.

I show my closed-mouth half smile and look around the room, making sure not to touch, not wanting to leave fingerprints behind. Anne told me her father isn't thrilled with her choice of friends, meaning me, which thrills her to no end. "What's Latin for 'seize the night?' "

"Chronic!" Anne says, handing me the pipe, but I'm too busy laughing to take it. "I wish Daddy dearest would get high and mellow out. He can be such an asshole sometimes."

"He was nice to me," I say. Anne and I meet at school. This is my first time at her house.

"To your face," she counters quickly.

"What do you mean?" I ask.

"Never mind, it's nothing I need to tell you," she says.

"We're friends, no secrets, right?" I whisper directions to that one-way street.

"He doesn't like you, Christy," she tells me, and I wish I had the pipe back in my hand. I don't say anything, but the big hurt in my heart's showing in my red eyes.

"He asked about you, and I told him the truth," she says slowly, almost ashamed.

I hide a laugh at Anne thinking she knows the truth of me. "What did you tell him?"

"I told him where you lived, and he rolled his eyes. Then he started with his 'people judge you by whom you associate with' speech. When he lectures, I don't listen," she says.

"You didn't tell him about Robert, did you?" I ask as I let one family secret slip.

"He knew, so he assumes, Christy, that you're like him," she says, handing me back the pipe, and then laughs her loudest laugh of the night. "You know, like you're a drug dealer."

I'm not laughing. I'm not speaking. I'm barely breathing.

"Christy, you're not a dealer, you're my friend," she says reaching out to me. I take a deep breath and accept the hug, even if her words—and my reality—feel more like a punch.

She releases the hug, readjusts the wool cap she's wearing, and sits on the floor.

"Should I go home?" I ask.

"No, you should stay. You should stay over as often as I want. I'll show him!"

"Show him what?"

"He's not telling me what friends I can have," Anne says. "He's so mean to me."

"I don't want to—"

"Christy, this ain't about you; this is about me and him," Anne says, stretching out on the floor. She motions for me to join her. The white carpet smells fresh and feels cozy.

"I don't understand," I say. I'm staring at the ceiling of Anne's room, taking in the details of the perfect white paint. I've memorized every crack, water stain, and tan paint chip in my own room. Everything in her room is perfectly organized, every book lined up, every piece of clothing flawlessly arranged, even in a closet that seems bigger than my tiny, dirty bedroom.

"Understand what?"

"How could you say that your father is so mean? Look at all the stuff he buys for you."

"This isn't love, this is a bribe," Anne says dismissively, then takes off her glasses and pulls her green wool cap over her eyes. Like a computer, she's in the process of shutting down.

As I look around the room, I'm taking in all of the details of the things that I will never have. The computer with a screen as big as our TV; the TV with a screen as big as my desk; the shelves lined with as many books as are in Ms. Chapman's room; the treasure chest disguised as a desk filled with toys like a white iPod, a shiny new silver digital camera, and a striking silver DVD player. The windows are covered with thin lace curtains to tease in the sun; mine is covered with an old black towel. The windows are clean and large, and I bet don't get covered with ice on the inside come wintertime. While Anne's closet is bursting with clothes, I worry that I'm just another outfit she's trying on for size, seeing if she likes my color or my style. I wonder what she sees in me.

Visiting Anne is like a dream in some way: the buzz from the pot making it even more so. Here are all the things that I've always wanted; here are all the things I know I'll never have for my own. So, this is my closet, these are my outfits I get to try on and learn they don't really fit me. I hope if they don't really fit me, then I will no longer want them. I want a place to call home that isn't my own. And I want more than that, I want the wealth of Anne's friendship. It's not just that she's smart, funny, and happy to capture the attention that I avoid. I know it is something else, something deeper, yet something quite shallow. But among all these things, the thing I want the most is not something to have or hold or horde, but something to hear: the sound of a door locking.

6

november 1, senior year

"So when did you start?"

I'm focused on the sorting-room shelves packed with the unorganized books that I, super shelver extraordinaire, will arrange in perfect order in a matter of minutes.

"So, you're the new girl," a deep but soft male voice says.

I turn to see a guy my age, and about my height, standing in front of me. He's got curly long black hair, a small scruff of beard, and gray eyes behind small silver-rimmed glasses. His white skin is dark, but not that weird orange store tan. "Last week," I mutter not to his face, but toward the camera hanging around his neck.

"You're Christy, right?" he says, sticking out his left hand. He leaves it hanging even though my hands remain by my side. His fingers have a couple of silver rings to match the small loops in his earlobes. "I'm Terrell, but you can call me Terrell."

I giggle, a schoolgirl giggle, which is okay. No matter what Anne or my ankle tattoo tells us, that's what we still are. I finally put my hand in his, overcoming the impulse to avoid skin contact with strangers. "Do you work here?" I ask, then quickly put my hand over my mouth.

He gives my hand a nice old school handshake. He didn't try to do some thugabe shake like most kids at school. Looking at his black jeans, green Converse All Star Hi-tops, and Bob Marley red-green-yellow on black T-shirt, I know from the get-go Terrell maybe isn't one to do things like other people, white, black, or tan. I don't like strangers touching me, but the press of his skin doesn't feel as odd as I imagined, even if he seems wonderfully weird.

"In art and music, but I can't paint or sing, only take pictures. How funny is that?" His arms are like windmills when he talks, and his words energize me. "You a shelver too?"

I just nod my head; I'm too embarrassed to speak.

"Everybody starts someplace," he says, then pulls up the empty book truck I was about to fill and sits on it. "Remember: even a journey of a thousand miles starts with a single step."

"I guess," I mumble, as I've gone from intrigued to afraid in a matter of seconds. I just don't know how to respond to boys. I guess because I don't have any idea of how they want me to respond. I assume leaving them alone is the response that suits them and me best.

"Do you know where I read that piece of wisdom that inspires me every day?" he asks. I shake my head from side to side, no doubt he can hear the rocks rattle around in there. "From a fortune cookie. How weird is that?"

"That's pretty strange," I say, guessing that agreeing works well with most boys.

"Where do you go to school? Central?" he asks, pointing in the direction of the school, which is across the library's parking lot.

"I'm a senior at Southwestern," I say, in a tone suggesting pride and surprise. My mouth is dry, my stomach is twisted, and

I'm biting into the groove on my lip. I want Terrell just to walk away now; he's had his fun showing off for me, but it's time for me to be invisible again.

"I go to Summit," he says, and I grin inside. I see Summit School every day with my view from the bridge. "I'm a senior too. So I guess we're both senior citizens."

I laugh, half from nervousness and half not. "Do you like it there?"

"I'll like it better when I graduate, and exit from Flint," he says.

I'm trying not to look at him, but it's hard to control my eyes. "Where are you going to college?" I ask. I know, unlike at Southwestern, every kid at Summit ends up in college.

"It's down to two: Kenyon or Oberlin," he says. I nod like I know what language he's speaking.

"How about you?"

"I'll probably go there," I say, pointing in the direction of University of Michigan-Flint, not that I've dreamed about it or planned for it for one second. The school counselors are off-limits, and there's no getting help at home from Mama. Only Ms. Chapman seems to care if I go to college. She's always dropping hints for Central Michigan, about fifty miles north of Flint.

"Really?" He's fidgeting with his glasses, and in doing so, making me more nervous.

"No good?" I ask, desperate for advice from anyone, even a stranger. Yet, there's a vibe between us. He's both a little strange and interested in me, which is even stranger still.

"I think of Flint as the land of opportunity," he says, then snaps his fingers. He's trying too hard to act cool. "And at the first opportunity, I'm getting the hell out of it!"

"That's funny!" I wish my bottom lip wasn't so chewed, so I could smile without pain.

"No, it's actually quite sad," he says, nervously thumbing a book he's lifted from the shelving truck. He's looking now at the book, not at me. "Where do you live?"

"Stone, off Fenton Road," I say. If he can't tell by how poorly I'm dressed, then my Stone Street address shouts out I'm not from the Miller Road mansions.

"I used to live in the north end, but we got out," Terrell says, and his gray eyes are magnets now. I know I'm staring at him, but I can't break free.

"Me too," I whisper, trying not to remember how we moved two or three times a year even when Daddy was alive. It was only just before he died that we settled south on Fenton Road and I finally started getting good grades. I guess you need security to find your true self.

"What are you going to study in college?" I ask, deflecting any more questions at me.

"Guess!" he says, snapping his fingers once more, then putting his palms faceup.

"Theater," I say, since he reminds me of Glen, or maybe it's just how I'm reacting that reminds me of how I reacted to Glen the first time I saw him. A rare good memory that lives on.

"Wrong answer!" he says, then makes a loud buzzing sound. "Want to guess again?"

"Poetry?" I say, even though I'm not even sure if you can major in poetry in college.

"Zero for two," he says, then glances at his watch, which is a lot fancier than mine.

"I don't really know what—"

"Last chance." Terrell stands up from the book truck, so we're eye to eye.

I don't know what to do: I get the feeling anything I guess is going to be wrong. He probably doesn't plan to go to college; he's just having his fun picking on the new girl. He'll tell his friends back at Summit about the skinny ugly girl from Southwestern who couldn't even guess what he was going to study in college, but couldn't stop studying him. Like these books demanding my attention, I'll be an entertaining story to be brought out, enjoyed, and put back on the shelf. "How about literature?" I say in a perfect library whisper.

He shakes his head slowly from side to side. The small silver hoop earring in his left ear seems to shine bright and beautiful as it reflects the ugly neon glow of the lights in the sorting room. "Christy, I'm afraid that's also incorrect, but a nice try," he says, then reaches out his hand once more to shake mine. His fingers seem longer, his skin softer, and his touch lingers.

"What is it, then?" I ask, as he pulls his hand away, then walks toward the door.

"Next time, next time," he says over his shoulder as he picks up a black leather biker jacket from the staff coat rack, then heads out of my day and joins Glen in my book of dreams.

seventh grade, november

"Please just look at me."

My eyes and unspoken words shout at Glen Thompson over the smashing sounds of music filling the crepe-paper-decorated McKinley Middle School gym. I'm straining to see him in the flashes of dark and light. I never thought, in the darkness of my life, that I'd dream about a boy like Glen. There's something about him; it's his gentleness of spirit that I don't feel at home or experience at school. It's not one thing he said or anything in particular that he's done; it's just who he is. Everything about him tells me he is kind, caring, even compassionate. Daydreaming about Glen, and planning a way for him to notice me, help get me through the long, lonely hours of my day.

Even though I can't and won't dance, I came back to school tonight to the Fall Dance because I guessed he would be here. Tonight is like any other day at school. I'm on the outskirts watching him. All year, I've seen Glen at school do what he's doing now: making rounds. He goes up to a group, boys or girls, black or white, and with nothing more than a look, he'll find himself on the inside. It's like magic, but I don't know the secret words to say to him.

"Please, look at me," I whisper again. Yet I could shout the words and no one would hear over the pounding bass that mirrors the sound and sensation in my chest as I stare at Glen. I've yet to speak

to him, but I've watched him every day this year. Since I'm not chained down by a group of friends like he is, I can come and go easily and unnoticed. I want to see his smile, which is wide and bright, and always sincere. I don't think he could smirk if you paid him, not that he needs the money. He's one of those Miller Road mansion types.

"Please, look at me," I say again to no one, since I'm sitting alone at one of the tables. I walked over to the dance with some girls who live on my street. I know they hang with me mainly so they can stop by the house to purchase product from Robert. They ditched me, or was it the other way around, as soon as we got here. They're all made up and ready to hook up, while I'm buried in a big black sweatshirt and wanting only one human touch. I normally try not *to sit alone at lunch or school functions because that attracts just as much attention, especially from school counselors. Since I don't say much to anyone, I can sit with most anyone at school.*

Glen's talking with some of the other artsy kids at school, and it looks like they're getting ready to leave. Glen's not super popular, because he's not a jock or a thug, but there's always a crowd around him, like he's some sort of magnet. All these people must have something that pulls them toward Glen, but then they must offer him something in return.

"Please, look at me," I say to myself as I follow him and the others out the back door of the gym, remain invisible as they walk over toward a Dumpster near the cafeteria, then disappear behind it. Seconds later, I see a quick spark, like lightning, followed by laughter. I take a few steps closer, but the Dumpster blocks my sight. Despite the stench coming from the garbage-packed container, my nose captures a recognizable smell that reminds me of Robert and Ryan.

I take a deep breath, inhale the familiar fumes, and join Glen and his friends in their secret spot.

"If you guys wanna buy some good shit, then I can hook you up," I say, knowing I can supply his demand. I know I can make sure that Glen does something tomorrow and the day after, something he does now for the first time ever—look at me.

7

november 13, senior year

"You sure you don't want a hit?"

I wave Anne off as she passes the joint over to Glen. I've got an SAT study class in the morning, then work at the library, so I need to be straight, since I probably won't be well rested. Aunt Dee has Bree tonight, so I'm free to attend this small Friday the thirteenth theater party at Glen's house, although I'm dreaming of good luck for once in my life.

I've got on my usual baggy black-hooded sweatshirt, keeping me warm and well hidden. Anne's wearing a pink "Love Bunny" T-shirt, tight and high, and her pretorn jeans, tighter and low, ready to flash her new lower-back-tattooed coolness. There are people dancing inside, but we're in the backyard on Glen's younger sibs play set, oblivious to the cold and the crowd. Anne and I are on the swings, while Glen gives us a gentle push. Anne could probably have Glen, but she's hands-off for my sake. I also don't think that Glen is different enough for Anne's rather interesting, if untested, tastes. He'd more amuse then enrage her father is my guess.

"Thanks," Glen says, then pulls and holds the smoke deep into his lungs.

"Is Mr. McDonald coming?" Anne asks. She's decided to pursue Mr. McDonald, after all. In the car on the way over, she was getting us pumped up, asking, "If not now, then when?"

"I doubt it," Glen replies.

Anne doesn't even try to hide the disillusionment in her face. She pushes her legs under her and sends herself higher into the air, wishing she could fly away from her disappointment.

"So, Christy, how's your job?" Glen asks.

"Okay, I guess," I say, since there's not a whole lot to say about putting books away, other than sharing the dream that one day my name and my picture will be on one of them. If I shared my dreams with Glen, then maybe it would be my lips not my weed he'd want to touch.

"Tell him about Terrell, that cool guy you work with," Anne says as she swings higher.

"Shut up," I whisper loudly, as I shoot her a look, but Anne just winks, then pushes herself higher. She thinks I need to make Glen jealous. I push my legs under me and try to swing higher and faster. When I swing like this, I feel like I'm defying laws of gravity and time.

"Higher!" Anne says, and Glen obliges with a big push, then does the same for me. The tips of his fingers touch my lower back, and I'm higher than even the best weed could make me. After more swinging and laughing, a sudden hard rain sends Glen hustling back into his house.

"Where's he going?" I ask Anne.

"Maybe Rani Patel arrived," Anne says. "I'll look for the red carpet."

"You're so mean," I say, but I'm laughing about it; there's

nothing else to do when I think about the uneven triangle of Glen, Rani, and Christy. "I'm sorry about Mr. McDonald."

Anne pushes herself higher on the swing, her feet pointed straight north. "Well, I don't think my dad would care for him, being that he's like twenty-five years old," she says.

"Not his type?"

"His type for me would be somebody like Alan Ackerman or David Lee." She laughs when she says their names. Alan and David are nice enough, smart enough, but they're the poster children for computer geeks anonymous. "Or maybe the son of one of his doctor friends."

"You could do worse, don't you think?" I say, knowing that with Seth Lewis as my only limited experience, there's almost no man alive that couldn't be better.

"God, if my boss Mr. Wallace's son is like him, that would be a lot worse," Anne says, her voice picking up pace with the slowly increasing speed of the rain falling on us. "He's such a creepy guy. He's like always hovering around me or doing some weird shit."

"What now?" I'm curious about her work life. I can't imagine doing what she does: serving people at a Country Club at weddings or other receptions. How could you not hate a job where everybody else is celebrating a joyous occasion and you're cleaning up their mess?

"You know we have to wear a uniform: white button-down shirt, black pants, real basic," Anne says, and given her somewhat provocative taste in clothes, the simple style doesn't suit her. "And I swear, Christy, that he drops stuff in front of me on purpose just so I'll pick it up."

"I don't get it," I say, swinging faster as rain hits my face like water bullets.

"Christy, when I bend over, he's looking down my shirt, I can feel it," Anne says slowly.

"That's gross," I say. "Why don't you say something to him?"

"Like what?" Anne says, for once not sounding sure of her words or deeds. "If I just avoid him, then maybe it will stop. I don't dare say anything because my dad would—"

I choke back what I want to say and instead offer: "Why don't you just tell your dad?"

"You can't tell the Good Doctor anything," Anne says, her voice rich with disgust. Both of our voices will be rich with mucus if we don't come out of this hard rain that's falling. "But maybe instead of dating one of my perve boss's sons, I'll bring home Tyrone Butler."

I might drown from laughing so hard as the rain pours down my throat, thinking of five-foot-two Anne Williams kissing six-foot-five, two-hundred-pound-thug-machine Tyrone Butler. Despite being a pothead, Anne's got a good chance to get named as the most likely to succeed; Tyrone's got a better chance of being named by a grand jury and joining Robert at Jackson.

"Not a good idea?" Anne says once I stop laughing.

"About as smart as staying out in this hard rain!" I shout, "Wanna go in?"

Anne and I both take big leaps off the swing, then head inside to warm up. As I open the door, I'm hit with the loud sound of rap music. Glen lives in Anne's neighborhood, so there's a music video projected on the big-screen TV, and everybody is dancing or grinding against each other. The cool thing about theater people is they don't really care what people think about them, so they are not afraid to act however they want. I want to be that way—so no words can harm me, no touch can destroy me—but I know that loneliness is my weakness. I want to be left alone, but I hate feeling lonely, which I usually feel in crowds like this. Everybody's having fun, but it's like something's holding me back, jerking hard on the link of chain tattooed on my ankle.

"Why aren't you dancing, Christy?" Glen says, moving closer and shouting into my ear.

"No reason," I shout over the booming bass. The vibration reminds me of standing on the bridge, especially when big trucks go under. I worry that bridge is going to collapse, but for one second my nerves forget, my fear leaves me, and the adrenaline rush is as addictive as crack.

"How could you not like this music?" Glen says, pointing at the screen. "It's so cold."

"I don't know, I just don't, okay?" It's so hard being around Glen and trying to say the right thing all the time. Besides, what would I tell him? That it's not so much the music I hate as the videos. The women in these videos are everything I'm not: they all have great bodies, fancy clothes, nice cars, and men panting after them. I know that Mitchell dreams of being the next Eminem, but if he made it, I just know he'd sing about women, not bitches or hos. Ryan and his friends, however, can't get enough of the skin and the sleaze on most rap videos. They don't just watch them, they sing along, spitting out bleeped words.

"That's cool, but I'm going to go dance. Catch you later!"

Glen says, with a goofy grin on his face, which is only partially drug induced. I can see just how much Glen likes having everyone watch him as he moves gracefully into the dancing crowd.

I stand with my back to the TV, knowing I don't really fit in even with this little band of theater and National Honor Society misfits. As I watch Glen dance, I wonder if I could find the courage to go over to him if a slow song came on. I wonder if he would dance with me. I wonder if he would hold me tight, wrapping his arms around my waist. I wonder how sweet he smells up close. I wonder if he'd whisper in my ear, look into my eyes, and then kiss my cracked lips. I wonder after that what would he do, and what I would I do. And it is then, always then, that the images stop in my head, like someone pulled the plug on the TV. I can imagine Glen loving me, but I can't visualize the image of us making love.

When no one comes over to talk to me, I'm consumed with loneliness, even in this crowded room. I know these people: some are customers, most are classmates, but none, except for Anne and Glen, are my friends. Every now and then, some part of me from my past wants to scream out, "Look at me!" but instead, I know that my role is not queen of the ball, life of the party, or homecoming princess, but the role I cast for myself: the invisible woman. I head out, alone, back into the cold rain. I'll let Glen laugh and dance it up with his real friends and future lovers; I'll let Anne circle the room waiting for Mr. Right for her and Mr. Wrong for her father to make his entrance; and I'll let myself drift back to chasing the tail lights of my memories, which are as elusive and all-consuming as Glen. Long ago, I picked Glen to be my white knight, even if he's told me directly, indirectly, and indiscreetly year after year after year that he just wants to be my friend. Still I dare to dream. But I've read enough books to know there can't be a white knight without a black one.

eighth grade, november

"So, who can tell me what a catalyst is?"

I'm struggling to stay awake in Mr. Sherman's science class, my first-period class. I couldn't care less about science, but this question interests me. I want to answer "Glen" to Mr. Sherman's inquiry, except I don't talk in class and that's not the right answer. It's been a year since I first approached Glen, but I'm still on the fringes. I'm his dealer, not his girlfriend. Yet I still dream that he can be my catalyst; he can be the one that changes my life.

Mr. Sherman looks around the room. It's November, and he still doesn't know any of our names, except for Seth Lewis, whom he can't abide. He's this weird new kid in school this year that nobody seems to like. I've seen him already a couple of times this year in detention: me for being late to school, him for using "inappropriate language" in class. I have two classes with him: this science class and music, which is a required class. In music, he's totally clueless and clumsy. I'm not much better, as I'm trying to learn to play the flute, but it doesn't come easy, since we can't afford to buy one, nor is there any quiet place to practice. About the only thing I want more than Glen's affection is quiet in my life: a silent house and a still mind.

A couple of front-row students jerk their hands up, then pump them in rapid motion to answer Mr. Sherman. Glen's arm moves into the air gracefully, like he was releasing a balloon to let it fly free into the sky. I admire how calm he is when talking or moving in front of others.

"I know!" I hear Seth Lewis, who sits next to me in the row nearest the door. I know better than to sit at the front, but also not in the back. The back's where the troublemakers sit, and that means attention. It's safer to be on the outside edge of class. It's much easier to be near the door, in case I need to make a quick exit to the bathroom or to head toward the office to deal with my "tardiness issue," as the school counselor calls it. It's much simpler because I never have to walk in front of any of the other students. It also makes the most sense, as I arrive late for first period most Mondays and Thursdays. On the edge, that's where I belong.

"Why don't you tell us, Mr. Thompson," Mr. Sherman says, pointing at Glen. I strain my ears along with my eyes to listen and watch as Glen starts to answer.

"A catalyst is—" Glen starts.

But Seth Lewis shouts over him. "The Cat A list shows where to find the best pussy!" There's some laughter, but Mr. Sherman doesn't crack a smile, not that he ever has in his life.

"Shut up!" Glen snaps, angry at Seth for stealing his spotlight.

"I mean best pussycats," Seth says, trying to avoid detention. "Get it? Cat-A-list."

Mr. Sherman frowns at Seth, but does nothing else. Instead, he goes back to talking, then explaining what he's talking about. He drones on; I start to doze off.

"Hey, Christy, take this," Seth whispers to me. He's got something in his hand.

I'm startled that he knows my name and shocked that he wants to talk with me. Note passing is something the cool kids in the center do, not us exiles on the edge of class.

"Take it," he repeats. I grab the folded piece of paper from him, successfully not touching his freckled skin. He's wearing torn blue jeans and a red sweatshirt, which barely fit him. I open up the top fold, and there's a badly drawn picture of a flute. Written underneath is the question: "What did the flute say to Christy?" I unfold the bottom part of paper, then hear Seth laugh loud enough for only us to hear as I read an answer a lot like the sound of Mr. Sherman scraping the chalk across the blackboard. It says: "Blow me."

8

november 14, senior year

"Got me *figured* out yet?"

I raise my eyes, looking away from the colorful romance paperbacks on the gray cart to see Terrell standing before me. Last week, he waved, but didn't say a word. This afternoon, he's back around, if not in, my face. I can't imagine what he wants or what game he's playing.

"My college major?" he says, then inches closer, but my mouth, like my feet, seems frozen under his warm, inviting smile. "I just wondered if you thought about it."

I'd like to tell him the truth: I'd thought, much to my surprise, a lot about his hanging question and his lingering touch, even if I deny it to Anne. I'd like to tell him that I've thought about him like I've thought about nobody else but Glen. I'd like to tell him that I think I might like him. But, I swallow the words, chew on my bottom lip, and let him fill the silence.

"So how's school?" he asks, but unlike me, I think he really wants to know the answer and isn't asking questions to deflect attention. I wonder now if last weekend was an unstated test. Maybe I was supposed to speak to him. I don't know the rules of romance. Even if I did, one almost imaginary and always unattainable lover like Glen is enough for my untried heart to handle.

"Okay, I guess." I don't want to give anything away since I haven't a clue why Terrell is asking me questions or paying attention to me. For the past two weeks he'll come around, talk at me for a while, then go on his way. I've got no experience talking with boys and I'm not sure I want to learn. Maybe he just wants to get out of doing his work, although I'm making him work hard to know anything about me. I look away and back down at the safe softcovers of romance fiction, then speak. "How about with you?"

He rubs his forehead, trying to scratch out an answer. Terrell's really verbal when he's talking at someone, I notice, but not as good when talking *with* someone. I'm not good at talking with people either, but I did learn two things in the past two weeks about Terrell from a coworker who goes to Summit: he's not rich and he doesn't have a girlfriend. Finally, he answers. "I'm alphabet boy. I got an A in two classes, B in two, and two Cs kicking my ass."

I frown, wondering how he plans to get into Oberlin or Kenyon with grades like that. Even with worse grades than me, he's going to land at a better school than I will, if I even get to college.

"How the hell do you get a C in photography?" he asks himself for my benefit.

"You like taking pictures, don't you?" the world's most camera-shy girl asks in terror.

"All the time," he says. "Maybe I could take your picture sometime?"

I shake my head, tiny little shakes, like I don't want him really to see. He'd need to promise any picture wouldn't land in my school yearbook. I've always managed to be sick on picture day, and I don't have any club or team photos. I don't want anyone to know that I ever went to Flint Southwestern or I even existed.

"You wanna see some of my photos?" Terrell finally says after looking through his backpack. Before I have a chance to answer, he shows off his camera. This one's not a small digital or a bright, shiny new one like Anne has; it's very old school. It leads me to believe that while Terrell may go to Summit, he doesn't belong there. The long, wild, untamed curly brown hair, the black System of a Down T-shirt, and those silver earrings shout out that he's someone who'd rather stand out than fit in anywhere.

He puts the camera back in the bag, then pulls out a binder. "Do you think this deserves a C?" he asks while opening up a photo album. The photos are black and white, each fills a half page in the gray binder. As I flip through the pages, I notice there are no people in any of the pictures. Yet, I can feel the phantom sadness of the faces who once lived in these forlorn places that Terrell has captured. The photos are of garbage-filled vacant lots, cold concrete walls painted with graffiti, buildings with broken windows, ruins of torn-down factories, and burned-out shells of houses. "My teacher said the photos were too depressing. What do you think?"

Before I can answer, I stare at the final page, puzzled by the last photo.

"You like it?" Terrell asks, his voice shaking with doubt. "It's the title photo."

"It's wonderful," I respond, touching the page. Other than filling the entire page, the photo isn't that much different. It's a black-and-white picture of a business with a hand-painted "4-Sale" notice in a broken glass front window, empty pop cans and beer bottles littering the cracked sidewalk, and the big tilted sign saying "Beauty Supplies" occupying most of the photo.

"My photography teacher didn't get what the project title means: 'beauty supplies,' " he says, softly now, like he's sharing a secret. "Christy, you understand what I'm saying, don't you?"

I think of all the times in school that I've known the answer to a teacher's question, but didn't speak so as not to draw attention. I've known the answer but held back, believing if Glen thought I was too smart, he wouldn't like me. I've known the answer, but swallowed it so I could remain just another poor white-trash girl passing through Flint Southwestern on the road to nowhere. But now I need and want a right answer to prove I'm not as dumb as I pretend to be.

When I don't respond right away, he comes to my rescue. "Beauty supplies! The photos show there is beauty in anything, even if you can't see it on the surface. Beauty supplies itself to all of us in different ways. It is up to us to find it. You get it, I get it, but my teacher, no."

"Where is this place?" I ask because the state of beauty isn't on the map of my life.

"North end, up off Stewart Ave., by my old house," Terrell says, his voice trailing off.

I leaf again through the notebook, wondering what else of his past is between the pages. I feel him staring at me as I stare at his work. We don't speak, and the silence is wonderful.

"Don't the two of you have work to do?" I hear one of the library people yell at us from a distance. I snap to attention, scared to death of losing this job. Terrell shoots me a guilty smile, then closes the notebook. He puts it back in his bag. Looking at his small yet crowded backpack, I know that he can teach me more than anyone, except maybe for Ms. Chapman.

"You know what interests me most about all these photos," he whispers.

"What?" I respond, and I wonder if he can tell that I'm interested in anything he says.

"I wonder how these places got like that," he says, readjusting his glasses. "How did these houses get abandoned? What happened to these people? What's the backstory?"

"Chasing tail lights," I whisper aloud, then push the book cart away from Terrell.

"What did you say?" Terrell asks, but I'm not ready to reveal myself to him. Yet.

"I'll tell you next time, Terrell," I say, safely moving away so I can't see the response, or maybe the rejection, in his eyes.

"Next time!" Terrell shouts, then laughs, and I actually smile. Not the usual Christy mouth-covering grin but instead, I smile wide and bright. I can still hear his laughter as I leave the back room. Looking at his photos and the person who took them, I understand that even in the ugliest parts of our lives, there's a reason to believe. And now I believe that beauty supplies.

eighth grade, november

"Put your fucking hands where we can fucking see them and come out of the house!"

For once, it is not the smell that wakes me in the middle of the night, nor is it my nightmare scream. It is real life and the flashing lights in front of the house. The lights flash in time, while the yelling voice seems to stop clocks. "Robert Mallory, we have a warrant for your arrest. Come out of the house now." I leap out of bed and look out the window. Behind the house are two men, pistols drawn, pointing toward the back door. I pull the curtain shut so fast, that it falls off the rod. There's a commotion outside, but the yelling in the front room distracts me. I can't make out the words, but the voices are clear: it is Mama and Robert yelling.

"Come out of the house now!" the voice seems to be coming through a microphone or maybe a megaphone. I crack open my door, but Mama shouts at me. Before I slam it shut, I yell out Mitchell's name, then run toward Bree's bed. She's asleep, beautiful and oblivious to the ugliness around her. She's seven, but she's lived enough to be seventeen. As the police yell louder, I wonder if her father will be alive for her next birthday and why he ran home, not away.

"Breezy, wake up," I say, shaking her bed, but trying not to scare her. I've got enough terror for the two of us. "Come on, right now, you need to come with me."

She puts her arms up, and I scoop her against my chest. I grab the Shrek-covered pillow from her bed, then wrap it around her ears so she can be deaf to the chaos around us. She's pressed up against me. I have one hand on the closet door, the safest place I think we can be in the house in case the bullets start flying, when a burst of light shoots through the darkness.

I cringe, but it's Robert stepping into the room. He kisses Bree, then whispers to me: "Protect her, Christy." He hugs me, maybe for the first time ever, then kisses his daughter maybe for the last. As we hide in the closet, Robert walks tall toward the front door and his fate.

9

november 21, senior year

"Who's the Chill?"

Mitchell's face is a triangle of surprise, shock, and shame jammed into his small brown eyes. He's silent, so our big, old, and mostly empty house fills with Ryan's laughter. I'm lying on the couch in the living room reading a novel, trying to block out the reality around me. I have no idea what's going on, but from the look on Mitchell's face coupled with the smirk of satisfaction on Ryan's, I know it's harsh, and there's nothing I can do to protect Mitchell.

"I said who's the Chill?" Ryan can barely speak he's laughing so loud. He's got a blue spiral notebook in his right hand. He's waving it in the air like some TV lawyer holding up evidence, although he's dressed more like a hood defendant than a defense attorney.

"That's mine," Mitchell finally says, his voice defeated and tired. He's in his grease-stained KFC uniform, and the strain, pain, and subtle shame of his eight-hour Saturday shift shows on his face. He barely got his coat off before Ryan attacked.

"Not anymore, Chill," Ryan shouts at him from across the

room. Ryan's sitting at the kitchen table shoveling down Halo burgers before he hits his Saturday night demon streets.

Mitchell's just standing there like a sad statue recently visited by birds. I've seen the blue notebook in Mitchell's room a couple of times, but never opened it. The fact that I found it when changing the sheets, because it was tucked under the mattress, along with some *Maxim* magazines, let me know it was out of bounds, but borders mean nothing to Ryan.

"Hey, little girl, didn't you know your brother's stage name is the Chill?" Ryan bellows at me, trying to draw me in when I'd rather be out of the picture entirely.

"You . . . ," Mitchell starts, but he swallows the words. Unable to speak. A statue.

Ryan tosses the food wrappers toward the trash, but misses. As the garbage smacks onto the floor, Mitchell makes a sound very familiar to me: a whimper of hurt and humiliation.

"Seems Mitchell's going to be the next Eminem or some shit," Ryan says, leaving the garbage on the kitchen floor, then taking center stage in the living room. "It's all right here."

I finally close my book and open my mouth, for what it is worth, to speak unfamiliar words. "Ryan, please, enough."

As usual, and expected, pleading and pleasing don't work, but then again, nothing does. When Ryan decides to be this way, the best thing to do is take it, turn your body off, let your brain find a safe place, and realize that even nightmares don't last all night.

Ryan opens up the notebook, while I can see Mitchell's spirit shut down. "Seems his first CD is going to be called *The Chill Effect*," Ryan says, showing me one of the pages. He's shoving it right into my face, and like a witness to a car wreck on the interstate, I can't manage to look away.

I take a quick glance at the page filled with Mitchell's handwriting. He's Scotch-taped his school class picture to it and written "The Chill" over the top of it. Below that is a badly drawn outline of the familiar mitten shape of Michigan, with the words "The Chill Effect" written in the middle in big bold letters. The image is in the middle of a square, so it looks like a CD cover. Next to the cover is a list of songs; the titles are all pretty lame. Below that is a list called "Chill's posse," which reads like a who's who of hip-hop. Below that is a quote from *The Source* calling Mitchell "the Chill" Mallory the next big thing. I take in the whole thing in just a few seconds, but it must seem like hours to Mitchell as his fantasy life gets revealed and ridiculed.

"Look, he's even got all these lame-ass rhymes," Ryan says, pulling the notebook away, then quickly thumbing through it. I avoid looking at Mitchell, but I can imagine all too well what's going on in his head and his heart. "Why don't you kick one out, Chill!"

Ryan laughs, louder still, then throws the notebook on the floor, like garbage. I gather my book to get away, but Ryan's hand clutches my shoulder, forcing me down. I bite into my bottom lip, creating a pain I can manage, and ignore the jabbing of his fingernails into my flesh.

Mitchell finally moves away from the door to retrieve the notebook. As he picks it up, he doesn't look like this smart college-bound kid who will do anything not to end up behind bars like Robert. Instead, he looks like a tiny, defenseless child whose favorite toy was destroyed.

"Come on, Chill!" Ryan shouts, removing his hand from me. He walks over closer now to Mitchell, shouting and probably spitting right into Mitchell's face. "Bust one out, bitch."

Mitchell screams, then dives into Ryan, grabbing his legs and they crash onto the floor. Mitchell's glasses, and the notebook, go flying. Ryan throws a couple of hard punches into Mitchell's head, but they don't seem to have any effect as Mitchell clutches onto Ryan's legs.

"What's going on in there?" Mama's rough voice shouts from the hallway. I want to shout back at her: why is your hearing so good only some of the time? When Ryan hears her voice, he manages to get his legs free and rolls away from Mitchell, laughing the entire time.

"Just TV wrestling," Ryan says, resting his back against a closet door. Even though he's breathing heavily, it's not enough to force the smirk from his face. Mitchell's got a trickle of blood coming from his forehead, dripping down onto the already stained KFC uniform.

Mama emerges from the hallway, angry at being woken up from her nap. She's already in her green home health aide uniform, getting ready for an overnight shift. Her eyes are heavy, as is her voice. She lights up a cigarette and stares at us all. "Mitchell, what are you doing?"

Mitchell looks quickly at me, but in speed of light time, I manage to avoid his stare. Ryan dusts himself off, steps over Mitchell, grabs his coat, and heads out into the night, like nothing happened. Mitchell, too, remains silent as he heads toward the bathroom; lucky for him the mirror is broken so he can't see his wet eyes. I pick up the notebook, feeling ashamed to have stared into Mitchell's means of escape. His notebook isn't his planning; it was his book of dreams.

When Mitchell comes out of the bathroom maybe ten minutes later, his eyes are red and his steps are heavy as he makes his way toward his room, which isn't really his own personal private space anymore, as Ryan just demonstrated. I bury my face into my book, so we don't have to talk about what just happened. There's a lot of that at the Mallory house on Stone Street.

"He's got no right," Mitchell says, then sits down near me. His voice is soft, to avoid waking Mama and her rejection. Like me, he knows that Mama's asleep even when she's awake.

"I know," I add weakly.

Mitchell throws his head back, looks at the ceiling, and up to heaven. He'll probably pray harder than ever at church tomorrow. "That notebook was none of his business, you know."

I reach beside me, grab Mitchell's dream book and fantasy life, and hand it back to him, although we both know it can never ever be returned to what it was. It's a dirty secret now.

He takes it from me, never making eye contact, then whispers, "It just takes my mind off stuff. I know I'm not going to be anything more than this." He points at his fugly KFC costume.

"Mitchell, don't talk that way." I try to assure him, but who am I to talk? He's at least got both a dream and a plan. He's got a shot at escaping; all I have are tail lights to follow.

"What gives him the right!" he says, tearing the cover off the notebook.

"Mitchell, don't—" I shoot back, asking him to save this bit of himself, but to no avail.

He's breathing heavy as he tears up the pages of the blue

notebook into smaller and smaller pieces. I watch in stunned and sad silence as the scraps of black ink, white paper, and gold-record dreams fall like dirty snow onto the carpet. One of us will pick up these dreams now turned to trash, look at the torn pieces, then throw them out with the rest of the garbage filling our lives.

sixth grade, november

"He scares me."

"Ryan?" I say to Mitchell, who just nods.

With Daddy dead, Robert on the streets, and Mama now working two jobs, Ryan's become a real menace. That's what Mitchell and I are talking about on the swings behind Cody School late on a Saturday night. We probably shouldn't be out this late; people might say it isn't safe, but they should come to our house and see the people Ryan's invited in.

"He's just so big, you know," Mitchell says, but it's more than just that. Although Mitchell is only one grade behind me, he seems younger. While he's shorter, Mitchell already weighs more than I do and is getting fat like Mama. Like me, he'd rather read or watch TV than hang out with kids on the block. That's okay for girls, but it gets him teased a lot by other boys.

I swing a little higher. "I know, I know," I say, then push myself higher still.

"He's always busting me," Mitchell says, and I know how upset he is. There's not a lot he can do when Ryan makes fun of him for being big, wearing glasses, and being a good student. Mitchell never cries when it happens; he just disappears into himself a little deeper each day. About the only time I see him laugh anymore is when he and Cousin Tommy get together.

"You tell Mama?" I ask, even though I know the hard-fact answer.

"I tried, but . . . ," he fades off, then swings himself higher. We don't know why, but Mama seems to think Ryan can do no wrong. Both Mitchell and I have tried to tell Mama about Ryan teasing us, about his low-life friends, but she gets mad at us, not at him. Like a child, Mama wants to play pretend. We realize there's nothing more to say, so we swing higher, at least pretending we're happy.

"Let's go," I tell Mitchell after a while, knowing we shouldn't be out this late, knowing that Flint streets aren't really safe for a fifth and sixth grader to be walking on an hour before midnight, but also knowing there's no place else to go but a home that doesn't feel like home anymore. There's no trace of Daddy left at all, save my Hershey Bear and all my best memories. Right after Daddy died, Mama put up photos of Ryan's long-gone father.

"Hey, little girl," Ryan says the second Mitchell and I walk through the front door. It's Ryan's new standard greeting for me and I hate it. Anger flashes in my pale green eyes, but it has no effect. He just laughs, which causes his three friends to laugh even louder. Mitchell takes advantage of Ryan's distraction and rushes to his room before Ryan can insult him.

"Pass her the pipe," one friends says, and they all laugh. A stoned, stupid laugh. I know better than to smoke weed, just by looking at the glassy eyes and stupid grins of these four guys.

"Don't you wanna wrap your lips around Cyrus's pipe?" another of Ryan's friends says, getting a bigger laugh. These guys are all Ryan's age and they're all dressed alike, with big basketball shirts, new bright-white kicks, and black pants showing off rather than covering their asses. I sense from the hard looks, numerous tattoos, and

the rank odor of weed, that these three guys, like Robert and now Ryan, don't just look the part of thug, they live it.

"Cyrus, pass it over," another says. Like Ryan, Cyrus is wearing new sharp threads. Ryan doesn't have a job, but he's always got new clothes. He's always bringing home clothes for Mama, while all I seem to bring her is trouble and tears. No wonder she likes him better.

"Bitch, Cyrus is talking to you," Ryan shouts at me. He's high, which is nothing new, but since Mama's working tonight, he figures he can hide it from her and stay the perfect son.

Staring down at the dirty carpet, I head toward my room to be alone. Mitchell asked if he could move into my room with me and away from Ryan, but Mama won't allow it.

"Couple more years and that girl's going to be fine," Cyrus says to Ryan, but for my benefit. The other friends all laugh the loudest yet, but Ryan just leers at Cyrus, then at me.

"No, she's an ugly bitch now and she's always gonna be an ugly bitch," Ryan says, directed at me, not Cyrus. When Cyrus starts to laugh, though, Ryan turns on him, putting his finger right in his face. "But if you ever touch her, I'll cap your ass."

I race to my room, realizing there's no state of mind beyond the sadness I feel. If earlier tonight I could swing no higher, now I feel I can fall no farther. As I crawl into bed, I pull the blanket over me, but I don't disappear, nor does the clatter from the other room. After an hour of loud TV, louder shouting, and loudest laughing, the noise in the living room finally stops, and I hear the front door slam a few times. I close my eyes tight, welcoming the silence, and try to sleep. My days are so sad without Daddy anymore that I welcome every night's slumber.

I awake slowly, struggling to figure out what woke me up. Was it the sound of footsteps outside my door? Was it the light from the door opening in the middle of the night?

"Who is it?" I ask, but there's no response. I don't have a clock in my room, but it seems too early for Mama to be home. When she comes home, her loud coughing almost always wakes me up. It could be Robert, but he's rarely seen anyplace but in his room downstairs.

"Mitchell?" I whisper, but again there's no response.

I pull the blanket up tighter.

The light grows brighter and the door opens a little more, but I don't need my eyes or my ears, because the smell invades my nose.

"Good night, little girl," Ryan says, sticking his head in the room. His massive frame fills the doorway, blocking out the light. He stands there, his nearly black eyes piercing the darkness.

I don't say anything. I'll just pretend I'm asleep. I grab my favorite stuffed animal, Hershey Bear, and squeeze it. It was the best Christmas present ever from my Daddy. I hold it tight, wishing it wasn't a stuffed animal, but a magic lamp. Then I could rub the lamp and make not a genie, but Daddy appear out of a puff of smoke. Maybe that smoke would mask Ryan's foul odor. Maybe Daddy could be here to tell Ryan to never set foot at my door again.

He laughs, then leaves the door open. I hear the warped floorboards in the hall groan as he walks away. I think about telling Mama about this, about how Ryan talks to me, but like we talked about at Cody, Mitchell and I know it's no use. I thought for a while that Ryan had one of those split-personality things like you see on TV. He's one person when Mama is around, all obedient and flattering, but another when she's gone. No wonder she doesn't believe us when we tell her things. Mama's living a hard life, and anything we tell her just adds to that burden.

I try falling back asleep, but it's hard with all the noise that Ryan is making in the bathroom next to my room. He's in there for a long time and it sounds like he's gasping for breath. Finally, I hear the toilet flush, the door close, and his heavy steps walk away from my room. The light from the hall shines through the still-open door, and I can't fall back to sleep. It is a realization, not the light that blinds me. I pull Hershey Bear closer and wish the heat in the house would kick on, since the chill isn't running down my spine, but all through my body as it all makes sense: Ryan isn't a person with two personalities; he's just a person without one human soul.

10

november 24, senior year

"So how goes that CMU application?"

I look up from the school lunch line to see Ms. Chapman standing across from me. Her plate contains a colorful green salad, while I stare down at drab yellowish brown cheese fries.

"Okay," I say, paying for my shitty meal with money from selling Ryan's shit at school to some kids who probably think I'm shit. That justice is as sweet as the can of Coke on my tray.

"You haven't started it, have you?" Ms. Chapman says softly, yet I can still hear her through the crazy lunchroom racket that is Southwestern feeding time. Between the laughter, the shouts, and the regular rapping, it's a wonder I can hear anything, but somehow my hearing is supersensitive, day or night, while my vision remains poor regardless of the hour.

"No," I say as my face melts like the gooey cheese covering my fries.

"I want you to come by after school today," she says. We're holding up the line, but it doesn't seem to matter to her at all. I'm terrified at all the pissed-off eyes behind me.

"I have to work," I tell her.

"The library, right," she says, although I don't recall telling her about my job.

"Right, so I haven't had time—"

"Make it," she says sharply, and it dulls my resistance to her offer of help.

"Okay," I say, then hurry off to meet up with Anne for conversation, and Glen for business. I manage to keep my eyes in front of me, never looking to see Ms. Chapman walk away in a huff, even though I'm sure she looks beautiful and perfect even when angry. I'm glad I didn't see the disappointment in her face, just as I'm glad she didn't see the blank Central Michigan application untouched but no doubt crushed at the bottom of my backpack. I asked for Mama's help filling it out, but it never happened. I don't want to ask Anne, since she helps me so much already, and I'd be too embarrassed to ask Glen. I could see one of the school counselors, like Ms. Pfeil, but the counselors don't just help with college plans, they also organize peer counseling and all of that kind of stuff. I don't want them looking into my past, my present, my future, or my family. I make my way through the halls, my stomach sick from the smell of the fries and the taste of disappointment.

"So, do you think he's gay or what?" Anne says before I can even grab some floor space.

"Who?" I shoot back at Anne, a perfect owl impersonation as I sit down with her at our usual perch outside the theater. I'm eating the fries one at a time, letting the salt-grease combo linger in my mouth and shoot instant after-lunch sleepiness through my over-shocked system.

"Mr. McDonald," Anne replies.

"Not biting?" I say, although the disappointment shows in her face. For despite her best efforts, she's failed to capture

Mr. McDonald's attention and has chosen to move on. She said she even tried thonging him and showing him her dragon tattoo, but he didn't take the bait.

"Maybe he and Glen were meant for each other," Anne says, then winks.

"Glen isn't gay." I counter Anne's new excuse for Glen's lack of interest in me, or her, as anything other than a friend. Glen's been my crush for so long, not that I can bring myself to do anything to move from friendship to courtship. Not doing anything is a pretty good way of avoiding disappointment or hurt: you want or expect nothing, then you'll never fail or feel like a screwup. There's something comforting in the pain you know rather than the pain you don't.

"He probably loves Juliet," I say, pointing at Rani Patel, who is talking to Mr. McDonald. She's playing Juliet in the school play, opposite my Romeo. She's cast in high school as the most beautiful girl at Southwestern, a title she proudly claims and shows off. While almost every boy at school would love to study her anatomy, Glen says they have no chemistry at all on stage, while my attraction to Glen defies the laws of physics.

"Hey, Christy," Glen says, tapping me on the shoulder, which scares and soothes me.

"Hey, Glen," I say as Anne breaks out in giggles.

He shows me a twenty-dollar bill, so we walk together to the back of the theater. I open up my backpack and pull out a brown paper lunch bag. I unroll the layers of aluminum foil from the sandwich-shaped square, and then hand Glen his weekly purchase of Ryan's product in a small plastic bag. Aunt Dee, Tommy, and Mitchell would kill me if they knew about this.

"Thanks," he says, and I feel my feet lift off the ground as

I look into his eyes. He snatches my glance, staring back at me. Anything is possible. If not now, then when?

"How's the play going?" I ask.

"It goes," he says, tucking the plastic bag into a thick book he's hollowed out. How he could treat a book like that hurts me, but not enough to say anything against Glen.

"Rani Patel is just terrible," Glen says. "She may look the part, but she can't act it."

"Why's that?" I ask, leaning in closer, hoping the hairs on our arms might touch.

"She's so stuck on herself," he says with anger, while rearranging the contents of his backpack for maximum protection. I nod my head at his comment, not that he noticed. In fairness, Glen himself is not immune to ego deficiency. I know he's both dreaming and planning for big things. I imagine him on the cover of magazines, appearing on TV talk shows, or starring in movies. I dream that I'm by his side as we're walking down the red carpet as the flashbulbs blind us. I think about being interviewed, telling the story of how the two of us met, ignoring these dirty dealings, and instead painting a different picture. If I'm going to tell myself lies, I might as well invent the best ones. Yet, I can't imagine it all. I can imagine Glen and me getting married; I see the family pictures of us with our beautiful children; I see us loving our children, but not the loving act of conceiving them. I have lots of dreams, but never any fantasies.

"Well, Rani is beautiful," I state the obvious, just to injure my deflated ego even more.

"And she always wants the two of us to rehearse together, just the two of us."

I frown, hating her for being so clever and me so consumed with fear. "Why?"

"She thinks we need to work together more. I know that I need to rehearse more in order to learn my lines, but not with her. I need to find—" but before he can finish, Anne's mantra of "take action" shouts from memory past my shy meter and out of my mouth.

"I could rehearse with you," I say in less than a whisper.

He pauses for a second that feels like an hour to me. "I don't know."

"I understand if you don't want to," I say, taking a step back. "I don't really—"

"Oh, it's not you. I think it could be fun," he says, laughing, then pantomiming like he was smoking a joint. "We couldn't tell Rani, though."

"I'm good at keeping secrets," I say with far too much modesty.

"I also probably couldn't tell my girlfriend," he says as my heart breaks.

"Your girlfriend," I mouth the words.

"She's at Northern. You'd like her," he says, but he's not looking at me. He's studying the simple patterns on the hall floor, while I'm listening to the complex quiver in his voice.

"My brother Mitchell goes to Northern, maybe he knows her," I say flatly.

"Well, she's new there, and it's a big school, so, maybe not," he says quickly.

"Where did she used to go to school?" I ask, gathering information for an obituary that I would like to write about this girl whose capital crime is murdering years of my dreams.

He pauses, like he's stumped for an answer; it's a position I've never seen him in during any class we've had together or any play I've seen him in, which is all of them. "What?"

"Did she used to go here?" I ask, trying not to be difficult. It's not that I'm trying to interrogate Glen, but I'm just used to asking questions. And this information, I need to know.

"No, she went to Grand Blanc," he says, pulling up his dark blue shirtsleeve to look at his watch. It's one of my favorites: the contrast of the dark blue of his shirt with the light blue of his lying eyes. I know the contents of his closet better than he does.

"What's her name?" I ask to prolong the conversation and his attention. "My cousin Tommy used to go to Grand Blanc, maybe—"

"Look, Christy, I really have to get going," Glen says. We've made eye contact once again, so Rani and the nameless probably nonexistent Northern girlfriend matter not. Liars like myself have a good sense of when someone is jerking our chain.

"So?" I ask, confused by his deceit, and yet delighted with it at the same time. I'm happy he doesn't really have a girlfriend, but also confused about why he'd make up such a story.

He pauses for a long time, running his thumb along his bottom lip. "What light through yonder window breaks?" he finally says, and I break out in a smile as bright as the sun. As my smile lights up my life and the darkness of the hallway, I chase my dreams like they were tail lights. I want to believe that Glen will lead me to a real human touch because Seth doesn't count.

eighth grade, november

"I just said that flute thing just to tease you. You know that, right?"

I'm staring at Seth Lewis, wondering why he's so mean to me, and why I'm with him.

"It's okay, I guess." I speak into the cracked concrete sidewalk, avoiding his creepy stare. I'm still mad at him, but we walk home from school together. It beats walking and feeling alone. I hear boys at school tease girls they like, but I can't imagine Seth likes me like that.

"I was just trying to be funny," he says, taking a step away. We're standing in front of his house, which is a few blocks from mine. There's an old rotted red sofa in the front yard. The lawn is covered in leaves that will never be raked. The house has a few broken windows and plenty of peeling pink paint. The driveway is as pitted as the sidewalk, the steps to the wooden front porch are tilting, and the street in front is mostly potholes. There's a broken-down brown Chevy pickup in the driveway next to a ripped-open trash bag filled mostly with beer bottles.

I blow on my hands to keep them warm and start to walk away, but stop when I see Seth looking at me with his sad puppy-dog eyes. I accept the overdue apology, then say, "I guess."

"So, you wanna do something?" It's Friday night, which I guess

is supposed to matter. I overhear my classmates talking about their big weekend plans. My guess is they're mostly telling each other lies, but the truth is there's nothing for me to do, especially if Ryan and his friends are in the house, stinking it up with smoke, swearing, and pornos. I guess that's why I'm here at Seth's house. He's a weird kid but he talks to me, even if it's mostly teasing. He doesn't talk to other girls, and I don't blame him. They all spend their time talking about boys, trying to make their breasts look bigger, putting on makeup, and fixing, spraying, gelling, and brushing their hair. Me, I don't talk about boys, I hide my body, I don't wear makeup, and I've chopped off my hair. It's a chicken and egg thing: was I always ugly or did I make myself that way? Do I believe Daddy's long-lost loving words or Ryan's hateful daily put-downs?

"Sure, like what?" I ask.

"I don't know," he shrugs, as clueless and lonely as I am. I guess that's why I'm talking to Seth. Just to fit in with someone, even if it's someone as rejected and unlikable as me.

"Wanna walk over to Cody?" I ask him. Sometimes I go there alone or with Mitchell, and hang out on the swings. Twilight's a good time: the younger kids are all in for the evening, and the older ones aren't out yet. The young ones play on the swings, pretending to fly, while the ground littered with matches, burned ends of joints, and beer cans show that the older kids swing higher a different way. I want to swing, even though the bars are rusted and the seats are torn, dirty, and frayed, not so much as to get high or pretend to fly, but instead to imagine that I can go fast enough and high enough to break through time. I don't have to be twelve; I don't have to turn twenty; instead, I could be eight forever. I can't plan a future, so I'll dream of the past.

"No, do you just wanna come inside and watch TV or something," he says after another long pause. If he's not teasing, he can barely talk to me it seems. "My dad's not home."

I just shake my head, and we're both kind of silent for a while. "Okay, fine."

I walk inside his house for the first time; it's a mess, even worse than ours, which I didn't think was possible. There are dirty dishes on a dining table and a thick layer of dust on everything, including the TV screen. There's a single lightbulb in the middle of the room, but the rest of the rooms are dark. It doesn't look like a house; it looks like a cave for humans.

"I can get us schnapps," he whispers toward my ear. His breath is like rotten apples.

"I gotta go," I say, turning back toward the door, knowing this is all wrong. Maybe it's watching my mom finish off a six-pack of Budweiser every night, but I don't want to drink. Getting high, however, makes me feel better and connects me with Glen.

"You're too good." He sounds both hurt and hurtful. "Or are you a bad girl?"

"Just leave me alone," I tell him, knowing this is a mistake, but my feet don't respond to fear by running. Instead, my ears take over as the word alone *just explodes in my brain like a bomb.* Alone. Lonely. *The words bounce off the empty beer cans then crash back into my ears, running like acid through my blood, then dripping out of my eyes. I lean up against the hard door. The doorknob jabbing into my back feels painfully familiar.*

In this dim light, with a glint of desperate loneliness in my eyes I take a good look at Seth Lewis: he's poor, he's pudgy, he's ugly, and I don' have the heart to knock his hand away from my arm. When he puts his dry thin lips against mine, I still don't push him away. I don't know why I let him kiss me, but maybe it was the same reason that Brutus got hit by a car. If you've been chained up for so long and you get a chance at feeling free, you take it without thinking.

"That's enough," I say, moving away from him. He answers by pushing toward me, trying to jam his rotten-apple-smelling tongue into my mouth and stuff his fat fingers under my baggy T-shirt. I wonder what he thinks he'll find there. If he would let his hand linger long enough over my heart, instead of frantically trying to get under my why-even-bother bra, he'd know everything. I pin his arm so he can't feel me, but then again, I can't feel myself. If he could stop his heavy breathing, if he could cease the loud smacking of his lips against mine, then he would know that my heart isn't beating, that my body isn't responding, because I'm not there. I'm inside my mind as he's inside my shirt. My arms try to push him away, while he presses his soft stomach against me. He's about an inch shorter than me, so he's standing on his tiptoes. I'm looking past him, down at the stained yellowish carpet. His kisses have hurt, not healed, my bruised bottom lip. The moldy carpet smell chokes off my breathing through my nose, since his tongue fills my mouth, while my ears fill with a screeching metallic noise.

"I'm going home," I tell him, then try to push him away.

"Come on, you tease," he says pushing me back up against the wall, his hand in my belt. I realize it's his own zipper undone, not mine. He presses up against me. "Blow me."

I don't say anything. Instead I see the terror in my face reflected in his eyes. I feel the familiar fright crawling all over my body, like maggots eating a decaying corpse. Even though he's a boy, I'm stronger and taller than he is, so I manage to free myself. As I'm running toward the door, he's yelling at me. "You tease, you whore," he throws down, but the words don't mean anything to me because I know the truth of who I was and who I am now.

"Don't ever talk to me again," I scream over my shoulder.

"I won't," he shouts from across the room. "Bitch, you're on my shit list forever."

I turn to face him, then scream, "You're such a loser."

As soon as I get outside, I wipe my arm across my mouth, but the taste of his tongue remains. I run faster and harder than I've ever run before. I get to the bridge in record time, but instead of chasing tail lights, I watch the vomit shoot out of my mouth.

11

morning, november 30, senior year

"Hey, you want some nice new Christmas clothes?"

"No thank you, Ryan," Aunt Dee says nicely, passing by the pile of brightly colored women's clothes with price tags still attached. Bringing home clothes to Mama is another way Ryan keeps his favored position, but Aunt Dee's not taking anything that wasn't paid for.

"But this is good shit, know what I'm saying," Ryan says, holding up a nice red blouse, only slightly rumpled from when Ryan lifted it from the rack and stuffed it under his long coat.

Ryan never steals anything for me, and that's just fine. I try my best to ignore him and the blaring TV, while I'm waiting for Anne to come pick me up this chilly Sunday November morning for us to go cruising in the PT Cruiser. We're going clothes shopping: well, she is shopping and I am going, which is our typical arrangement.

"Sorry, nothing for you, Cuz," Ryan says, pointing at Tommy who is standing by the front door. It's the first time I've seen

Tommy since he got out of Genesee County Juvenile Hall this September. He doesn't look that different: he still looks like a person in charge with his over-six-foot frame and penetrating brown eyes. Still, he looks harder and older than his eighteen years. It's weird how just nine months can age someone, even outside the womb.

Tommy doesn't say anything, just shoots Ryan a look that could kill, and I wish it would. Aunt Dee and Mitchell are taking Bree to church. It's a Sunday ritual that isn't adhered to by all in this household. Mama says she wants to go every Sunday, but instead she ends up with some girlfriends driving down to the Detroit casinos to worship slot machines and blackjack tables.

"Don't be dissin' me, Cuz," Ryan says through his always present smart-ass smirk.

"Mitchell, see if Bree is ready?" Tommy asks Mitchell, who has stepped from the bedroom wearing his brown churchgoing suit, which is much nicer than his fugly uniform. Bree is spending time at Aunt Dee's over this weekend, which fills me with dread. I've wanted to spend nights there, but since Tommy is around my same age, Aunt Dee won't allow it. She knows how screwed up our family is without two cousins hooking up, not that I've ever once thought about Tommy in that way. So Bree spends nights in a nice warm condo in Grand Blanc, while I'm trapped in the cold cell of Stone Street. I should thank the god that I don't believe in for Anne's red car and her restlessness, which allow me a few hours of escape.

"She's almost ready. You sure you don't want to come with us, Christy?" Mitchell says as he buttons up his coat and heads outside. He asks out of habit, knowing I'll always say no.

"What are you looking at?" Ryan suddenly shouts at Tommy. I'm standing in the corner of the room, but Ryan looks like he's having trouble standing. I never look at my watch when I smell him enter the house, but I knew he came home late last night. He's acting so irritable not because he had to get up early, but because I don't think he's been to bed yet. I smell the stench of his cologne, vodka, and dope smoke even from across the room.

Tommy shrugs, turns on his heel, and starts walking toward Bree's room when Ryan grabs his beefy arm, spinning him around. "I'm talking to you, loser!"

Tommy pulls his arm away, looks at Ryan, shakes his head in disgust, and then starts laughing. "I'll get Bree," Tommy says, walking away from the insult and attack. He knows too well the consequences of not walking away from trouble from his stint in juvy jail.

"Loser, what the—" Ryan starts.

"That's enough, young man!" Aunt Dee says with her best authoritative flight attendant voice. She always dresses nicely, wearing clothes that she bought, which are nicer than any Ryan steals. Like me, Aunt Dee's tall, but the resemblance ends there. She's got a curved, shapely body, long, dyed-blond hair, and wears more jewelry than I own. She's one of these women everybody calls striking. She's another human tail light in my life. I still dream about living with Aunt Dee rather than at my home. But I fear the nightmare of Mama's likely response if I asked to leave. She'd probably say, "Go ahead, Christy, I don't want you here anyway."

Ryan heats things up by lighting up a small cigar, blowing the smoke in Aunt Dee's direction. "I don't take orders from nobody," Ryan says, knowing having her against him is more points for him in Mama's eyes.

"And that's why you'll never leave here," Aunt Dee says in the most dismissive voice possible. Ryan used to try to play Aunt Dee like he plays Mama, but she's never had any of it. "Don't speak to me again until you learn how to speak correctly. Your language is disgraceful."

"Chill, Aunt Dee, I was kidding, you know what I'm saying," Ryan says, pulling smoke into his lungs and trying to blow smoke up her ass.

"Ryan, you'll never change," Aunt Dee says, then walks away. Ryan's smiling, not understanding Aunt Dee has dissed him. I'm smiling, realizing she has. I put on an old green cap and two pairs of gloves, since the holes don't overlap, and join Mitchell on the snow-covered sidewalk out front. Aunt Dee, as always, tells me to have a blessed day before I leave.

"Ryan's such a disgrace," Mitchell says, pacing back and forth, trying to keep warm.

"What do you mean?"

"Did you see how he dresses?" Mitchell asks, adding a furious headshake underscoring his disapproval and disgust at Ryan's attire.

There's nothing unusual about it; it's pretty standard stuff for north of Bristol Road: oversize basketball shirt, baggy pants hanging down around his thighs, a bunch of gold chains, and expensive sneaks. His wardrobe is mostly stolen, or purchased with cash from other stuff he's stolen, and then pawned. That's yet another reason I won't wear his hand-me-downs. I even hate to wash his clothes, because the smell of cologne, vodka, and smoke never washes away no matter how hard I scrub.

I'm hearing Mitchell with one ear, listening for Anne with the other. "What do you mean?"

"He's living proof of every negative thing folks with money think about poor people. They don't see people like me, they're too busy fearing the Ryans of the world. Every step I take forward, people like Ryan kick me to the back of the line," Mitchell says sharply and sadly.

I nod in agreement.

"Let's get going," I hear Aunt Dee shout from the front door. Bree looks so cute in her new blue dress, a present from Ryan's fast fingers.

Mitchell heads toward the car, while I look down the street, waiting for Anne.

"Christy, long time no see." I turn around to see Tommy just behind me. "I wasn't ignoring you in there, but I just don't like talking around Ryan, know what I mean?"

I nod quickly in agreement. "How you doing?"

"It's nice to be out, Christy," Tommy says softly. For such a big guy, his deep voice is almost always soft and warm, like a loud whisper. "I ain't going back."

I nod in agreement. When Robert ended up in Jackson, everybody had known it was really a matter of when, not if. But no one thought Tommy would end up behind bars, especially him.

"I know this sounds crazy, but it was the best thing ever to happen to me," he says.

"What do you mean?" I ask.

"It gave me a chance to slow down, to think, to plan, and to decide," he says, each word very deliberate.

"You got your GED too, right?" I ask, remembering the pride in Aunt Dee's voice, since unlike Robert or Ryan, Tommy at least graduated from high school, even if it was done behind bars.

"Yeah, so I can go to college and learn something useful, not like in there," he says.

"That's great, Tommy, just great."

"I mean, I could have learned useful stuff in there, except it would all be how to become more like Ryan and Robert," Tommy says, then laughs for no reason. "If Robert could get out, he'd be made. Best thug education in the world is behind bars. It's like a college for criminals."

"But you were never a thug," I remind him.

"Well, maybe not, but I did a violent thing, and I got punished," Tommy says. "But I also learned I've got to stop thinking about what I want; now, I'm thinking about what I need."

"Tommy, let's go," I hear Aunt Dee shout from the window of her car, a new dark blue Volvo, and just as she's backing up, I see Anne's car cruise in front of the house. I blink quickly, hoping I could make my family disappear, but Tommy's still standing next to me.

"Wake up, sunshine!" I hear Anne yell, followed by the sound of her honking the horn. I wave to Anne and start toward the car. Anne's never been inside my house and never will. She doesn't need to see the leaking roof, the pillows jammed against broken windows, and the rented furniture. Mama works long, hard hours, but somehow there's never enough money to fix the house. There's just enough to make the rent.

"So who is that? Tommy asks as he follows me down the sidewalk.

"That's my best friend, Anne Williams," I say, proud to label her as such.

"Hey, Christy," Anne says, a big smile appearing on her madeup face. I notice Tommy staring at Anne. She's wearing a black fake fur coat and a funky yellow ski cap: she's got a bad hat habit. I climb in, then blast up the heat. It's always too cold in my house.

Before I can speak, Tommy turns into Mr. Manners. "Pleased to meet you, Miss Williams." He flashes his best smile, piles on all the charm he can summon, and fixes his eyes on her. If she wasn't wearing gloves, it looks like he'd be ready to kiss her hand.

"This is my cousin Tommy," I say, trying not to giggle at what I sense are some serious vibes jumping between these two people.

"My pleasure," he says with total confidence in his voice, the same kind of confidence that Anne seems to have. Tommy heads back toward the car to join Aunt Dee, Mitchell, and Bree for church, but looking at the almost glaze in Anne's eyes, it looks like she's found her savior this Sunday morning. As Anne pulls away, Tommy keeps our attention with an oversized wave filling the rearview mirror. Watching my house disappear from Anne's rearview mirror is always the sweetest sight of any day.

before seventh grade, august

"Can I come live with you?"

"What's wrong, Christy?" Aunt Dee asks.

"Everything." Since Daddy died, everything is wrong. The house is filled with nothing but sadness and chaos. The sadness mainly from Mitchell and me; the chaos courtesy of Ryan. Robert's not around enough, since he comes, goes, and does as he pleases. Daddy couldn't control him, having a child didn't change him, and Mama doesn't even try. With Daddy gone, Mama's not just ignoring me—it's almost like she's punishing me for having been Daddy's little girl.

"I'm sorry, but I've got my hands full," Aunt Dee says, pointing across the park toward her son, Tommy. Tommy, Robert, Ryan, and a bunch of other male cousins are playing basketball. Mitchell's on the sidelines, watching Tommy's every move. Everybody's on the skins team. We're out at Kearsley Park on a baking-hot August day for the annual family reunion on Daddy's side.

"Okay," I say, accepting her answer and my fate, just that simply.

"I know you miss your daddy," Aunt Dee says, wiping the sweat from her brow. She's in her Sunday best, even at a party. She reaches across the table toward me, but I pull back.

"This is so crazy," I say, shaking my super-short-haired head in

slow disbelief. It's weird to think that everybody's laughing, listening to music, eating, yelling, and drinking, like nothing happened. Like Daddy's still alive. Like everything was still the same.

"What's that?" Aunt Dee asks.

"Just how everybody's having a good time," I say, unable to join in, but that's something I'm growing used to more every day it seems. Next year at school, I just want to figure out how to go from class to class without being noticed, spoken to, or bothered. Or touched.

"I know it's hard," Aunt Dee says, her voice gentle and soothing.

"Why couldn't Ryan come live with you or somebody else?" I ask. Robert couldn't care less about Ryan, other than using him to sell shit and run his errands. The only thing Robert seems to care about is his daughter, Bree. If Ryan was out of the house, I think everything would be okay.

"That's complicated," Aunt Dee replies.

"But . . . ," I start, then stop. I'd like to tell Aunt Dee more, but to talk about it makes it real, to deny it means nothing is really happening. It's like I have an imaginary enemy.

"Christy, I don't know. Your mama doesn't talk with me much, you know that?"

"I know," I say, looking away, embarrassed. Aunt Dee made something of herself, while Mama just makes it through every day for herself. Everybody knows Dee's son, Tommy, is going to college someday; everybody knows that Robert's going to prison or to an early grave. Everybody knows these things, but nobody talks about them.

"You know how I invite your mama to church all the time," Aunt Dee says.

I shake my head. Every Wednesday and Sunday, whenever she's in town, Aunt Dee comes by the house to take any of us to church.

Daddy never went, but he did insist that all of us go. Mama talks about Jesus a lot, but she never seems to have time for him either.

"I know that Ryan's father wasn't a very nice man to your mother or to Ryan, so maybe your mother feels guilty about that," Aunt Dee says.

"What do you mean?" I ask, looking over my shoulder for Mama. I know I'll catch hell if she catches me talking to Aunt Dee like this. To Mama, Aunt Dee isn't real family.

"I don't mean to be uncharitable, but your mother hasn't led a very Christian life, so maybe loving Ryan unconditionally is her way of returning to God's good graces," Aunt Dee says. I don't say anything. Instead, I look over my shoulder again. Mama's sitting with a group of women smoking, drinking, and playing cards. She takes a break every now and again to fuss over Bree, like I can't imagine she ever fussed over me. Love in my family skipped a generation.

"Christy, just believe in God, and everything will be all right," Aunt Dee says, then crosses herself. To her, every day is a blessed day. To me, every day has become a cursed one.

"But it's not all right," I mumble.

Aunt Dee doesn't say anything, and I know there's nothing else to say. She's found her savior; I've yet to find mine.

"Come on, let's go see Breezy girl," Aunt Dee finally says, and we both get up from the table. We walk by the basketball court, walk by Robert's tattooed body, walk by Tommy's winning smile, and walk by Ryan's losing leer. We walk by all of those things over toward where Mama is sitting. And when I see Mama, I know there's nothing to say or do. And I know when I look at her, I will see the scariest sight of all: myself in twenty years.

12

afternoon, november 30, senior year

"Let's just chase some tail lights for a while, okay?"

"And pass up the mall the weekend after Thanksgiving?" Anne says sarcastically.

We've just finished a fast-food breakfast, which Anne generously paid for, and have climbed back in the car. The mall means Genesee Valley, Flint's oldest and biggest mall. Maybe because I've never gone there a lot except with Anne, I've never felt comfortable there. There are lots of places in Flint like that, like this morning at breakfast at the Miller Road McDonald's. I have to sit in a booth; I just hate sitting at a table in the center where everyone can look at us.

"Pick a truck," Anne says, as we pull back out onto Miller Road.

I nod, but pickings are slim for this time Sunday morning. After a bit, I spot one with Texas plates turning onto the entrance ramp to I-69 West. "Chase him!"

Anne quickly cuts across a lane of traffic, almost killing us both. She's a terrible driver, but she's better than I am, since my only real solo driving experience almost ended in arrest.

"You wanna get high?" Anne says, steering with one hand, opening her purse with the other, all the while keeping her eyes glued to the Texas plate in front of us. I don't like when Anne smokes and steers.

"No, I don't need to." I wave her off.

She laughs, that deep, rich, laugh. "I don't need to either. I asked if you wanted to.

"Do you know why I like to get high?" Anne asks. Before I can answer, which would be to guess it's for the same reasons I do, she starts in. "Because it feels good!"

"Sure, but—" I counter.

"No but, even though I got plenty of butt," Anne jokes. She seems as comfortable in her body as I am uncomfortable in mine.

"You're right, it is a great escape and—"

"That's not it at all," she says. "For me, it's not an escape, crutch, or any of that other DARE crap they taught us in school or the scary stuff that my dad always says when he launches into one of his endless antidrug lectures."

"What do you mean?" I love to hear Anne talk: she's so passionate about stuff.

"Face it, for lots of things, there's just no reason to do it other than it feels good," Anne says in full argument mode. She'd make just as good a lawyer as she would a doctor, I bet. "It doesn't hurt anybody and makes your own body feel good. It's kind of like sex, I guess."

I shift uncomfortably in my seat, wondering when we'll see a rest stop.

"You know you never answered me about that?" Anne reminds me.

"About?" I reply, but I know.

"Are you still a virgin?" She waits, giving me plenty of time to finally answer the question, which, of course, I won't. We'll talk about boys and crushes, but I don't want to talk about what happens next. Instead, I just stare ahead as our Texas trucker picks up speed.

"It's okay if you don't want to answer," she says as a batch of heavy gray November Michigan clouds appear. "You know what I'm talking about. About sex stuff feeling good."

I turn away even from the truck, stare out the side window, and shut my eyes. Anne's not only the one who always steers the car, she's always the one steering the conversation.

"Don't you even, you know," Anne says, quickly taking another hit.

"What?" I reply, giving in.

"Well, it's something you do when you are alone," Anne says, raising her eyebrow while I shift my embarrassed body uncomfortably in the seat. "Christy, don't you, you know?"

I avoid the question by closing my eyes and my mouth.

The conversation stalls as the speed of the truck in front increases once we get out of Flint. Tired of waiting for my answer, Anne clicks on the radio, and I start to drift off to a relaxed sleep. With the background noise of some thrash band filling my ears, my mind fills with the clashing sounds of a thousand thoughts slamming against each other.

"Welcome to Lansing!" Anne shouts, giving me a light poke.

I look at the clock on the dash; I've been asleep for

about an hour. I'm feeling refreshed, since I rarely sleep peacefully at home. Mostly, I rely on short naps at school to keep me sane.

"You ever been to Lansing before?" Anne asks.

I wipe the sleep out of my eyes. "Never," I say. Except for school field trips and a funeral in Ohio, I've never been out of Flint, except to visit Robert in Jackson.

"My uncle lives here. He's a chemistry professor at Michigan State," she says as we start to exit off the expressway. "I said good-bye to Mr. Texas a few miles back. Sorry."

"It's okay," I say.

"We're going to this upscale Meridian Mall, to get you something nice," Anne says.

"Thanks, doctor," I almost whisper. There's a New Year's Eve party at Rani's for all the theater students that Glen invited us to. I want to wear something other than some ill-fitting dress purchased at the Salvation Army, which never seems to have anything in my awkward size. Anne insisted on buying me a nice dress as an early Christmas present. I'm thinking about making her a homemade collage with photos of famous people so it looks like they are talking to Anne in her senior picture. I would put myself in the collage, but senior pictures are something else I can't afford and really don't even want.

"What are friends for?" Anne asks, and I don't have an answer for that query either.

"You don't really need to buy me a present," I say, but not protesting too loudly.

Anne pauses for a second, sprays the car with an overwhelming pine-scented air freshener, then cracks open the window.

"Okay, then, I won't buy you anything. Instead, why don't you sell me something and then we'll be even."

"You bought it already," I say, pointing to the ashtray we've yet to empty.

"No, I had something else in mind," she says, pulling her hat over her eyes.

"Okay, what do you want to buy?"

"Your cousin Tommy's phone number," she says with a laugh, then gets out the car.

The Meridian Mall is packed with shoppers going to stores I've never been to, like Aeropostale and Hollister Co. It's a little overwhelming, since I hate big crowds, but also interesting to see all the different faces, even if most of the girls look like Barbies. We don't have a lot of time. Anne needs to get home to work tonight. Since we have probably an hour drive in front of us, it seems this trip was mostly about the driving, not the destination.

"Look at that dress!" Anne says, pointing to a simple, elegant yet sexy white dress in the window at Victoria's Secret. It can't fit me, since it is the anti-Christy: I'm complex, ungraceful, and blue most of the time. I feel out of place in the store: everybody dresses like a model and comes from money; I look lost in my long black Tupac T-shirt covering my black big-pocket pants, while Anne's not quite nerdy, not quite Goth trendy style fits right in. She insists, so we barge into Victoria's Secret, like wild women on a mission. "That's for you!" she shouts.

I look at the dress's plunging neckline and shake my head furiously. "That's your style."

"I might buy one for myself as well, but not as a dress," Anne says.

"Then what?" I ask, wondering if Anne knows how uncomfortable I feel right now.

She reaches into her purse and quickly pulls out her Visa card. "A weapon!"

"A what?" I reply, adjusting my ears from the din of the mall noise to the pounding techno soundtrack of the trendy shopping experience.

"If I wore this dress in front of my boss, I think he'd have a heart attack from all the blood rushing from his body to—"

"Got it," I shoot back.

"I've got to do something. We've got all these holiday parties, and I just can't take my boss hovering around me and making these sly little sexual comments. It's so strange."

"Maybe we should switch jobs," I offer weakly. Then I could save Anne from the leers of her lecherous boss, and she could save me from Terrell's attention, followed by his eventual rejection.

"Maybe," Anne says as we cruise around the store jammed with holiday shoppers. Every time I see a couple holding hands, I'm envious.

"Can I help you?" this way-too-thin college-age girl asks almost the second Anne takes one small step away. I just shake my head, and start looking for the dress in the window.

"I'm going to look at some lingerie; be right back," Anne shouts as she walks away.

"Can I help you find something?" another clerk asks; she looks a lot like the other one.

"I'm fine," I say again, unaccustomed to so much attention. About the only store Mama and I ever shop at that sells new stuff is K-Mart, where nobody helps you.

"Are you finding what you need?" This one is a little older with jet-black-dyed hair, and her name tag says manager. Her manner also tells me she's in charge.

"No, I'm just looking," I reply. I don't know why, but I hate asking for help. In almost every part of my life I'm so dependent upon others that anything I can do for myself, I will.

I finally spy the rack with the dress in the window and start toward it.

"Find what you needed yet?" It's the first girl, the stick figure with skin. She's standing right next to me as I pick through the dresses, vainly trying to find one in my odd body size.

"I think I found it," I say with pride, but I see there's a couple of dresses on the same rack I want to try. So unaccustomed to buying new clothes or even having the chance to shop in a nice store like this, I decide to take advantage of the opportunity and pick up a couple of different styles and sizes. I'm undecided about how much of my athletic legs and how little of my anemic cleavage to show to get Glen's attention at the party. I pick six dresses, and walk toward the back, no doubt with a goofy grin on my face.

"I'm sorry, you can only have two items in the dressing room," the manager says, holding out her hands to me. "You'll need to put four of those back."

I'm just about ready to respond, when I suddenly take it all in. I look around the store and it is filled with other people shopping, but none of the clerks are asking them if they need help.

No one is talking to Anne. Other people—all college girls in hundred-dollar dresses or high schools girls wearing pearls with cashmere sweaters—are going into the dressing room with five or six articles of clothing. I see this big white sign with small black letters asking people to limit the number of items in the dressing room to five. Not two, but five. I turn around and look behind me to see the manager staring at me, not like I was a person, but like I was garbage. Like I was trash. Poor white trash. I toss the dresses on the floor, then I run like the track star I know Ms. Chapman believes I can be. I race from the store crying and knowing no matter how fast I run, I can't accelerate time to turn myself instantly from an ugly moth to a beautiful butterfly.

"What's wrong?" Anne says gently when we meet up outside a few minutes later. I'm drying my eyes and leaning up against the window of the passenger side of her mom's car. SUVs, Hummers, and other cars circle the parking lot, shoppers walking by with bags in one hand, cell phones in the other. All around me is the wealth of the world. And inside me is a wasteland.

"I hate this," I say, then look down at my tattoo, wishing I could get free from being me.

Anne opens the door for me, and I crawl inside. Before she can even start the car, I've lit up our last joint. I inhale deeply and let the dope drown me. "Are you okay?" she asks.

"No, I'm not okay, Anne," I shout at her. "Did you see what happened?"

Anne shakes her head, but it doesn't open her eyes at all.

"Never mind," I say, the anger burning away with the rolling paper and weed.

"They said you left without buying anything, so . . . ," Anne says, and it's then I notice she's holding a Victoria's Secret bag.

"Thanks, Dr. Williams," I say, hating myself for taking the bag, but happy for a friend like her. I wish I was like Anne and able to stand up for myself rather than need her support.

"Well, maybe you can put in a word for me with your cousin, you think?" Anne says, then smiles. I offer her the joint, but she waves it away.

"I think," I say, then pull the dope again into my lungs. I'm smoking green, and it makes perfect sense as I'm green with envy. If Anne hooks up with Tommy, then I'll never see her. I'll be friendless again, but it will be worse because she'll be in love and I'll be alone.

"Now what?" Anne says, as we start out of the parking lot.

"If not now, then when," I mutter, half hoping she won't hear me.

"Glen?" she asks, and I nod. I look again at my ankle, then look at my sad green eyes in the car's mirror. I think about all the beautiful girls in the store and the pain it causes. Pain I must give a name and a shape and a place. "Anne, do you mind getting to work a little late?"

"Not really," Anne says, then shrugs.

"Do you remember where that tattoo place was?" I ask, as calm as terror can sound.

"I think so, why?" Anne says, trying not to laugh.

I take a deep hit from the joint and feel the lack of fear and hurt and life float through my body. "If I'm going to be treated like a freak, I might as well look like one."

"Are you sure?" Anne says, so unaccustomed to my taking the first step.

"Bring on the pain," I say, then rub my hands along the virgin flesh of my ears and nose. I stick out my also virgin tongue, capturing my reflection in the side mirror. I'm sucking in this last image of this version of myself before I dance on its grave.

sophomore year, december

"So what did you think of the book?"

I'm sitting in the unfamiliar desk in front of the class clutching Ms. Chapman's copy of Speak, *trying to keep tears from falling from my green-and-white ovals. In exchange for taking a grade demotion, she let me do my oral report after school for an audience of one.*

"Christy, come on now, tell me what you thought of the book," she prods me again, but the words remain buried in my throat. I hold my notes in my hand, clutching them like life itself.

"Can't I just hand this in," I ask, in the smallest voice I can imagine, offering up my handwritten notes and hoping she's not noticing that my hand in shaking.

"No, this is an oral report, so . . ." she leans back in her chair, and I watch her mouth: frown, smile, or whatever expression she flashes my way, it's like a traffic signal.

"I don't want to disappoint you," I say, waiting for a go sign, but I'm shut down.

She shakes her head, then stares right at me. "That's playing to lose, Christy."

"What?"

"If you want to please me, that's one thing," she offers, not knowing how true that is. I'm not sure why, but since day one in her class

I've wanted her approval. Even if I've continued my invisible woman impression, I've fought the urge to sleep almost every morning. "That means you want something, but if you don't want to disappoint me, well that's something else."

I bite my bottom lip until it bleeds. She hands me a tissue. "Sorry," I whisper.

"My blood type is 'be positive,'" she says, then smiles. "Now, let's talk about the book."

"I liked it, but it's hard to explain," I finally offer, moving down in my chair.

"What did you like about it?" she asks, and my eyes dart back to floor.

I look down at my notes, the product of my hand talking to my head. I feel the pressure in my chest, my heart coming alive. I bite again on my bottom lip, but my mouth won't open.

"What did you think of the main character?" she says, causing more pain as my mouth fights to form words. What can I say about Melinda, the girl in Speak*? A girl suffering in silent sadness? A girl shunned by her classmates? A girl without friends and without much of a family to support her? What do I think about a girl who has been a victim? What do I think? I don't think and I won't feel. I so badly want to answer, but I can't bridge the gap between what I want to say and what I need to swallow.*

"Christy, I'm willing to meet you halfway, but you have to give me something; if not, then I have no choice but to give you an F on this assignment," she says.

"Whatever you want to do," I say, able to breathe again as I try to hide in plain sight.

"No, Christy, I don't have a choice, but you do," she says. "It is what you want."

I finally start to talk, and it's a familiar feeling. I hear myself saying these words, talking about this book like it was any other book, when it's not, and I wonder if Ms. Chapman knows that. I suspect she knows more than that, so I make sure that I tell her nothing. After I finish, I hand her my notes, then sit down, exhausted from the effort.

"Pretty good, but you can do better," she says, handing me another book. I look at the tattered paperback of Dreamland *by somebody named Sarah Dessen. I read the description, then sink back into my seat even more. "Christy, sit up straight and—"*

"And?" I say and she lets the words hang free, like a life saver or maybe a noose.

"Walk tall," she finally says, then hands me back my notes. Written at the top is more than a grade. Written at the top of the paper is this: "B positive."

13

december 6, senior year

"You look tired, Mama."

As I get a few steps into the house, I realize the floor isn't shaking from the booming noise from Ryan's basement room but the windows are rattling from the blaring TV. Mama's plopped down on the broken-down coach, towels covering the many holes, and watching TV with her eyes closed. I wonder if one of the reasons everybody in my house always sounds like they're yelling is because we compete with the noise of all these loud reality TV shows. I mumble my words to her, but she doesn't wake up, just like she doesn't hear footsteps at night.

I'm waiting for her to shout at me: "Surprise," but the words don't come. Balloons don't come pouring from the ceiling, friends don't come charging from hidden spaces, and there's no cake with eighteen candles on the table. My eighteenth birthday vanishes like all the others, just another day in my life unnoticed by most. Anne has bought me an iPod, sort of. After her most recent fight with her father about her job but also explaining to him who Tommy was, her mother made the peace by buying

Anne another piece of electronics, which she then gave to me. A used gift from Anne is more than I got at home.

I head to my room to start on my English homework. Breezy is reading a book, body buried under a blanket, and her ears buried under headphones. Even in my room, the TV blares, so I also put on my old twisted black headphones to test out the new-to-me white iPod.

The headphones hurt pressed against the four piercings and small mock-silver studs lining each of my ears. My ears still hurt, but more from my mother's reaction to me when I came home with my new look. She didn't yell about the holes in my ears or the silver stud in my nose; she just laughed at me. I didn't open my mouth, so she has yet to see the tongue stud. I just let her reaction bounce off of me, or better still, slide over my now black hair with only a streak of red remaining. Mitchell told me I looked "cool" while Ryan just sneered with icy contempt at my trying to change something. Most of the kids at school turned, looked once, and then looked past me, like they've done for three years. Seth said I looked like a freak, while Glen said nothing at all, which hurts the very worst. I wonder if Terrell at work will notice when I see him tomorrow.

I get up from the desk—the English assignment is a pretty easy one about vocabulary—and look in my mostly bare closet. My stacks of jeans and T-shirts lay on the floor, while a few sweatshirts join the dress Anne bought me at the mall. I wonder if there'll ever be a day when I'll need to buy hangers for a closet, when I'll have nice things, and when I'll just stop wanting.

I hold the dress up against me, imagining what it will look like. There's no mirror in the room, which Breezy hates, but there are some things you don't want to see reflected in glass. As the soft fabric tickles my skin, I think about Glen touching and holding me. I try to think about more, but those thoughts won't come. I need to stop wanting; I need to plan to stop dreaming.

"Get the phone!" I hear my mother shout from outside the door, then she coughs loudly.

I put the dress back in the closet, then take my headphones off and head toward the kitchen. There's no phone in my room, the reasons Mama prohibited it lost, like this birthday, into the fog of history.

"Hello?" I answer, picking up the receiver Mama has left lying face up on a kitchen counter. Whoever is on the other end got their scream-and-shout-TV quota filled.

"Happy birthday eighteen times," the male voice says on the other end of the phone. I press the phone closer. The earrings dig into my flesh, but my tongue's weighted down with doubt; I'm too embarrassed to admit I don't know who's speaking. "Christy, is that you?" the voice asks.

I mumble some nonresponsive noncommitted sound.

"It's your birthday right?" the voice says, overflowing with excitement.

Another mumble from me. Rocks in my mouth and in my head.

"Well, since I wasn't working today, I didn't get a chance, so."

I laugh, smile, and almost cry in a single sound. "Hi, Terrell."

He's silent now, embarrassed for both of us that it took me so long to figure out his voice.

"How did you know?" I ask. Other than Terrell, I hardly talk to anyone at work. I come in, shelve my books, dream my dreams, and come out with my life untouched. I'm also curious about how he got my phone number; I'm even more curious about why he's calling me.

"Can I trust you?" Terrell asks.

No words again, just my laugh, smile, and cry sound, which he takes as a green light.

"I was looking up your phone number in the computer a few days ago, and I noticed your birthday, so I just thought I would call." He sounds different over the phone: less sure of himself and his words. He doesn't sound like Glen; he sounds a lot more like me in that way.

"Thanks," I say. I'm trying to listen, ears distracted by the TV; nose disgusted by the smell of Mom lighting up a smoke in the other room.

"So, what did you do to celebrate?"

Even over the phone, I notice I'm looking at the floor, avoiding eye contact, like some dog that's been hit too much. "Nothing much."

"Really?" He sounds confused, and I realize I must sound pathetic.

"Well, my friends and I will probably do something this weekend," I throw out quickly, wondering if by saying it there's any chance it increases the possibility of it happening.

"Me, I'm going to have a monster party. Why aren't you having a party?" he asks.

"When's your birthday?" I ask, both interested and avoiding further interrogation.

"Don't laugh, okay, promise me," he says, even as he's more laughing than talking.

"Okay," I reply, realizing he's already offered me his trust and his promises.

"It's on Valentine's Day, how lame is that?"

"Does that mean your girlfriend just gets you one gift," I say softly, but he knows what I'm asking. It's his turn to pause. Music, which sounds like old Motown, fills up his end of the phone.

"Well, I just wanted to call, so . . . ," he finally says. His voice sounds strange, yet he doesn't sound like a stranger. Not a friend, yet certainly nothing more. I decide to take a small step.

"Thanks, Terrell, maybe I can call you on your birthday," I almost whisper.

"Maybe you can get me a present," he whispers in reply.

I'm shaking inside because this small step's landed me on unfamiliar ground. "Maybe."

"You know what I want?" I'm straining to hear even the pauses between his words.

"What do you want, Terrell?" Like a leaf lost in the wind my words float to him.

"To take your picture; would you let me do that?"

I want to tell him why there's no mirror in my room, I want to tell him he shouldn't waste his film. I want to tell him the truth, but inside I lie and take another small step. "Sure, Terrell."

"Great, that's great, I'll start thinking about locations," he says. I think I hear him smile.

"I'll start thinking outfits," I say stupidly, ignoring my closet of orphan clothes hangers.

He laughs. "Doesn't really matter either way."

"Why's that?" But as soon as the question exits my brittle lips, the answer enters my mind.

"Because beauty supplies," he says as I mouth the words slowly, softly, smoothly. "You know, Christy, I think that—"

"Get off the damn phone!" Mama shouts from the kitchen door.

"I have to go now," I say slowly, softly, sadly.

"I heard!" Terrell says. "See you soon."

"Now!" I don't even slip in a good-night wish over Mama's now booming voice. I hang up the phone, take a breath, and let the new stud in my mouth be the magnet for all the old rage.

"Mama, what do you want?" I ask stupidly. I know there's nothing Mama needs that I can provide, unless I become a psychic and tell her the numbers or slots to play.

She uses her cigarette to point at the stove, then heads back toward the couch. As I start to heat up the leftover macaroni and cheese she brought home from her job at Harvest Crest, I remember, back when Daddy was alive, how different my mom was: she was funny, always telling stories, just full of life and energy. When Daddy died, that part of my mom died too. Not so much out of grief—I think in some ways I'm the only one in my family who still misses Daddy—but out of what she had to do to survive and raise us kids. She's worked at small factories and other jobs, but has never managed to be anyplace long enough and is always the first to lose her job when hard times come, which come often in Flint. Now, she's breaking her back not on an assembly line, but assembling enough hours between two jobs to pay the bills. It's almost Christmas, and no gifts are present, but that happened when Daddy was alive too.

"Breezy, dinner's almost ready!" I shout. Because Mama is working all the time, I do most of the cooking, cleaning, and laundry in the house even though I have a job too. I'm not so good at the cleaning, so the house is a mess, but we've all just gotten used to it. Cooking is the hardest because I never know how many people are going be around for dinner.

"Thanks, girl," Mama says. Kind words are few and far between, so I settle for any. This is one of those rare days where I actually see Mama, although she's too tired to let me do much more than just see her. She'll eat in front of the TV; finish off her six-pack of Bud then fall asleep with one of those unreal reality shows still booming. She works at Harvest Crest from 7:00 a.m. to 5:00 p.m. five days a week, getting only Monday and Sunday off. Her other job is working three to four overnight shifts as a home health aide, which is crazy, since with her drinking, smoking, and fifty-plus extra pounds she's packing on her small frame, she's the last person in the world who knows about good health. But the work isn't that hard, just degrading, as she helps this old rich man do everything, including wipe his ass.

"Grammy!" I hear Bree shout in delight as she runs into the room. I'm jealous, because even though I can't see her, I know that Mama's face just lights up, that old smile of hers returning again. For Bree, she'll find the energy to tell a story or let her feel loved; for me, she has only the time to hand off leftovers and make me feel like one. She'll find the energy to cuddle Bree on her lap, which she never did for me unless I was bent over it to get a spanking. She rarely raised her hand to hit any of the boys, especially not Ryan, so she took out her frustrations on my backside. I knew she was afraid of Robert, and I didn't blame her; everybody was, and in some way, still is. Now, he's really got nothing to lose.

"It's ready," I announce as I set the bowls on the table. Along with the leftover mac and cheese, there's two-day-old green beans and white bread from the bakery outlet store. I butter the bread enough so they won't notice it's stale, and I salt and pepper the beans so they actually have some taste. Thank goodness for leftovers; sometimes that's the only food in the house.

"Get your grammy some," Mama instructs Bree, who loads up a plate for Mama, and then a smaller one for herself. Bree takes both of the plates into the living room, while I sit down alone at the table. From the distance and over the clatter, I hear my mama say, "That's a good girl, Bree." I don't know why, but those words always crush me; as if I'm not a good girl, even if I'm doing most of the work in the house. My dinner now tastes bitter, not salty.

I open up my latest Ms. Chapman recommended book, *The Color Purple* by Alice Walker, to read during dinner, but it's hard to follow: why write letters to God because, like Santa, he doesn't seem to answer. I won't tell Ms. Chapman I won't finish it because she might stop talking to me or recommending books. While I tire of her trying to recruit me for the track team, I'm flattered that somebody wants me for something, other than to be a beast of burden.

After I finish dinner, Bree brings in the dirty plates from the living room. She hands me the dishes, then opens the refrigerator, pulling out a beer for Mama. The sight of this little, innocent girl carrying a twelve-ounce can of Budweiser makes me want to laugh, cry, and scream at the same time. I wish that Bree wanted me to read aloud to her or help her with her homework, but instead she goes back into the living room. From the light of the blaring TV, I can catch a glimpse of Bree crawling up next to Mama. Bree's too old for this, but then she didn't really have much of a childhood, so I leave her alone.

I wash the dishes by hand. The dishwasher broke months ago, but Mama hasn't gotten it fixed. Ryan keeps saying he'll do it, but I don't believe him. After doing the dishes, I need to start on the laundry. Since Bree is curled up in the living room, I strip the fading old Shrek sheets from her bed, and gather up her clothes, most of them hand-me-downs and Ryan's five-finger discounts. I want to dress Bree in pink skirts with pretty bows in her braided hair, not old sweatshirts. I want for her everything that I never had, everything that I am not, and nothing I have ever felt.

While I wash Bree's clothes, I decide to bathe my body. I lock the bathroom door, but also jam a mop handle against the knob. I don't understand how the other girls parade around naked during gym class. I sometimes wonder if that's yet another reason I don't take Ms. Chapman's offer to try out for track. The water feels as good and clean as my body feels sore and dirty. No matter how hard I scrub, I don't feel any cleaner, and the foul odors of our house cling to me. As I clean between my legs, I'm gentle. Yet even if I'm thinking about Glen, I can't imagine what Anne said, about sex feeling good. My body must be numb.

After I dry off, I throw an old yellow cloth robe on over my pajamas. I'll need to pull out another blanket, since I noticed ice inside the window even before sunset, and with the small cracks in the window and the tears in my pajamas, it's going to be a long, cold night. I'll bring Bree into the bedroom with me, close the door behind me, and wait for morning.

"Hey, Christy," I hear Mitchell shout from his room. He must have sneaked in while I was in the shower. He sounds bone tired. "Can I ask you something?"

"Sure," I say, standing next to the door, waiting for an invite inside that doesn't come.

"How did you get through your junior year? It's so hard," he says, pushing his glasses up on his nose, then looking down at the math book in front of him like it was a map to buried treasure.

"I don't remember," I say, as drops of water from my wet hair drip onto my shoulders. I shiver at the sensation and at the thought of telling Mitchell more lies. He doesn't want the truth; he needs a reason to believe. "You're smart, Mitch. You'll do fine, probably better than I did."

He looks up, adds a smile to his face, and takes a deep breath. "I doubt that. You—"

"What's busting you?" I ask quickly, turning the attention away from me.

"All of it, that's the problem," he says, then coughs. His voice is heavy from too little sleep and not enough dreams. Ryan kicked away Mitch's dreams, leaving him nothing except planning and praying.

"If I can make it, then . . . ," I start, then my voice fades away, since surviving isn't really success. But if Mitchell can avoid becoming another casualty and make it out of Flint to get to college, then he has a chance, although he doesn't need honors math to figure the odds are long.

"Thanks, Christy," he says, then goes back to work. The walls of his room are empty now. The Eminem posters were ripped down the day after Ryan ripped open Mitchell's secret life. But in some way, I think, that's a blessing to have the burden of unreachable dreams disappear.

I walk on, throwing Bree's clothes in the dryer while I finish my English homework at the kitchen table. In the other room, I hear Mama's snoring broken up by her hacking cough over the soundtrack of reality TV contributing to the decline of Western civilization. A full ashtray and six empty beer cans form a circle around her. In English we're studying words that have two meanings depending on how they are used. We're supposed to come up with illustrations from our literature textbook, but my example is from my life. I'll use the word *mother* because in my house "mother" is just a noun; it's never been a verb.

first grade, christmas

"Santa?"

I whisper the words as I open my bedroom door on Christmas morning. But when I walk into the main room, I see there's still no tree, no presents, nothing. I woke up early, silently hoping during the night that Santa had visited our house. But with tears in my eyes, I see that everything on TV is a lie. I walk into the kitchen. Mama's smoking, sipping coffee, eating oatmeal, and not saying a word. I grab a bowl, take some oatmeal, and go back toward my room.

As I walk through the living room, I look at the TV. For once it's not on, so the dark dusty screen is like a mirror. I see my reflection in the glass surrounded by the empty room. I look down at my breakfast. A deep anger overtakes me as I hurl the oatmeal at the TV screen.

"What the hell," I hear Mama shout from the other room. I set the now empty bowl on top of the TV and retreat into a corner, but there's no place to hide. She jerks my right arm, which seems no bigger than one of her fingers, and pulls me toward her. I don't fight back, instead I let her drag me across the floor to her chair. I'm over her knee by instinct and I barely even cry as she turns my skin black and blue. She beats me so quickly she doesn't take time to pull down my pajama bottoms, or maybe she wants to avoid the loud sound of skin on skin.

I crawl off her after the last smack; I lost count at ten. She storms into the kitchen, while I creep into the corner and curl up on my side against the heating vent, pressing up against the metal grating, which bites into my skin. I'm shivering from cold and shaking with tears. She tosses a roll of paper towels at me. I look at the white oatmeal dripping down on the TV screen.

"I'm sorry, Mama," I lie to her as she towers over me.

"You clean that up," she says. "Or I'll make you lick it off the floor, you hear?"

I nod, eyes to the ground, avoiding her cold, angry look that only I seem to inspire. She coughs loudly, then walks into the kitchen, leaving me alone on Christmas morning. Daddy's still sleeping, so are Mitchell and Ryan, while Robert never came home last night. Christmas or not, it's just another morning at the Mallorys on Stone Street.

I take the paper towels and wipe away the mess. Every day after school I had come home and watched TV for a couple of hours. Every day for months I'd seen the Christmas commercials with all these people smiling, dancing, and singing songs. The TV showed me all these pictures of happy families together and presents around the tree. But those faces, feelings, and presents are missing in our house. I scoop the oatmeal off the screen, then go into the bathroom to throw it away, so I don't have to face Mama again.

"Good morning, my most beautiful one!" I hear my father shout out as he enters the bathroom. I hug him, accept a kiss on the forehead, and savor the feeling of his rough beard against my skin. I throw the mess away and then wait outside while he finishes in the bathroom.

When he steps out, right away he knows that something's

wrong. My eyes can't lie, and since Daddy's home so little, I tend to stare at him whenever I can. "What's the matter?"

"Mama's mad at me," I tell him.

"Well, she's mad at me then too," he says, then winks. He reaches out his hand and I take it. His hand is wrinkled and scarred, with twisted fingers, but he's still strong.

"Daddy, where's Santa?" I say, all innocent, but I know better. Still, I just want desperately to believe.

He yawns, then bends down next to me. "Santa must have missed us this year, again."

I don't say anything; instead I lean into Daddy. Time with him is my real present. He hugs me back, then touches the top of my head. He fingers my long, dirt-brown hair and smiles. No matter that he's missing a few teeth, it's still the biggest and brightest smile I've ever seen.

"If he didn't come to us, we'll go see him," Daddy whispers with his hoarse voice.

"Really?" I reply, as he gently wipes the tears running down my cheeks.

"Go get your coat," Daddy says, as he walks into the kitchen. I try to be quiet so as not to wake Ryan or Mitchell, although there's little quiet as I hear Mama and Daddy yelling.

I dress quickly, grab my coat, and race for the door, but Daddy is still in the kitchen with Mama. After a few minutes, Daddy meets me at the door. We go outside and climb into his car. It's a cold morning and the old car strains to start, coughing like Mama. He puts me on his lap, my hands on the wheel, his resting on top, and we steer the car together on the snow-covered streets. "Let's go chasing the tail lights of Santa's sleigh," Daddy says, then softly kisses the top of my head. The kiss moves down my long braided hair and touches my neck.

"Honey, next Christmas, things will be better. I'll be working again," Daddy says.

"It's okay," I tell him, my small hands turning the wheel as my mouth turns out lies.

"It's not all right," he says. "I'm going to do something about it."

I sit on his lap as we drive the streets, which are mostly empty. The party stores, drugstores, and bars that line Dort Highway are all closed. With my help, Daddy turns the car into the parking lot of a Mobil gas station, which seems to be open. He leaves the car running, although the heater barely works, and goes into the store. After a few minutes he returns with a big Hershey's chocolate bar and a small stuffed chocolate-colored bear.

"Santa wanted you to have this," Daddy says, breaking the candy in two pieces and giving me the larger one. Then he hands me the small stuffed bear. "And your Daddy wants you to have this. He's like you: tiny, beautiful, and sweet. Let's call him Hershey."

My face is too small to hold my smile. I know that Santa isn't real; but this moment is.

14

december 30, senior year

"Aren't you supposed to be at work?"

Anne shrugs, then coughs way too loudly, which slowly dissolves into her even louder laugh, both of which I can barely hear over the blasting music. "I'm sick."

"Sick?" I ask as I trade the cold of my house for the warm comfort of the PT Cruiser.

"Sick and tired of my boss," Anne responds, then leaves some tire rubber in front of my house, adding to the overall noise level of a Stone Street Saturday night.

"What now?" I hide a sigh, wondering when Anne is going to either quit her job or at least quit complaining. Sometimes I wish she'd be more like me and suffer in silence.

"Tonight, I get into work, and he says he needs to talk to me alone," Anne says, teeth clenched and tone caustic. "He takes me to his office, tells me to sit down, then shuts the door."

"What did he want?"

"He said he wanted new employees to wear name tags."

"And?"

"And he leans over and presses this name tag on my shirt,"

Anne says, sounding like she wants to throw up. "I don't think I need to tell you where he put his hand, do I?"

"Disgusting."

"He did it really quick, but it seemed like forever," Anne says. "I can still feel it."

I let her confession dangle. I keep wondering when Anne will stand up to her boss. I can't bring myself to ask her. If she reflects the question back at me, then I'd be blind as well as mute. I shift in my seat, chew on my bottom lip, and change direction. "Where we going?"

"Chillers, you know it?" she asks, but she knows the answer, since I rarely go anywhere, except with her. And of all the places I would go, Chillers, a teen dance club about a half hour away in Lapeer would be last on my list. But since Anne's only seventeen, it's our only choice.

We drive down I-69, faster than a burning joint, not that we have one. Anne's agitated, since I didn't have any weed, and she couldn't stop at home to get some. We'll have to move our feet without shuffling our brain cells. I don't think Anne knows how much I hate dancing and hate being in crowds. The only thing I hate more is what she saved me from: Saturday night home alone until Ryan stumbles in, his smell my personal alarm clock. Anne spends most of the drive talking about Tommy, whom she's now dating. Good thing she tells me details; Tommy's not much of a talker. We find a place to park, but Anne's PT Cruiser sticks out in the lot, which looks like an SUV dealership. We walk past cars with music booming out of them, and past groups that have gathered in the lot. We walk by two beefy security guards, who let me pass without a look, but I hear a murmur when Anne passes by.

New hair and holes regardless, I'm expecting the same disinterest in me inside.

The music smashes into us the second we enter, not even the churning bodies absorbing the loud techno sound. The beat's like a drill, as Anne heads quickly toward the crowded dance floor after we drop our coats. I follow her, but then look straight at the floor in front of me as I push myself into the swirling mass.

"Where's the dress?" Anne asks, pointing at my oversize CMU hooded sweatshirt that Mitchell got me for Christmas. It's nice to see somebody thinks I might have a life after Flint. I bought him a new blue notebook to show him he's got the right to dream again.

"What dress?" I shout back at Anne. I haven't a clue how people hook up at places like this, since they can't hear each other, but maybe the only talk that matters here is body language.

"The dress from the Victoria's Secret in Lansing?"

I smile, knowing it will go unseen in the strobe-lit darkness. "I'm saving it for Glen."

"Why bother?" Anne says, then sighs loudly.

"What do you mean?" I shout back, the waves of sounds make every word quiver.

She shrugs her shoulders then leans into me. "It's not like you're going to show him."

"I will, I'm just waiting for—"

"Carpe diem, Speedy," Anne says, but I deflect her words. I turn away from her and pull the hood up over my head.

"Listen, you gotta do this thing," she shouts, then drives her point home by tightly clutching my wrist like she's looking for my pulse.

"I know," I respond, but she tightens rather than loosens her grip. To the onlookers we're holding hands; to me, she's holding my barely dancing feet to the fire I feel for Glen.

"Then do it at Rani's party tomorrow," Anne shouts louder and grabs even tighter still.

Anne's a friend, but I don't like anybody touching me like that. "Let go!"

"See how easy it is to ask for what you want." Anne laughs, and lets my hand fall free. She takes her free hand to flip her hair. "You just gotta ask."

"Maybe," I mumble. Anne's still in her work clothes, although she's let her hair down, unbuttoned one button too many on her white shirt, and added eyeliner blacker than her pants. Looking around the room, I see the too pretty, too tanned girls in their short, sexy dresses, and I know that Anne is right. Glen is never going to ask me; I need to take the first step. Even changing my look didn't change his reaction to me. Why did I think seven piercings would change five years of Glen only showing an interest in me as a friend or a supplier of weed? Since I know the end result will be rejection, there's no use delaying the inevitable anymore.

"Come on," Anne says, pointing deeper into the crowded dance floor. The song's changed, but the smashing beat, the crushing volume, and the booming bass rumble like an earthquake. While the room shakes, I won't. "Look, like you said: 'let go!'"

"What do you mean?" I shout, even as the words *let go* form a groove in my brain.

Anne moves us near the boys' bathroom, which gives her plenty to look at, since talking is out of the question under the techno cloud. I finally take a risk and do what I've never done before. I let go.

"That's it," Anne shouts, laughing with me not at me, as I let the rhythm move me. She's kicked off her shoes; I've kicked off the chains, if only for one night. Every time a new song comes on, I hear loud cries of "That's my song!" from a group of four blond girls on the other side of us. They're dancing with each other, but trying to impress a group of boys who seem superglued to the wall. Each of them has one leg up behind them, suburban flamingos.

Five songs later I'm dancing strong, but Anne needs to catch her breath. I know that Ms. Chapman was right: there's a finely tuned athlete buried in this damaged body. I'm wishing I had long hair again so I could shake my head and feel it on my shoulders. I'm wishing I'd come here before. I'm wishing I'd always be the person I feel like right now.

"Keep calling me, Daddy," Anne says, dancing over to shout in my ear.

"What did you say?"

Anne smiles, then points toward her pocket. "My boss probably called my dad, and now my dad is calling me," Anne says, as she pulls the cell phone out of her pants, then laughs way too loud. "He keeps calling, but it's cool, since I got it set on vibrate."

She looks at the phone, then moves toward the wall of flamingos, who look more like buzzards to me now that I'm alone. I turn my back to them. I know Anne's not talking to her father or mother, and if it was Tommy, she'd have mentioned it.

That means she's talking to another friend, probably one of her Honor Society buddies. I'd like to think I'm Anne's only friend, but I know that's not the case.

"Nice moves," a deep voice shouts from behind. I'm shocked, not by the voice but by the fact that I didn't hear it coming. A combination of my hoodie and the techno din.

Even engaged in conversation, I see Anne manage to slip out a sly smile. I turn around and there's another smiling face greeting me. I take a step back, my natural stranger reaction.

"Don't stop," the boy says, moving closer. His mouth is too near my shiny left ear, but despite my discomfort, I just do as I'm told. I keep moving to the loud music, avoiding his eyes, and silently questioning his intentions. He's dressed pretty nice and neat, like he just came from work. He looks Indian: light brown skin, short hair on top, and maybe some brains up there, too, since he's not wearing expensive kicks. Seems the sharper the shoe, the duller the brain, but then again, why should I care? I'm sure, like most boys, he's come to talk with Anne, not me.

He's leaning toward me, but other than some cologne, there's no stench of smoke, weed, or booze, so I let him step closer. He's about my height, and while he's not skinny like Terrell, he's not thick. "Are you bald or something?" he says, pointing at my hoodie-covered head.

I put my hand over my mouth, another natural instinct, and then shake my head. By now, he must be wondering if I have any brains, even though I don't have nice shoes.

"You go to CMU too?" he asks, pointing now at my sweatshirt, and I've got to think quick in this instant game of old-school truth or dare. Do I tell him the truth: that I'm in high school, unlike him, or do I dare to lie and see where that takes me? Or maybe he's lying as well. I'm trying to catch his eyes, but he's looking me over. It feels creepy, maybe how Anne's boss makes her feel, but somehow it kind of feels fine to think he wants to look.

He takes a half step closer. I don't pull back; I don't lean forward. I stand up straight, and I take the low road. "I'm home for break, you too?"

"U2? I don't like U2," he shouts, then leans back to enjoy the puzzled expression on my face, which I can't seem to hide despite the hand in front of the mouth, the eyes looking down, and the covered skull. "I'm just busting you. So, what's your name? What dorm you in?"

My brain's smashing cells hover between saying "My name is why don't you leave me alone" or saying "My name is whatever you want it to be." But my words remain in my mind, so he speaks again.

"Derrick," he says, but he doesn't offer his hand, instead his fingers brush against my hand. The touch sends shivers of fear, which I know, and an unfamiliar shiver of optimism.

"Christy," I tell him. I'm not sure if he'll hear me, since I'm talking to his hands, which remain mostly at his side, the tips of his fingers just making contact with me. I know that I'll lift my head up again to tell him Anne's name, since that's the obvious next question.

"You're a fine dancer," Derrick says. "How come I haven't seen you at clubs at CMU?"

"I don't go out much," I say, reintroducing myself to the truth.

"Well, Christy, that's a damn shame," he says in a loud whisper. "You wanna dance with me?" I'm fighting back a smile and losing the battle, so I decide to lift my head. He's not really dancing, just kind of swaying now to the slow R & B song. I think how earlier I told Anne "let go," and now I take that advice, letting him pull me gently into his human touch.

He presses against me, but I don't react, either running away or holding him closer. He seems like a pretty good dancer, but I suspect as his hands move farther down my back that dancing isn't what he's really interested in doing with me. "I gotta go," I say as the song ends.

"You should lose the hood unless you're from it," Derrick says into my ear. The music has stopped spinning, but he hasn't. "And lose that big-ass gangster sweatshirt."

"Excuse me," I say, finally taking a step back.

He leans back into me. "I'm just saying, you look really cool, don't know why you're hiding it." He speaks with the confident tone that Anne owns. I look at him and see something strange: someone telling me a truth with their eyes, since my ears refuse to believe.

I take a step back, then with shaking hands take the hood off my head, but the sweatshirt stays no matter how smooth his talk, or how awkward my response. "Really?"

"Sweet hair," he says, then he takes a step back, if only to get some distance so he can dance to the now booming beat that sounds almost as loud as the pounding coming from my chest. As I watch him dance, with more freedom and fluid movement than I'll ever know, I notice his group of flamingo friends behind him aren't laughing. As the dance club speakers push out shouting song lyrics I can't understand, I hear instead my own voice telling myself "let go."

Anne's still talking wildly on her cell, but I'm struggling with words. I guess she's called Tommy to tell him of this strange occurrence, a positive freak of nature: his cousin Christy looking happy. As the next slow song oozes across the club, I let Derrick hold me a little tighter, even if I need to keep his hands from moving a little lower. Nothing's going to happen between us, which is what I want, but thinking that something *could* happen, that's what I've needed for a long time.

"So, could I call you sometime back at CMU?" Derrick says quickly between songs.

I again pretend not to hear, as I try to remember my made-up college life. "What?"

He makes a motion, like he's talking on the phone; he's a better dancer than mime. I finally answer even as I'm asking the question to the test: does he really want me? "I'm never home, why don't you give me your number, okay?" I say, thinking that's what Anne would do.

He smiles and I can't help but respond in kind. He turns and shouts something to his buds standing behind him. One of them throws him something, which he catches. He very gently takes my left hand and starts to write on my palm with a black magic marker. "This is my cell."

I wish I could tell him that these numbers were the combination unlocking the belief that someone could want me, but before I can speak, Anne taps me on the shoulder, then whispers, "Let's cruise, lover girl."

As Anne and I head for the parking lot I feel like I'm walking a little taller. While I know the security shock troops won't be whistling or craning their necks when I walk by this time, now, I think they could.

sixth grade, december

"What are you doing in my room?"

I can smell the stink of him, even across the room, standing by my door. He doesn't answer; instead he walks slowly toward me. I open my mouth to scream, but nothing comes out. My locked jaw forces the terror down my throat. I pull the thin blue blanket over my head, but he rips it away, tossing it onto the floor. I try to push him away, but he's too strong. I try to resist, but even in the darkness, his cold, dark eyes hold me in place, like some science fiction movie death ray. I curl up against the back of the bed, since there's nowhere to run. He presses up against me, his legs against my body, pinching my skin through the thin pajamas.

"Shut up," he hisses, then puts his left hand across my mouth. I try to bite him, but the force and mass is too big for me. He moves his hand up slightly so it also covers my nose. I struggle to breathe, my lungs frantically pulling in the air, including every odor molecule of his stinky body. I try to fight, but he's too big, too strong, too everything.

"Take that off," he says, tugging with his right hand at my top. When I pause, he slams his arm across my throat. "Now!"

My eyes consent. He takes his arm away, and I remove my top, then throw it on the floor. I cover my barely existent breasts with my hands, then I close my eyes. My ears bleed hearing the loud grating metallic sound of a zipper. My stomach churns as the bed shakes from his rapid arm movements. His breathing gets heavier, until . . . He lets out a harsh sound as I feel the hot, wet sensation on my chest. He sighs, then leans into me, his tongue almost in my ear. "Ugly bitch, I knew you'd like it," he says, then slithers from the room leaving me on the now stained and forever unclean sheets.

15

december 31, senior year

"Is he here yet?"

Anne surveys the room; she's the appointed Glen spotter. "No sign yet, Speedy."

"I'm sure he'll be here," I say as I breathe out a sigh of relief, but breathe in a feeling of fright. I should first get from Anne's father those drugs they use when they transplant organs: I need a dose of an antirejection drug to get me through this party. I've decided that "when" is now.

"Unlike Tommy," I say, twisting the knife a little. My cousin is now a cautious man—the thought of a graduate of the juvenile correctional system hanging out at a teen party wasn't a smart idea. Glen invited us to join him at this New Year's Eve gathering at Rani's house. She lives in Anne and Glen's neighborhood on the other side of the bridge. I'm on edge in this house, knowing that I can't live another year, or even day, without Glen. I look at Anne. While she's alone at this party, she's no longer alone in her life. I'm so happy for her; I'm so damn jealous.

"How do I look?" I ask Anne, thinking how Derrick made

such a question possible. My freshly showered hair is still wet, and the water causes my ear candy to glisten in the light. Despite the shower before Anne arrived, some days and nights, like this one, I can't feel clean.

"Like a gold medal!" The loud music has been making my head spin; my running legs feel the need to unwind and dance. I kick off my shoes as I try shaking out the nerves; instead, I rearrange the too-tight-for-Christy white dress and the stress swimming in my blood.

"Tonight is the night," Anne says, coaching me toward the finish line of unfulfilled love. She's called in sick again for work and is risking another grounding by coming out with me. I begged her to come to the party with me, asking the rare favor. I'm desperate for Glen and to get out of the house. Mitchell's spending time at Tommy's, while Aunt Dee and Breezy are visiting relatives down in Cleveland. Mama's off playing the slots, while I've spent the day at home with Ryan. Anne arrived late to my house, but any time wouldn't have been a minute too soon.

I stare at the floor. "I like Glen so much."

"I know, Speedy, I know," Anne says, which is nice. She doesn't laugh at me, which is nicer. Looking around the room, I think how I've gone to school with most of these people for four years, but they're all strangers to me. I stand behind Anne as she talks randomly, all the while watching the front door.

"Twelve o'clock high!" Anne shouts excitedly, pointing at the door as Glen walks in, along with Tristan and some other theater folks. He's wearing a long black trench coat, black gloves, and a long red scarf that touches the ground. He's growing a beard, at Mr. McDonald's suggestion, for the part of Romeo, and that makes him look even more handsome. "Remember, if not now, then when?" Anne whispers as she walks away.

"Hey, Christy," Glen says, those blue eyes cutting right through me. Even though he's surrounded by people all wanting his time, for this moment, I'm the most important person.

"How was your Christmas?" I ask, desperate for conversation.

"Check it out," he says, then shows me a watch that costs more than the entire contents of my closet. He's talking to me, but his eyes are darting around the room. "How about you?"

"Okay. Anne got me this dress," I say, pressing the dress down against my body, forcing those blue eyes to look at the white fabric and the paler white skin peeking out from underneath.

"Cool," he says with an indifferent shrug. Obviously I'm losing his attention and my opportunity. Tristan, one of his always present theater toadies, is tugging on his arm.

I open my palm to show him a virgin joint. "Wanna hit?" I ask.

"Sure," he says, pulling himself away from Tristan, who is one of the straight-edge types.

I take the lead, and we head back downstairs. Glen's always acting: he wants people to think he's cool, but he's never wanted a rep as a pothead with his high school theater-artsy pals. We walk into the basement bathroom. I open the door, flip on the light and the fan. "This okay?"

"Sure," he says, as we walk inside. I close the door, hand him the joint, then light it for him. He takes a hit, coughs, and holds in the smoke, while I'm finally ready to let it out.

"So do you think Rani knows you're rehearsing without her?" I whisper, even though the locked door protects us from the outside world peering into our business. We've only run lines a couple of times, and it was during lunch at school.

"I haven't told anyone," Glen says. "I know how to keep a secret. That's what friends are for, right?"

"I can keep a secret too," I say in the sexiest voice I can summon, a voice that sounds nothing like a friend or friendly dealer. "You know there's one scene we haven't rehearsed yet."

"What's that?" He seems nervous, less charming than his normal self.

"The scene where Romeo and Juliet kiss for the first time." He's inhaling again, so I have the floor. "Although you'd probably want to rehearse that with Rani."

He laughs, then checks to make sure the door is tightly closed. "She's such a bitch."

He hands me back the joint, but instead of taking a hit, I decide I want something else up against my lips. I touch his hand, hold it tight, then lean into him, dizzy with desire.

He takes a step back, but I take a giant leap forward. I toss the joint into the sink, toss caution to the wind, and risk it all by wrapping my hands around his neck. "Christy, please, don't do this," he says even as I push my lips against his. My kiss is tiny and tentative.

I take another step up, trying to focus as my head and life spin out of control, the high of the weed and low of my life crash together. My mouth has failed me again. Even with my anger-inspired manic makeover, Glen sees me as Ryan does: an ugly bitch. Knowing now that Glen finds me unlovable, I realize all that's left and all I'm good for, is to be fuckable. I reach behind me, quickly unzip, and then let my dress fall to my feet. "Glen, don't you want me—"

"It's just that . . .," he starts, but finishes the sentence by exiting the bathroom.

I look in the mirror and think how ugly I am when I cry. I grab the dress from the floor, then stare again into the mirror. Instead of putting the dress back on, I wrap it around my right hand, form a fist, then smash it hard into the mirror. My self-image shatters as the mirror breaks, and another seven years of bad luck come my way. I put the dress back on, the bloodstain from the cut on my hand my reminder of this evening, and pick up out of the sink the biggest, sharpest piece of broken mirror. I slip out of the bathroom, then just as quickly run out the back door. Anne yells at me, but I'm too far gone, leaving my coat and my ride, along with my dignity, my blood, and my reason for living, back at the party. I'm off the chain, sprinting through the streets of Flint in bitter winter weather. I know for once exactly where I'm running: to the bridge to chase tail lights for the very last time. As I'm running, I know I won't win a gold medal, but instead I'll reward myself by raising my hand high in the air in victory to make the vein in my wrist easier to see and sever.

fifth grade, september

"Daddy, please don't die."

I'm holding Daddy's limp hand, but there's no answer, not even the sounds of the machines, which stopped beeping. Mitchell's beside me, but he's too little to offer comfort.

"He can't hear you," Mitchell tells me softly. He's trying to be tough and not cry. It's how I would imagine Robert would react, if he ever would have come to visit, but he's nowhere to be seen. He and Daddy never got along once Robert started to go bad; the more Daddy yelled, the more Robert stayed away, even now. Ryan is outside the room consoling Mama.

"I know," I say, feeling sick to my stomach. The hospital smells of ammonia, metal, laundry soap, and piss. It smells like nothing else; it smells like death.

I'm holding onto Hershey Bear with my right hand, and touching Daddy with my left. I'd like Mitchell to hold my hand, or hug me, but that's not his way. Same with Mama.

"Let's go," Mitchell finally says, no doubt so he can cry by himself. Like me.

We walk out of the room, but I take one last look. Daddy's gone, I wonder if he'll chase the tail lights all the way to heaven. Outside, I look into Ryan's dark eyes, then down the hospital hallway, and he looks different. He smells unusual, like something worse than death.

"Things is gonna be different now that that miserable bastard is dead," Ryan tells Mitchell and me, while Mama watches, listens, and almost nods in approval.

I start to say something, but Mama turns her back and leaves us trapped inside tears that she doesn't share. She waddles toward the elevator, and we follow in our zombie state. As we climb in the elevator and start our descent, the fears rise within me as Daddy's soul rises up to heaven, leaving me behind in hell.

16

january 1, senior year

"How are you feeling?"

I'm a little groggy; it's hard to get my eyes to focus, but I can smell the unmistakable shiny steel odor of a hospital.

"Christy, it's Anne's father, Dr. Williams," the voice says again.

The light shining overhead blinds me, as does the whiteness of the room. I try to raise myself up, but I can't move. "What happened?" I remember only the sight of the blood.

"Anne found you," he says softly. "She called 911, covered you with her coat, and then called me. You cut yourself and went into shock. But the cut wasn't deep. You will be fine."

Can you laugh in a hospital? Can I laugh at this man who hates me assuring me that I will "be fine." I wonder if he knows exactly how deep my cuts are and how they'll never heal.

"Anne and your cousin Tommy are outside to see you," he says, and it must be the hospital drugs making me super-sensitive, but I hear disapproval in his voice as he makes his way toward the door. "But first, some other people need to speak with you."

After Dr. Williams leaves, I'm all alone and that seems right. The last time I was in a hospital was the night Daddy died.

"Ms. Mallory, can I come in?" a voice says on the other side of the curtain.

I don't want to answer. I'm looking around the room for a glass, a vase, or something to help me finish the job, but there's nothing.

"Ms. Mallory, do you want me to come back later?" the voice asks again. I'm thinking I would like to come back later: in about ten years, after high school, after college, after I've made all my stupid mistakes and talked some sense into myself.

"No, it's okay." More untrue words were never spoken.

"I'm Mrs. Grayson, a social worker here at the hospital," the woman says as she sits down beside me, clipboard in front of her, her eyes staring into mine. I don't say anything as I take her in: her light blue suit, her dark black skin, and her fake painted smile.

"Dr. Williams has given you some of the details, right?" she says.

I nod my head, then instinctively turn away from her, her questions, and her caring.

"I'm here to help you any way that I can. You can tell me anything, and it doesn't leave here," she says, reaching up and closing the curtain behind her. "Where do you want to start?"

"I don't," I say firmly, then half smile at her. "Well, can you take these straps off?"

"Will you promise me you won't try to hurt yourself?" she says, and I nod in agreement. Hurting myself solved nothing. Changing my look solved nothing. There's no solution for me.

"Do you want to talk about what happened?" she asks, pointing at my bandaged wrist. But they might as well have stitched up my mouth too.

Mrs. Grayson sits looking at me, waiting for an answer she'll never get. "Christy, I understand if you don't feel like talking now, but you'll need to talk with me or they won't release you. Perhaps I should set up an appointment with your mother for—"

"My mother's dead. I live with my Aunt Dee," I say, my brain becoming a spinning wheel of lies. I can't stand to think of Mama learning about this; scared to death of not knowing whether she'd be angrier at me for trying to kill myself or for messing it up. "I don't want to talk now."

"Very well," she says cautiously. "I'll be back later. I know you don't want to talk, but there's a police officer outside. She needs to at least get a statement."

"A statement?" I'm feeling drugged, but not in a good way, as she releases me.

"We couldn't get one last night. The police collected what physical evidence they could."

"What are you talking about?" I'm confused, just like I was when they brought me in and probed me like a biology class frog. She doesn't answer but, instead, goes to the door. As she leaves, a middle-aged white policewoman enters holding a notepad. She sits down, then pulls out a pen and a look of concern at the same time. The badge says "Officer Kay."

"Christy, who did this to you?" she asks, just as serious as the cops you see on TV. I'm thinking for a second this is like some sort of bad dream sequence, but the bright lights of the hospital room and the stink of antiseptic lets me know I'm still restrained in a living nightmare.

"Did what?" I reply while squirming, still strapped to the bed.

"Your friend Anne says you were last seen entering a downstairs bathroom with a Mr. Glen Thompson. Shortly thereafter, Miss Williams witnessed you running away from the party. Is that correct?" She's looking at her notepad, not me.

"Yes, but I did this," I say directing my eyes toward my bandaged and scarred wrist.

"But before, did Glen attack you?" she asks, her voice concerned and serious.

"What are you saying?" I want to die again, wondering how many people at school know about this, thinking that Glen probably told the truth to the police, and knowing that few things that happen at my school stay secret for long. My cause of death: not suicide, but humiliation.

"Look at me, Christy." She takes a deep breath, like a person about to go underwater. "There was blood on your dress. You were in shock. I know you're lying to me."

"Glen didn't touch me." I tell that truth and it hurts too hard to remember.

"You don't have to lie to protect him. People say the two of you are friends," she says, really turning up the heat as I shiver in cold fear. "If he did this to you, he should be punished."

"Did what?" I say, hysterical tears held back.

"Raped you." The whispered words explode in my ears.

I want to run to the bathroom, but her chair and these restraints are blocking my path. All I can do is shake my head in denial.

"Then who?" she says, leaning closer. "Who did this to you?"

"Why are you saying this?" I say, but I know. I know and I run inside myself.

Officer Kay shakes her head sadly, then speaks. "Because your rape kit came back positive."

sixth grade, new year's eve

"Don't move."

His elbow is digging deeply into my neck, his mouth pushed up against my ear, but it's not his words that wake me from sleep, it's not his body pressed up against mine; it's his smell. The room is totally dark. I start to cry out, but barely a sound emerges, before the point of his elbow cuts deeper. I bite my bottom lip in pain as he pulls my long hair back like a leash. I try to kick him, but it's no use. He grabs onto my legs and pulls my pajama bottoms down. Then comes the familiar grating metallic sound of a zipper. My right hand shoots out from under me, knocking Hershey Bear onto the floor, while my left hand grabs onto the end of the bed. With my arms in front of me, he quickly pulls them together, as his knee jams into my back.

"I said don't move." His full weight is on me; his full force pushing into me. Then his breathing is heavy, heavier, heaviest, and then normal. Silence returns for a moment, since my tears make no noise as they soak into the pillow. "If you say anything, I'll kill you," he says into my ear. I can feel my stomach racing upward and sense the blood dripping down my legs. His elbow returns to my neck, the point of it cutting into me while his other arm snatches Hershey Bear off the floor.

"I'll kill you like this," he sneers, then jabs a pair of silver scissors into the middle of the bear's brown chest.

17

january 11, senior year

"Happy belated New Year!"

"Hi, Terrell," I mutter, as no year could start more unhappily than this one. I nervously tug at my oversize Detroit Pistons sweatshirt, making sure the tiny bandage on my wrist remains invisible, and wishing that I could be. Ten days off from school and work wasn't enough.

"I made a significant New Year's resolution," he says, acting all serious. After that time showing me his photos last November, he's joked around with me, but nothing more.

"What is it?" I ask, knowing I can't tell him my resolution was to simply stay alive.

"Not to make any more resolutions!" he says proudly. "How about you?"

I busy myself thumbing through a book on the sorting shelf as nothing emerges from my legally chemically altered mind. I left the hospital after a few days, gaining antidepressant meds but giving no truth. Mrs. Grayson still wants me to see her, and the police have their questions, but my mind is made up and chemically modified.

"Come on, Christy, you have to want to change something," he says, taking a sip from the oversize white Styrofoam coffee cup I've noticed is his constant winter-morning companion.

My eyes scream "to be left alone" but my mouth won't comply. "To shelve these books."

He smiles, but doesn't move, instead he picks a book from the sorting shelf, then shrugs his shoulder. "I thought maybe you'd wanna write a book, rather than shelve them."

"I don't think so," I say, grateful he's not asking me to explain my two-week absence.

"I bet you have a lot of stories to share," he says.

"I'm not really that interesting," I tell him as if he hasn't figured that out.

"Don't do that to yourself," he snaps, but with a smile. " 'Nuff people in this life to put you down, don't be doing it to yourself. You don't say much. I bet you're like an iceberg."

"An iceberg?" I ask, wondering what he could possibly mean, or if he's being mean.

"You only see about one-third of an iceberg," he says. "The rest of it stays hidden."

My thumb should be bleeding from the paper cuts I'm inflicting upon it as I nervously move it back and forth across the top of the book in the my hand. "I should really shelve—"

"I bet you have lots of stories you tell your boyfriend," he interrupts with averted eyes.

I shrug. "I don't have a boyfriend."

"There you go," he says, all confident and energetic. "That's Flint's problem!"

"What do you mean?" I ask, unsure what my boyfriendless state has to do with the city.

"Flint's loaded with people with really bad judgment and poor taste," he whispers. "Maybe we could go out some time, then?"

"Maybe," I whisper.

"Maybe? How vague is that?" he says, laughing. A nervous, shy laugh. Same as mine.

I take a quick hard look at Terrell, and I suddenly don't see this cool guy I work with who's always joking with me. I don't see someone who seems older, wiser, and more secure. I see someone not so different from me—from a part of myself that I don't hate.

He offers me his coffee, then speaks. "I'm sorry, Christy, I didn't mean to—"

"Okay," I say, then I can breathe again as I push the coffee away, but not Terrell.

"Okay, that was my second resolution," he says. "How weird is that?"

"Really?" I ask in shock and awe.

He pulls out a piece of paper from his pocket and pretends he's crossing things off a list. "Don't make New Year's resolutions—check. Ask Christy out—check. Only one thing left."

"What's that?"

"Rescue the city of Flint," he says, laughing at his words. "That might be more difficult."

"Good luck with that, Terrell," I say, managing a little half smile.

"So after work tonight?" he asks, sounding as shy as I do.

"I can't. I have to watch my niece." I have to watch Bree this evening, since no one in my family expects me to have something to do on a Saturday night. I hope I don't have to explain anymore. I don't know anything about romance, but I'm pretty sure that most first dates don't involve explaining about your incarcerated family members.

"Well, then I'll have time to work on my plan to save this city," he replies, then buries his eyes into the floor. "So, how about some other time?"

I dig my hands deep into my pockets, so my shaking hands are well hidden. "Okay," I say.

"Okay!" He shouts to the chagrin of the other staff, most of whom have started working hard, wondering when and if either of us will shelve a book. Terrell gets this real embarrassed look on his face, then walks slowly over to his section to start shelving, while I think of how sad a feeling it must be for a book to be shelved, alone and unwanted, just like I used to feel. Used to.

"Are you ready?' Terrell says, tapping me on the right shoulder. I try not to jump, and I realize this isn't the right time or right place to tell him that I don't like to be touched by anyone.

"Ready," I reply.

He points at the clock in the reference area, which reads 12:30. Even though I like my job, some days the time drags, but today I've barely noticed a second pass by, maybe because I've hardly shelved a book.

"You said some other time," he says, tapping me again on the shoulder as I hide my discomfort. "And as you can see, this is some other time, so."

"But, I—" I start.

Terrell pantomimes a whisper, then speaks, "Lets run down

to Angelo's. We can take my wheels. The wheels are actually about the only thing that work on my not-so-Grand Am."

I shove my hands into my pockets, looking for loose change. With no work for two weeks and no Ryan income, I've got only a bus pass to my name. "I don't—"

"Have any more excuses," Terrell says, then raises his left eyebrow.

"Okay," I mumble as I walk with him toward the door. My digestive system roller coaster leaves me sweating, sore, and seriously terrified, but I press on. I can't decide if I'm more terrified of Terrell's attention or afraid of his rejection.

Things are pretty quiet on the short drive over to Angelo's, an old Flint diner. He turns on an oldies R & B station, which is what I listen to whenever I have a chance, which isn't often. Whenever Mitchell or Ryan drive, it's loud rap, while Mama listens to a Christian station.

The parking lot is pretty empty, just a few old pickups. The rusted red of Terrell's Grand Am adds to the beaten-up and beaten-down look of the lot. There's a line of guys in work clothes getting take-out, and the counter is packed with older white men, surrounded in the haze of twenty-four-hours-a-day cigarette smoke. When we walk in, Terrell leads us toward a table, but I move us quickly to a booth.

"Two up and a cup of Joe," an almost blue-haired waitress says to Terrell as soon as we're seated. He looks embarrassed by her attention. "Um, I come here a lot," he says shyly.

There is a layer of grease on the scratched-up Formica table, matched only by the double layer of grit on the filthy floor. My restless feet stir the debris of uneaten fries and ketchup packages tossed under the table. My left foot yearns to run away, but the right one wants to stretch out and pin Terrell into place. Another waitress comes over with a cup of coffee for Terrell, which he starts to sip even before he unzips his leather jacket, like it was life itself.

"What's two up?" I ask, curious about the greeting he received.

"That means two hot dogs with everything," he says, pointing to the food being delivered to the table next to us to two overweight fifty-something guys wearing work clothes and scowls. I look quickly for the cheapest thing on the yellowed wall menu. I have found a dollar in change in my coat, so Terrell won't have to treat me and I won't owe him.

"So, what'll it be?" The waitress ends the sentence with a loud snap of her gum, although whatever the mint flavor it isn't enough to overcome the smell of smoke clinging to her bluish hair.

"Just toast," I say, fingering the coins. I'm not toasted, but I'm still desperately hungry. My stomach is churning, full of anxiety at the thought of eating in front of Terrell.

"To drink?" she shouts back. Yelling seems to be her normal tone of voice. "Coffee?"

"No, um, just water," I say, noticing a slight frown from Terrell.

"Bread and water. It ain't that pretty in here, but this isn't prison," he says, then laughs, and I hope he didn't see my eyes close tight. "Give her a pop and one up. I'll pay. This time."

I'm looking around for the bathroom, but seeing the condition of the floor, tables, and smoke-hazed windows, I decide not to run into the bathroom. "So, it seems they know you here," I say softly.

"My mom works a lot. She's not home much, and I can't cook. So . . ," he says.

"What does she do?" I ask, trying my best to hear over the constant yelling of the waitresses who shout out the orders from halfway across the room, trying my best to breathe through the lung-blocking layer of smoke, but mostly trying to say, do, and be the right things.

"She's a nurse at McClaren," he says, followed by another sip. "What about your mom?"

"She works in health care too," I say, kicking myself for telling so many lies. He doesn't ask about my father, so I won't ask him. I learned not to do that. Like Tommy said, people always tell you their dads are dead, even if they've just run off. Like Tommy's did.

"She works a lot of long hours, and so I don't get a lot of home-cooked meals. We just live off Franklin, and this is so close," he says, sipping his coffee. "She's so busy, you know, I don't want to ask her to do stuff for me. Probably the same thing with your mom."

I nod my head in agreement, trying to remember how many lies I've told. "You must be busy, too, working at the library, and going to Summit. That's a real hard school, right?" I know Anne's father pushed her to go to Summit, which is how she pulled into Southwestern.

"It's tough, sure, but it needs to be. I want a good education so I can get into a good college," he says, sipping his coffee again, although I can't imagine there's any left in the cup.

"What are you going to study in college? You never told me."

"No, you never guessed," he says, then laughs. "Okay, last

chance. Consider all the clues I've given you, consider this place, our fair city of Flint, and then it's double or nothing."

"Double or nothing?" I ask, trying not to appear totally dense, but I'm clueless.

"That means if you get it right, you win double, but if you get it wrong you win nothing," he says, smiling at both his statement and the food arriving on the table.

"What's the prize?" I ask, pulling the hot dog loaded with onions, mustard, meat sauce, and more onions closer. The same aroma is ingrained in the torn green vinyl seat I occupy.

"Me, although I realize I'm not much of a trophy," he says, leaning closer. "You get it right, then we'll both forget my pathetic date attempt, but if you get it wrong, then I get a second date. Okay, Christy Mallory, double or nothing. I plan to study what at college?"

I take a deep breath, which in this air is a mistake. I start to cough, which kills time as I try to figure out what I want to do, what I know about Terrell, and if I want to know any more.

"So?" he says, leaning closer. The fact that I don't want to push him away is my final clue.

"Chemistry," I say, which I hope is the smartest sounding wrong answer I can give.

"Incorrect answer!" I wonder if he suspects that I missed on purpose. "Urban planning."

"Urban planning?" I ask, unsure even what it means. "Why urban planning?"

"You ever heard of the computer game Sim City?" he asks, but I don't get a chance to answer, which is fine.

"Every other computer game is about killing things, Sim City is about building stuff," Terrell says, then pushes a napkin in front of him. He pulls out a pen and starts drawing little squares on the napkin, like some secret code he's been waiting to share. I nod and he continues.

"You get to be mayor of the city, and you decide everything. It's a lot of fun, but get this," he says, more frantic drawing. I notice his legs are in constant motion when sitting. "In one of the old versions of the game, they have this scenario where you get to be the mayor of the city and save it after a disaster, like Chicago after the fire or San Francisco after the earthquake."

He pauses long enough to sip some coffee, not that he needs an energy boost.

"Well, one of the scenarios in one of the old games is saving Flint, a city with high crime, no jobs, and lots of poor people living in the city because all the rich people moved the money to the burbs," he continues, and I think about Aunt Dee living in Grand Blanc, not rich, but not poor like us. "I've played that scenario hundreds of times, but I can't win and save Flint."

"But it's just a game, isn't it?" I say weakly, compared to his now booming voice.

"Not to me, Christy, not to me," he says.

I don't know if it's the mix of anger and hope filling his answer, the scent of the onions filling my nose, or the toxic air that causes my eyes to tear.

"I want a world where poor people don't go hungry while rich people drive Hummers."

I lean in toward him and whisper, "How are you going to change the world?"

"Like I told you, every journey starts with one step, and my step's here."

"At Angelo's?"

"No, here in Flint," he says with more conviction in his voice than I've ever heard from anyone. "I'm like this city: half black, half white. If I can get it together, then so can Flint."

"What do you mean?" I'm overwhelmed by his passion in my passionless life.

He zips up his leather jacket as he speaks, covering up the old school Public Enemy T-shirt but not the outlook. "I'm going to be the person who saves Flint. I want to be the person to help this city rise up and be great again." I don't say anything; instead I think if every journey starts with one step, then maybe Terrell can save Flint one person at a time, starting with me.

18

january 15, senior year

"You have to tell your mother."

The tone in Aunt Dee's voice is as angry as I've ever heard. I want to crawl under her table and escape her, as well as Tommy and Anne's caring if somewhat appalled stares.

"I can't," I say softly, wishing there was another slice of pizza to fill my mouth. The four of us are having dinner at Aunt Dee's, so I don't have to be at home with the commotion of Ryan's so-called friends watching football and creating a mess that I'll need to clean tomorrow. Anne and Tommy are sitting next to each other, holding hands, and sharing those silly in-love looks. Bree's upstairs, curled up in Aunt Dee's bed reading books from the library. Mama's at the Detroit casinos, while Mitchell's spending his Sunday praying to God, frying chicken, and studying science, hoping one of the three will save him.

"I don't like keeping secrets, especially from family," Aunt Dee whispers to me, even if she's engaged with the rest of us in this conspiracy of silence against Mama.

I slowly swallow some Coke, which gives Tommy time to fill the silence. "She's going to find out when the hospital bill comes," he says all serious, then winks at his mom. "Go ahead and tell her, Christy. Moms always find out the bad stuff anyway."

"That bill's been taken care of," Aunt Dee says softly to Tommy, contradicting her earlier statement: families do keep secrets. It was Aunt Dee, not Mama, who met me at the hospital and arranged with the hospital to pay the bill. Aunt Dee also covered for me with Mama, telling her I'd spent those days at her house. Mama doesn't need to know about what I did. My loud, lonely cry for help stayed a secret to most. But for all of her gentleness, Aunt Dee can be tough: she made me agree to see Mrs. Grayson and to take the medication another doctor prescribed. Like most things, I've turned my words into a half-truth. I see Mrs. Grayson, but I don't say anything. I sit there with my arms crossed over my heart, biting my bottom lip and playing with my tongue stud in order to keep my mouth shut and my mind tuned to a different wavelength. I'm seeing Mrs. Grayson, but I'm just not letting her look into my life.

"Hey, Tommy, how's college?" I say, turning the attention to a safer place. Tommy started classes at Baker College last week, in their physical therapy program.

"It's hard, but I'll make it," Tommy says confidently.

"How can you be so sure?" I ask, wondering if there's a magic formula for self-belief.

"I've survived worse. I'll get along just fine," he replies, then starts clearing the dishes from the table. I know he's talking about his time in juvy, which is a subject he doesn't like to touch on. Remembering the past, Tommy says, is to relive it, and reliving it is just too hard. He says he won't forget what happened, but by forgiving himself and those other kids, it frees him.

Anne's silent. She doesn't know what Tommy's talking about, but I'm under orders from Tommy to remain mute—like that's so hard—about his crime. He'll tell Anne when she's ready to hear it. Yet another conspiracy of silence in our small, splintered, screwed-up family.

"Let me help," I say, but Tommy waves me off. He knows I clean up enough at home.

"I'll pass; I clear too many tables at work," Anne says, then laughs.

"How's your boss?" I ask, but Anne shoots me a look. Her boss remains a problem, but one that Tommy doesn't know about. He's left the room with the dirty dishes, but I bet she's afraid of what he might hear or what he might do to her boss. I swallow my words, as my head fills with thoughts of how all of us would rather suffer in silence than talk about the things that shame us. It's as though if we don't mention the shackles around our ankles, then no one else will notice them.

"Speedy, it's gonna be fine—end of story," she says firmly.

"Why do you call her Speedy?" Aunt Dee asks, my secret name revealed. I wince: this is like when Mitchell's fantasy life as "the Chill" was exposed, but not as devastating. Even though I gave Mitchell a new blue notebook for Christmas, I doubt if he can return to those illusions that used to sustain him. What Ryan took from him that day, another notebook can't replace.

"Because the school's track coach thinks she could be a superstar!" Anne offers.

"Christy, I didn't know you ran track," Aunt Dee says.

"I don't," I say firmly, to put the matter to rest, if only Ms. Chapman would.

"I did sports in high school. I played basketball, but I've got to admit that I wasn't very good," Aunt Dee says, and it strikes me as odd. She's the most successful member of our family, so I can't picture her not being good at something.

"Tell them how many points you scored," Tommy shouts from the kitchen.

"Forty points!" Aunt Dee replies.

"In one game?" Anne asks.

"No, over four years!" Aunt Dee says quickly, and we all laugh. "Well, that's not totally true. I actually tipped in a basket once for the other team, so maybe my career totals should be thirty-eight or maybe forty-two points."

"My mother was the Shaq of her generation!" Tommy shouts. I can sense his smile even from the other room. He and his mom get along; add Tommy to my envy-hate list.

"But I was a star. Think about it: all those girls God blessed with natural talent, it came easy to them, and while there wasn't the WNBA then, they knew they might be rewarded somehow for their skills," Aunt Dee says, sounding a lot like Ms. Chapman. "But girls like me, who went to every practice, did our best with the ability God gave us, and came off the bench only for a few minutes so the best players could rest. I think we were the real stars of the team. How much dedication does it take to show up when you're already a starter?"

"None," I answer.

"But how much dedication does it take when you were like me, a benchwarmer, who will never start, never star, and not even play enough to get a letter. I don't care if I scored forty points or four points; you ask me, I was one of the stars of that team!"

"I would have just quit," I mumble.

Aunt Dee shakes her head, half in anger and half in humor. "That's Ryan talking, not—"

"Speedy," Anne says.

"Here's to Speedy Mallory!" Tommy says, coming in from the kitchen, holding up his glass. Everybody holds their glasses up, and for once, being the center of attention feels good. This feels like home, and I wish it was.

As Tommy, Anne, and Aunt Dee talk, laugh, then talk more, I melt in the seat, thinking about our Christmas visit with Robert a few weeks ago. Meds or no meds, there are also some memories, dreams, and plans that I can't let go of.

senior year, january

"Robert, aren't you scared?"

It's a stupid question to ask Robert, but I can't resist it. While this is our late Christmas visit, there's certainly no telling the season from the cold concrete of Jackson State Prison. This is a place without seasons; time doesn't stand still, it just doesn't exist. The air isn't filled with holiday spirit. I'm almost choking on the thick dust that swirls in the air and the stale smell of the cracked gray floor in the visitor's area. The rest of the family waits in the parking lot. I've stayed behind, but I'm not sure why. Robert was never a brother to me, or part of the family. He was always for himself and by himself.

"I ain't scared of shit," Robert replies, then runs his hand over his now bald head. He looks so strange in the ugly orange-and-blue MDOC outfit; stranger to see him look so small, but that's a trick of the grayish light filtering in through the small barred window.

"Bree misses you," I remind him. "You should write her."

"I know," he says, while I swallow hard. It was a dumb thing to say. Robert can barely read or write, one of many reasons he bailed on school like his daddy bailed on him. I don't know how he and I could be so different just because we have different dads. "You watch her."

"You watch yourself in here," I say, trying to add some gentleness to the harsh air.

"No problem," Robert says, looking around the room. "You tell Mitchell to keep his shit together and not to end up here. If he does, I'll fucking kill him when he gets here."

I nod, more than eager to pass along Robert's death-threat warning, if that's what it takes to save Mitchell from taking the same road and saves us from taking the same trip to Jackson over and over. "I'll give Mitchell the message."

"Lot of dead men already in here," Robert says, but he's smiling, like it's funny.

"What do you mean?" I ask, my knowledge of prison life limited to watching the movie The Shawshank Redemption *on TV, although I doubt now I'd watch it the same way again.*

"Two kinds of guys don't live long in here, and I ain't either," Robert says, that cocky swagger back in his voice. "Stupid fuckers who snitch end up dead."

He pauses to look around the room, before he looks at me. "Who else?" I ask.

"Baby rapers," he says. "Anybody touch Bree like that, I'd break out just to kill 'em."

"But Robert, wouldn't you just get into more trouble?" His loud laughter stops me dead.

"I'm in hard-ass Jackson State Prison. I'm probably never getting out." He rubs his right hand against his chest and leaves it lying over his heart, a muscle he rarely exercised on the outside. "What are they going to do? You can't kill someone who's already dead."

"But Robert—" But before I can say another word, a loud ear-busting buzzer goes off. I say good-bye, then walk with the family members visiting other prisoners as we exit back to the free world.

It's so cold you can see, smell, and taste your icy breath. The air out here, although frozen, still makes you feel alive. I keep my head down and make sure not to talk to anyone as I try to find Ryan, Mama, Mitchell, and Bree. As I watch the other visitors climb into their cars, I can't help but wonder if one of them will come back next week to find their man dead. Dead because he ratted or someone found out he raped children. Robert's right, you can't kill a person who is already dead, but he should have added something about the other set of marked men inside those walls: you can't really murder a person who doesn't even deserve to live.

19

january 23, senior year

"Nobody knows, are you sure?"

Anne and I are walking from school at the end of the day. We're headed toward the parking lot, not the bridge. It's not just the arctic weather keeping us from chasing tail lights and getting high, but Anne told me that Tommy's pressuring her to stop getting stoned. It's too bad Anne can't tell her dad this fact, then he could find at least one thing that he likes about Tommy. The list of what he doesn't like is long; no doubt his relationship to me topping the list.

"Not that I've heard," Anne replies, blowing on her hands to keep warm. We're talking about the New Year's Eve party, my disappearance, and the broken mirror. Anne's listening for gossip, but it seems nobody knows—or maybe cares—about my stupid desperate act.

"That's good news," I say, knowing the bad news, that I have an appointment with Mrs. Grayson in about an hour. Aunt Dee's threatening to tell Mama if I don't keep showing up for these appointments. Since Aunt Dee is more a mother to me than Mama, I can't afford to get any further on her bad side. I've taken a step in that direction by helping Anne and Tommy hook up; a coupling Aunt Dee's not thrilled with either. She wants Tommy focused on his future, not on anyone in his present. I'll keep my word to Aunt Dee and see Mrs. Grayson, but that doesn't mean I have to say anything. Just like I won't talk to Officer Kay, who called to press me about pressing charges. I told Officer Kay the same true story: Glen didn't touch me, and I don't want to talk with her. All these people say they want to listen, but none of them hear what I say.

Anne shoots me a little half smile, which breaks out into a full-blown energy-generating grin when Tommy's old Toyota pulls into the parking lot with music thumping through closed windows. "Sure you don't want a ride?" she asks through lips ready to be kissed by my cousin.

"I'm good," I say, which is only half true. I'm not good about Anne riding to and from school with Tommy most days. I'm not good about him spending time with Anne that used to be mine. I'm not good about Anne getting close to a member of my family. I've kept a lot of stuff from Anne, best friend or not, so I'm not good about her knowing more about me.

"He's so cool," Anne says, giving my too-thin-for-winter jacket a pinch. "I owe you."

I laugh, thinking how much money I owe Anne from the past three years, thinking how maybe I owe her my life for following me at the party when she saw me race out, and thanking her for being a better friend to me than I've ever been to her. "No charge."

"Hey Cuz," Tommy yells at me out of the rolled-down window. "Jump on in!"

I shake my head, shoot them a big wave, then walk down toward the city bus stop on Twelfth Street in front of school. As they drive past, Anne already cuddled against his chest, I feel like splitting down the center. Seeing the two of them together, I feel so left out. I feel so alone. Yet, no more than three weeks ago, I did something really stupid because I just wanted to be left alone. I didn't want to die; I just didn't want to live in the foul air that I was breathing.

While the air still stinks, I feel I can breathe again. Three weeks into my meds, I don't feel like I'm walking on a road full of trapdoors anymore. I don't feel much better, but I don't feel much worse: the door to despair seems stuck. It took falling as far as I did, as well as finally seeing a doctor, which I haven't done for years, to realize I had options. When you're so used to having no power in your life, the idea of making changes is blacked out. I don't have to worry about one possible side effect of these meds, loss of sex drive, since I've never had one.

The bus toward downtown is pretty crowded, but I find a vacant seat in the middle. It's hot and loud, so I unzip my jacket and open up my mind. I remember dreaming about Glen sitting next to me on a bus, in a car, or at school, but I know now it's only dream. Deep down, I guess I always knew he was too smart, too funny, too popular, too handsome, too rich, and also too normal to be with someone like me, but the dream kept me going. It was also a safe dream: dreaming a dream of the unreachable means you'll always want, but never really fail. But Glen is a lost dream now: I can't ever speak to him again. I'm so embarrassed and ashamed that if I see him at school, I'll walk in the other direction. He doesn't want to talk to me either: just like Romeo and Juliet, our ending is tragic, full of misunderstandings, with a bloody final scene.

"Hey FUBU," a voice says. I'm wearing one of Robert's old FUBU shirts, since the sleeves are long enough to carefully cover up the last remains of the scars on my wrist.

I look up to see that the voice belongs to Seth Lewis, standing over me, then sitting next to me.

"So, Christy, I always wondered, what does FUBU stand for?" He pushes against me.

"Leave me alone," I say, almost wincing in pain from his mere presence.

He presses closer against me. The rotten apple smells still cling to him after all these years. "Let me guess; FUBU stands for "fucked up bitch ugly."

I want to get out of the seat, but I'm pinned against the side of the bus. His leg is blocking any chance of escape. I can't fight back; I can't answer; I can't do anything but beg for him to stop, which makes me even more powerless. "Please, Seth, leave me alone."

"I keep thinking, you've had six years to change your mind, but I guess not," Seth says, pressing against me, almost talking in my ear. "Maybe it means "furry untrimmed bush."

"Leave me alone," I say loudly. There are other people on the bus from our school. Several look over, but none of them move a muscle to help me.

"I see Anne getting all lovey-dovey with that guy. I heard he's your cousin, so I guess you and Anne aren't cleaning each other's carpets. Too bad, 'cause I'd pay to watch some of that action."

"Let me go or else." I'm chewing on my almost healed bottom lip again.

"Or else what?" He's not backing down.

"Or else," and then I stop because there is no or else. There is nothing to do but run. I take a deep breath, then push against him. He's surprised that I'm fighting back at all. He's more amused than angry, so rather than holding me back, he lets out a loud laugh as I crawl over him. He puts his fat hand on my ass as I escape. I pull the cord, then run toward the front of the bus. I don't know where I'm getting off, but it's got to be a better place than this.

"FUBU! I got it," I hear Seth yell at the top of his lungs for everyone to hear.

"Please, stop now!" I beg the driver.

"Christy is a frigid uptight bitch ultimately!" Seth shouts as I exit the bus.

I walk the half mile toward Mrs. Grayson's office, stopping long enough at the downtown Halo Burger to throw up the remains of my lunch, wishing Seth's face was in the toilet. The detour makes me late, which means less time sitting in silence in the brightly colored waiting room. I sign some papers, then sit with my head almost hanging between my knees, Seth's insults hanging around my neck like a stone, and my ugly coat hanging on a gold antique rack. A few minutes go by before Mrs. Grayson opens a door, then says, "Come in, Christy."

She's dressed in another blue suit, complete with pearls. I sit my torn-blue-jean-Seth-infected ass down on her colorful couch covered with flower patterns. There are flowers in a vase, as well as a picture of sunflowers on her wall next to all the diplomas.

"Christy, how are you today?" she asks, and smiles. She doesn't know that not only do I live on Stone Street, I'm made of it. I will not speak or cry or crack. "Would you like some water?"

I shake my head. My eyes are cataloging her brightly lit office, not catching her stare.

"Well, we need to know each other a bit better," she says, then opens up a big black notebook. She could use a Post-it note for all that I plan to tell her.

"Why don't we start by you just telling me a little bit about yourself," she says.

"I don't know," I mutter at a barely audible volume.

"What do you mean you don't know? You don't know anything about yourself?"

I understand the question, but that doesn't mean I'll answer it, so I say, "I don't know."

And it goes on like that for another half hour with her asking me question after question, lecturing a little in between about how I need to answer, telling me she knows what I must be feeling, always followed by more questions. When she says we're done for the day, I let out a loud sigh of relief, which causes her to ask, "Christy, are you going to talk to me at all?"

I finally give a full and loud answer. "No."

"Fine, if you don't want to talk with me, I can't make you," she says, then leans in a little closer. She's wearing perfume, but I have no idea what kind. It might smell nice, except the stink of Seth on me overpowers her scent. "I spoke with Officer Kay, you know."

I jam my top teeth into my bottom lip, hard and fast. I feel blood forthcoming.

"She says you don't want the police to follow up on your attack. On your r—"

"I just want people to leave me alone," I finally speak, actually more of a shout.

"I could have the police visit your house if you like," she throws down.

"Is that supposed to scare me?" I snap back.

"No, Christy, I don't think that will scare you," she offers. "I don't think much scares you. Kind of the way people who lived in castles with high walls and moats weren't scared. You've got all your defenses up, I can see that. There's maybe only one thing that scares you."

"What's that?" I shoot back.

"The truth," she says, then closes up the notebook she's been writing in. She puts down the notebook, then hands me a single tissue from the flowery box. "Your lip is bleeding. Here."

I don't say thank you, I don't say anything. I take the tissue, wipe away the blood, jam the bloody tissue into my pocket, then get up from the couch. I don't look at her as I head toward the door.

"I'm sure you've heard the truth will set you free," she says as I open the door. "It's not just a saying, Christy. I'll see you in two weeks."

I resist the urge to slam the door behind me and in her face. I grab my coat, then head outside. I don't zip it up, instead I let the cold January air push into my lungs. I'm not thinking about Seth or Glen or even Mrs. Grayson, I'm thinking about Breezy. I'm remembering a year or so ago us putting together a jigsaw puzzle that Mama bought for her at Goodwill. We got most of the pieces together, but a few were missing. As I wait for the bus to my house, I think how I'm like that damaged and used puzzle. Anne holds some of the pieces from New Year's Eve, so does

Glen. Mrs. Grayson might be able to figure something out, and Officer Kay thinks she already knows something. Everybody has a piece, but as long as they never talk to one another, they'll never put the pieces together. The truth is the missing piece; the truth is me.

20

january 30, senior year

"What's going on with you and Glen?"

I don't say anything. I remain locked in the stillness that overwhelms me even amid the cafeteria clatter. This is not shyness; this is about being strong enough to survive in silence. We're sitting in the cafeteria away from traffic and my Glen perch.

"Does this have to do with New Year's?" Anne knows the end of the evening, not the start. And she never will.

"Anne, I don't want to talk about it," I say as harshly as I've ever spoken to Anne.

"Some friend," Anne says, trumping my harshness with spitting anger.

"We are friends, but this is my business, not yours," I say, then stare at my feet.

"Look at me, Christy," Anne says, but I don't turn an inch.

"Fine, you won't look at me, but you will listen to me," Anne snaps off the words. "We go to a party together, you disappear, and next thing I know you're on a bridge barefoot with blood on your dress. I call my dad to meet us at the hospital, I sit with you, and I don't ask you anything. I've let it slide. I've let you slide, but this morning was too much."

"What happened?" I ask, then yawn. It's a Thursday morning; I'm feeling pretty tired.

"Glen called me and asked me to ask you a question, since you won't talk to him."

I put my left foot over my right; I tie my tongue to the roof of my mouth.

"He wants to know why you hate him." Anne's talking right into my ear.

"I don't hate him."

"Then why are we here, and not by the theater? Why don't we drive by his house anymore?" Anne's anger is boiling over. "If you don't hate Glen, you gotta funny way of—"

"Enough," I say. Beg. Plead. Demand.

"I'm good at math and I can add. You like Glen; something happens to you at a party. Now you're avoiding him, while he's wondering why you hate him. Did Glen do something to you at the party? Is he the reason you ended up in the hospital. He didn't—"

"No," I want to shout, but it comes out as no more than a whisper.

"Then what?"

Anne's good, but if I didn't answer Mrs. Grayson or Officer Kay, I won't answer Anne. I will run. I will hide.

"Nothing." I'm fighting both with my meds and with my best friend, but I stay silent.

"Then at least you and Glen have to talk," Anne says, taking French fries off my tray.

"I know," I say. I can't stand the way Glen glares at me, like I once stared at him.

Anne's playing with a gold bracelet that Tommy gave her, trying not to look me in the eyes. "I'm sure Glen is as worried about you as Tommy and I are. I'll set it up with Glen."

"Why bother?" I hiss, wondering where the laughter of lunches past has gone.

"Because he's your friend," she says. "And because I'm your friend and I'm asking."

I shake my head no, yet I know she's right and I need to correct this wrong somehow. "He used to be my friend, I thought," I say after a long pause.

"Ironic, isn't it?"

"What's that?"

"You've spent almost five years practically stalking Glen," Anne says, releasing an almost now rare memory movie in my mind, "and now you do everything you can to avoid him."

"I just want to run away from this," I say as I rub the sleep out of my eyes, clearing room for tears to flow. I get up to leave, but Anne grabs hold of my oversize T-shirt. "Let go!"

"No, Christy, I won't let go," she says. "I won't let you run away from this, from Glen."

"Screw you, or is that Tommy's job now?" I say, then turn on my heel and run to prove her wrong. But my meds are like a chain, and I don't even make it as far as the front door.

Ten minutes later, I'm sitting alone in the school library. My face is buried in the book *Ellen Foster* by Kaye Gibbons, another Ms. Chapman pick. The bell for sixth period rings, my history class with Anne and Glen, but there's no sense going. It seems as if I'm never going to learn from history, so why bother at all. Someday I'll face Glen again; this isn't that day.

"I'm sorry," I hear Anne's voice whisper behind me.

"Me, too," I say, as she sits across from me. Unlike me, she's got a pass to be here.

"This thing is so hard to figure out, you know?" Anne, the smartest girl in school, says.

"I've got an answer," I whisper to avoid drawing notice from the librarian, Mrs. Sullivan.

"What's that?" Anne replies, and I swear she's almost glowing she's so filled with love.

"I'm dropping out of school," I say without any emotion in my voice.

"You can't do that!" Anne says instantly.

"Why?"

"Because," Anne says, then pauses. A pause you could drive a semitruck through.

"Who am I kidding?" I say these words that have rattled around in my head for so long.

"You won't be able to go to college, if you drop out," Anne says, reasons returning.

"And do what?" I counter quickly, telling Anne the fate of most poor kids like me of every color in Flint. "Be a doctor like your dad? Or a college professor like your mom?"

"You can be anything that you—"

I cut her off. "You don't really believe that, do you?"

She answers by not answering.

"Never mind," I counter. Anne might kiss my cousin and share her secrets with me, but she's not part of the family. "I've decided."

"No, I won't allow it," Anne says, reaching across to grab my arm again, but I retreat.

"You're not my mother," I shoot back, thinking how my mother isn't one either.

"Maybe not, but you can't do this," Anne says. "Promise me you won't drop out."

"I promise," I say after a while. I know I'm just dreaming, not planning. I'm thinking how hard it is to break free of anything, even something you hate. We sit for a while in silence.

"About Glen," Anne finally says while flashing an out-of-place smile.

I fidget in my seat. "I just can't face him, and I'm sure he doesn't want to talk to me."

"Yes I do," Glen says from behind me.

"How long have you . . ." I say, turning to look at him, then glaring at Anne.

"I heard most everything," he says. Anne smiles, then exits. She gives her chair and pass to Glen, but I can't look at him. The brightness of those blue eyes seems faded, and I know I'm the one to blame. He's no longer my Romeo, and I was never ever his Juliet.

"Glen, I'm sorry about everything," I say, my words falling short and stale.

"I'm not angry at you, Christy," he says and I believe him. I always believe him.

"About the police, about everything," I say, not wanting to go into detail.

"I don't want people to think I'm some rapist. You have to tell them the truth," he says.

"I have, I have." I've told the police it wasn't Glen, but they don't believe me. They won't believe me until I reveal the truth behind their evidence. "But don't you understand how humiliating the truth is?"

"I'm sorry about that night, about what happened," he says, as if that is comforting.

"That's not what hurts," I confess and unclench my jaw. "Why don't you like me?"

"I'm sorry, Christy; I like you, but I just want to be friends," he says as gently as possible.

I close my eyes tight, holding back tears. Glen doesn't love me and never will. "I don't blame you. Who could love someone as ugly—"

"It's not you, Christy. Don't you know how funny and smart and beautiful you are?"

Then he stops speaking, and my heart stops beating. I wipe the tears from the corners of my eyes, then he takes my chin in his hand. I stare him down and I realize he might be telling the truth. I know now Glen will never kiss me, and I doubt if Terrell ever will, but Glen saying these words delights me. I'm strangely at peace from the damage of his final rejection.

"Thank you," I say as he releases my head from his hand and lets my soul soar. I wish this moment was recorded for Terrell to know he was right: beauty supplies. "But why, then?"

"Can I trust you?" Glen asks, and agreeing with him comes instantly and instinctively.

"Always."

"I don't want you to think that I didn't, you know, because it's not about anything about you, it's me," he says. He looks around the mostly empty library, then leans across the table, so he's almost whispering in my ear. He lets out a sigh, like a weight lifting from his chest. "Christy, I'm gay."

21

february 12, senior year

"I want you to knock this crap off!"

Tommy tells me that the second that Anne heads outside to take a call from her dad. We're sitting in a booth at Angelo's. I'm hoping that Terrell will somehow just show up.

"What do you mean?" I say, sounding stupid, but wishing I was stoned.

"Working for Ryan and selling his shit at school," he says forcefully.

I'm more pissed at Anne for telling than Tommy for talking. I know Tommy didn't learn about this from Ryan, since they exchange only angry glares, not words. "But—"

"I'm serious; you don't want to end up inside," he says speaking from experience.

"I'm not a dealer," I might as well confess, since he knows. "I sell to Anne, Glen, and a few other people, that's it. I sell to the good kids who are afraid to buy from the bad kids."

"Like you," he says, pointing his fork in my direction. What he doesn't know, of course, is I've tried to quit before. But when Ryan points his anger in my direction, he might just as well have a gun to my head or scissors to my throat. I can't get myself free of this chain either.

"I'm not like one of those people," I say, thinking of Ryan's hangers-on.

"Neither was I, but look what happened to me," Tommy says, looking over his shoulder making sure that Anne remains in the dark.

"Wrong place, wrong time," I say.

"Yes and no," he replies. "But I still made a choice to be in that place. That was my choice. If you blame everything on fate, then you're not responsible for anything."

"When did you get righteous?" Tommy was never like Robert, but he wasn't any angel.

"When I spent nine months living, eating, and going to school with the future Roberts of the world," Tommy says. "I ain't ever going back. It is the worst place in the world."

"How did you get through it?" I ask.

"I read, then read some more," Tommy says. "I avoided trouble and made sure that trouble never found me. And I prayed to God for strength. But I'm not perfect, you know."

"What do you mean?" I ask.

"I never had trouble with the other residents. I took their crap but it didn't stick, and they let me go my own way," Tommy says, talking faster now, not just to tell his story before Anne gets back, but because I think he just needs to tell it. Telling the story makes it real, not just a story. "But some of the staff, that's something else."

"Tell me, Anne's not coming back soon," I tell Tommy. "She's gotta argue with her father for at least twenty minutes every day about something or even nothing. You'll learn."

Tommy takes a deep breath, then speaks. "When I first came to the facility, I was scared. I wasn't catching on to what was expected of me. I'll follow the rules, I just have to know what they are. But this one dried-up CO always hassled me, I don't even know what for, and I finally yelled at him: 'Just because I'm in a cage, doesn't mean you have to treat me like an animal.'"

"What happened?"

"After that, he owned me because he knew he'd got to me. He'd see me in the hall and make sure to hassle me in front of the others. One time I was running late for class, he stuck his leg out and tripped me, but acted like it was an accident. He never laughed, he just smirked."

"How terrible," I say, thinking instantly of Ryan's perma-smirk.

"Then one day, I just didn't let him get to me anymore. I'd had enough. I can't say why or what caused it, but I said to myself, this son of a bitch doesn't own me. And he saw that in my face the next time he tried something on me. I told him that, and after that he left me alone."

"That's great," I say.

"Except for the kid he started picking on instead of me," Tommy says.

"That's not your fault."

"That doesn't mean I don't feel guilty about it," he says. "And the kid who he picked was like me, from the burbs, not from the hood, so he learned the same lesson the same hard way."

"What lesson is that?" I ask

"I tell you, Christy, one thing I learned inside is that if you're poor, young, and live in Flint, you just get used to people in uniforms, suits and ties, and other costumes pushing you around," Tommy says. "And I don't want that for you."

"So," I whisper.

"Stop slinging for Ryan," he says again.

"But it's nothing. Why would the cops even bother to—"

"Because that's how it works. They know the whole thing is a pyramid. They start at the bottom, bust the smaller dealers or the big users, then get them to snitch on somebody else to get less time. Even Ryan, he's small time, a punk. He'd snitch in a second to avoid hard time."

"Okay," I say, realizing Tommy is becoming a tail light in my life. "But you tell him."

Tommy laughs, but it's cut short when he sees Anne returning to the table. "No, it's up to you to tell him. If you don't tell him, then you'll never get free of it."

I think about Brutus, then touch the tattoo on my ankle, and grab my coat.

"Where you going?" Anne says.

"Home," I say strongly. Not just because I don't want to be a third wheel, but because I want to ride free. Maybe this tail light I can chase, and it will actually get me someplace. I say my polite good-byes, zip up my coat, and walk outside to catch a southbound bus.

"Bitch, where's my money?" Ryan shouts at me almost the minute I come in the door.

He stands at the door of my room, blocking out the light from the hallway. Bree is with Aunt Dee, while Mama and Mitchell are both working tonight.

I pull the bills from my jeans. I put my hand out. He takes the cash, counts it quickly, but his touch lingers, like a snail's slime. "You're light."

I've been cutting into his profit since Glen confided in me. While it healed my rejected heart, carrying a secret that large is one heavy stone. "Too bad, Ryan, that's all I got."

That laugh, that stinky smelly laugh oozes across the hall. "Too bad for you."

"I'm not dealing at school anymore," I say, taking baby steps at age eighteen.

"Little girl, you do what I tell you," he says, a step closer now.

"I'm afraid I'll get caught, get kicked out of school," I counter, hiding Tommy's role.

"You act all stuck up and smart like you're too good for us," he says, and I can taste his hot breath from a distance. I'm silent, my chewed tongue and rough bottom lip trap in words. "Ugly bitches like you are good for three things. You can sling shit, steal stuff, or suck dick."

I turn around and slap his face. As he tries to wipe my hand print away, laughing as I stumble past him, finding my lost speed again. As I run toward the bridge, I don't hear the sound of cars, but of the smack of flesh, and it reminds me of when Anne and I ran away. I use the sting of Ryan's words to fight through my meds and remember how I learned two years ago that running away is easy; staying away is the hard part.

sophomore year, february

"I'm sick of this!"

Anne's fuming mad at her father for telling us, for what he said was the hundredth time but I only counted ten, to be quiet and go to sleep. Anne and I are spending the evening of Valentine's Day at her house rather than at the Friday school dance or out on a date. It's past midnight when we finally turn off the lights.

"What do you want to do?" I whisper. It's funny that Anne so hates it here at her home, while I wish I could move in. My almost regular weekend stayovers are not enough. If I could live here instead of my house during the week, then I'd be awake for school and not laying in the darkness of my own room. I'm here so often, I probably should pay rent.

Anne crawls out of bed and across the floor, and shoves some towels under the door. She flicks on the small light near her bed, then opens the window. The cold air blasts into the room, but Anne just wraps the thick blanket around her, pulls her bone white pipe from beneath her mattress, fills it, then lights up. "Do you know how to drive?" she says after inhaling.

"Not really, why?" I ask, thinking that good memories of sitting on Daddy's lap and steering hardly qualify as driving.

"Let's run away," Anne says, very definitively. She hands the pipe and the decision over to me. Her eyes are bloodshot, but not

from the dope; it's our first taste of the night. She's tired from constant fights with her parents, mainly her father, and mostly about my being her friend.

"Anne, why does your father hate me so much?" I ask, ready to swallow the acid of her dad's loathing. I can't just feel good; sometimes I think rejection is my real drug.

There's the expected awkward silence, although silence is rarely one of Anne's best qualities. "Because he's an arrogant asshole obsessed with money," she finally says. Even though we're whispering, since her parent's bedroom is across the hall, in my ears she's shouting.

"What do you mean?" I ask. Since her father barely speaks to me, I don't know him.

"Here's how the world works according to my father," Anne says. Even though the room is cold, I've moved myself from the confines of the sleeping bag to sitting on the floor, leaning against Anne's big white oak desk. She hands the pipe back, then uses her free hand to jab me lightly in the arm. I still flinch; Anne's become my best friend, but I still feel allergic to human touch. "He says you hang with trash, you end up stinking yourself."

"What does that mean?"

"What do you think it means, Christy?" she says. But I know, and it makes me sick.

"You're my friend no matter what he says," Anne says, putting the subject to rest, even if we are not. At these almost weekly weekend sleepovers, we stay up much later than she's allowed, then sleep late the next morning. It's the freest feeling in the world.

"No matter what anyone says," I say, taking a deep hit on the pipe.

"So, let's go, what do you say?" Anne says, moving toward her closet. She starts throwing some clothes into her normally stuffed monogrammed bright green L.L.Bean backpack.

"Where are we going?" I ask, gathering up my own belongings, which barely fill my bag.

"I guess we'll have to finally do it," Anne says as she removes the towels from the door.

"Do what?" I respond, the click of the door unlocking distracting me.

Anne opens the door, the hall light shines in, and darkness, at least for the moment, disappears. "Chase tail lights."

Anne hands me the car keys as we slip outside of her house unnoticed. We open the garage door; every little crack and pop sounds like gunfire, but the chain reaction doesn't occur. The sounds outside don't cause the lights inside her parent's bedroom to click on. We open the doors to her mom's PT Cruiser and almost leap for joy as we land in the seats.

"Where to?" I ask, trying to find where the key goes to start our journey. Anne expertly lifted the keys, along with all the money from her dad's wallet, before we crept clear of her crib.

"I don't know. None of my relatives would let me stay with them. They'd turn me in. One big happy family," Anne says sadly, realizing the obstacles ahead. "How about you?"

"Maybe Aunt Dee," I respond, unsure but looking for any out I can find.

"Then let's get going," Anne says, pointing out the ignition slot. I turn the key. When the car starts, classical music bursts out of the speakers, which Anne quickly turns down. I look into the rearview mirror, then into my memory of driving with my daddy. For once, a

good memory conquers all my bad sad ones, as I slip the car into reverse and we exit the garage.

I almost take out the mail box, but do a last-second correction. I get the wheel turned the right way, and we are on our way. I decide not to get on I-69. Instead we take Miller Road out toward the mall, which is where Anne and I started the evening. We took the bus there, much to her parent's chagrin, watched a movie while Anne filled us with soda, popcorn, and candy, and then got picked up by her mother. Her mother doesn't seem to dislike me as much as her father, but as Anne says, her house isn't a democracy. Even if it was, she says, her dad's vote is worth two of her mom's. Anne doesn't even get one.

"I want to dye my hair blond, what do you think?" Anne says out of nowhere. "Do you think there's anyplace we could do that tonight?"

I shrug again, keeping my eyes on the road. Even if my hands are slightly shaking, my feet are steady on the pedals, and the driving is becoming less terrifying. "Why would you?"

"I hate how I look," Anne says, as she pulls down the mirror on the visor.

"Anne, you're gorgeous," I say, wondering even as the words slip out of my mouth if I've said something wrong. People at school, no doubt, think I'm a lesbian, since I've never had a boyfriend. I don't seem all that interested in boys, and I look a lot more like a boy than a girl.

"I don't think so," Anne says, staring at the mirror not at me. "I hate how I look."

"You're too smart for that," I reassure her. Anne's got plenty of boys at school who want her, and I think she enjoys that more

than anything else. She doesn't like them, she just likes them liking her. For all her bluster, Anne's really pretty shy around boys, just like me.

"Well, so are you, Christy, but you don't believe it," she says, but I know it's just to be nice. Sometimes I think, in those dark places of my mind I visit far too often, that Anne only likes me because I'm not beautiful, so she can be the center of attention. But I let these dark thoughts vanish as we cruise by the mall, then turn around. If Anne's going to try to tell me I'm beautiful, I might as well believe her rather than Ryan's constant "ugly bitch" comments.

"Where does your aunt live?" Anne asks, knowing full well the answer. She lives in Grand Blanc, south of Flint, but we're headed in the opposite direction.

"You caught me," I say, driving carefully so we don't get caught. "We're going—"

"To Glen's house," she says, then we both laugh.

We continue to laugh, listen to music, and laugh some more as we just make a loop from Glen's house, back to the mall, and back to Glen's over and over again. It's unsaid, but somewhere in the middle of the night just before the light of day, both Anne and I know that we're not going to Aunt Dee's to stay. We know that we're not driving across the state to Lansing to relatives of Anne's that she reconsidered and thought might let us stay, and that we're certainly not going to stay the night at Glen's. Just like my daddy said, chasing the tail lights sometimes takes you home, which is where we both decided we're probably headed. Running away seems like a good idea, until you realize there's no place else to go. As we drive deep into the night, I realize while you can run, you can't hide from your secrets.

"We should get home," Anne finally says. While the sun isn't rising yet, it's close enough. We've both been yawning more than talking for the last hour. I'm used to sleepless nights, but it's never been because I was having so much fun that I wanted an endless night.

"Now what?" I ask, knowing Anne has all the answers.

"How about a little revenge?"

"What do you mean?" I ask as we cruise very slowly through Flint's battered streets.

"Let's go pay a visit to Seth Lewis, or should I say Seth Loser."

"I don't know," I reply, my voice wavering between fear and fearlessness.

"Why do you let him treat you like—"

"I'll make you a deal," I say to stop her from telling me what I already know too well.

Anne moves in her seat so she's kneeling, not sitting. "What's that?"

"You stand up to your dad and I'll stand up to Seth," I say, delaying the inevitable.

"Define 'stand up,'" Anne says. I'm focused on the road, but I know she's smiling wide.

"I can't, but you know what I mean," I say, thinking of my home, not hers. "Tell him that he doesn't control you, that he doesn't own you."

"Nice speech," Anne cracks, since she normally dominates 90 percent of our conversations. "But until that day, why don't we take something from Seth."

"He doesn't have anything," I remind her.

"Then, fine, Christy, let's leave him something," she shouts, as we drive to a twenty-four-hour Meijer's. The bleary-eyed clerk never

even flinched at two fourteen-year-old girls buying two cans of spray paint at three in the morning. Instead, he had the look of Flint, slightly battered, tired, and wondering when better days were coming. Anne pays with cash, and we're in front of Seth's house in minutes.

With no streetlights or stars above us, a lonely half-moon guides us as we spray-paint "Seth Loser" in his driveway. I'd never tasted vengeance before, so I didn't know I had been starving.

The energy rush of revenge doesn't last long. It's not long after we're back driving in circles that Anne falls asleep. I drive past the mostly deserted parking lot of the GM Truck Assembly plant. It's lit up with this strange neon glare. Yet, there's something in the light, or this night, that hits me like a bolt of lightning and makes our evening spent driving in circles a simple straight truth: you can't really run away from anything, because whatever you think you're running from is always with you.

When I turn onto Anne's street, I see the lights on in front of her house and the police car. Unlike my neighborhood, a police car in front of the house at five in the morning isn't part of the normal scenery along the Miller Road mansions.

I wake Anne up before we pull in the driveway, where her father awaits. He's wearing a long black satin robe over pajamas. She sees him, and I watch as Anne quickly calculates in her head, like doing a math story problem, the duration of her grounding. The rest happens so quickly, almost in superspeed, as Anne walks toward her house, head down, and the police walk toward the car, staring at me, eyes up. I don't say anything as I leave the safe warmth of the car for the cold uncertainty of the police cruiser. They protect my head, just like they show on TV.

"Are you taking me to jail?" I ask in a small voice, almost cringing as I speak.

The one cop laughs loudly, which is better than swinging his nightstick at me. "If we put every kid in jail who stole a car and ran away, we'd need a jail as big as a mall."

"We're taking you home," says the other cop, also white, also overweight, but a little angrier. "It's up to your folks to deal with this mess."

I don't say anything as I listen to the crackle of the police car radio. It's because of my family that I'm in this mess. I'm guilty, I want to shout, but I'm not to blame.

As the car starts to pull away, I look over my shoulder at the scene taking place at Anne's front door. It's a good thing the car window is closed, the radio is crackling, and the big cop car engine is racing, because if not, I'm sure I could have heard—even from this distance—the sound of Anne's father's hand smacking against the skin on her face.

22

february 13, senior year

"So, Speedy, who will we get our weed from now?"

I'm laughing too much to answer Anne's question. I took a small bag from Ryan's private stash as my retirement gift, and we're sitting in Anne's bedroom making the most of it. The fact that I'm alive proves that sometimes Ryan is more bark than bite.

"How about somebody at your job?" I ask, thinking I don't want to do business with strangers in the strange land of getting high. Anne is braiding her hair, just like she's twisting the truth with Tommy. We both told him we'd stop getting high. We both lied.

"I don't think so," Anne says, then giggles for no reason, other than the fact we're both incredibly stoned. "How about your new boyfriend Terrell, can he score for us?"

"He's not my boyfriend." Terrell and I flirt, make each other laugh, but nothing more. Our hands remain by our sides. "Maybe he's one of those straight-edgers."

"At least he is straight," Anne says, but I don't react and Glen's secret stays safe.

"Shouldn't you be working tonight?" I ask, to change the subject. Anne's parents are out at some society occasion, so we created our own high society event.

"All work no play," she says since we're talking about her job, then passes the joint, of which she's smoked more than her share. "Work makes Anne a dull girl, just like Daddy likes it."

"So did you quit your job or what?"

"No. I want to, but Daddy would stroke out," she says, then hurls herself onto the floor, twitching like a fish, and we laugh even more. She seems comfortable on the floor, so I fling myself off the sofa and curl up next to her. We've got everything we need: a big bag of Cool Ranch Doritos, a small bag of weed, a liter of Coke, and a lifetime supply of air freshener. There are pine forests that won't smell as natural as her room by the time the doctor returns.

"Let's smoke out!" I say, then inhale like life itself depended upon it. Sometimes it does.

"My boss is getting creepier. The other day he accidentally on purpose put his hand on my ass," Anne says, with less laughter.

"Like Seth Lewis creepy or like—"

"Well, my boss is a little older," she says. "And my boss is at least part human."

"Maybe he's also part zombie," I crack, then do a zombie impersonation. We laugh like our mouths are disconnected from our minds as we shovel down chips. "*Mmm*, brains."

"His brain is about two inches long, I think," she says, holding her thumb and forefinger barely apart, and placing them between her legs.

"You know this how?"

"He's always hovering around me; it's just creepy." Her fingers are now closer together.

"Want Tommy to get medieval on his ass?" I ask, striking a thug poser pose.

"Christy, would you tell me something?" she asks, stuffing chips in the vicinity of her mouth. "What did Tommy do? He didn't kill somebody, did he?"

"What do you mean?" I say, then roll over so my back, not my mouth, is facing her.

"I know he's already done time in jail, but he won't tell me why, Speedy. Will you?"

"No way, Doctor," I say coldly, even as the warmth of the weed works its wonders.

"You tell me, and I'll tell you something," she counters.

"Like what?" I say, turning back now to face her.

"It's big," she says.

"Not like your boss!" I say as we both chant "little dick, little dick" until we're laughing so hard the sounds from our mouths are recognizable to no one, not even people as stoned as us.

"Deal?"

"I really shouldn't," I say, but I'm also too stoned to really care, and she should know.

She takes a hit off the joint, then hands it to me. "And you don't do anything you're not supposed to do, do you?"

"Okay, but swear you won't tell anyone else, okay?" She does a cross my heart motion as I nail Tommy up on his. "About two years back, he came by the house and picked up Mitchell. It was a really hot night and they were cruising in Aunt Dee's car, trying to look real cool."

I pull too much smoke into my lungs and start to cough, worse than Mama's hack.

"So they end up over on the north end of Flint, and something happened," I say slowly.

"So, what did he do?" Anne says impatiently, and I don't blame her. I'm not a good storyteller, mainly because most of the stories in my life are like this one, not worth telling.

"He almost killed a guy."

"What happened?"

"So, they're driving around, and somewhere on Pierson, they got a flat tire. It's like one in the morning and you got two young kids way out of place on the north end."

Anne pulls closer to me, as I force the words out.

"A carload of kids pulls up. Four of them in Mount Morris varsity jackets. Tommy says they were drunk, but I don't think that matters. Tommy had changed the tire and was putting the jack back in the trunk. They were ready to leave. If they'd got done a minute earlier, or if these kids had stayed at their party a minute later, none of this would have happened."

"Wrong place," Anne says, then shakes her head.

"Tommy says he doesn't remember a lot of the details. He says when people talk about stuff seeming like a bad dream, that's what it was like. Tommy said they were going to rob them or steal the car, but he didn't give them a chance. One of the guys got in his face and shoved him. Then another one of the guys pushed Mitchell down and knocked the glasses off his face."

"What did Tommy do?"

"Nothing until it looked like the guy was going to kick

Mitchell, then Tommy lost it. He grabbed the jack and smacked the guy right in the head. Said he went down like he'd been shot."

"Then what?"

"The other guys came at them, so he defended himself, then got the hell out of there," I tell her, remembering only some of the details from what Tommy said in court. "Because of how bad he beat down the rest of the guys—one lost an eye—they said the attack was too violent to claim self-defense. Me, I think there comes a time when you do what you gotta do."

The story has almost sobered up Anne with shock. "How'd he get caught?"

"Tommy turned himself in," I say with a strange mix of sadness and pride. "He figured it would be better for Mitchell that way, and it was. No doubt Aunt Dee talked him into it as well. Aunt Dee is big on doing the right thing. And if you do wrong, then you pray for forgiveness."

"But Tommy's so sweet and gentle to me," Anne says, almost in tears.

"I know. He'd never been in trouble, did well in school, and then this," I say softly, but it quickly turns into a loud shout. "He's a good kid, not a convict. He just fought back."

"What's wrong?" Anne asks, unaccustomed to my showing anger or any raw emotion.

"He's not like Ryan or Robert," I say, although mentioning Ryan's name starts to kill the buzz. My mouth is running too much but I don't seem to be able to shut it down.

"What did Robert do?" Anne says, trying at last to unlock all of my long-held secrets.

"Cops said he killed a guy, gang stuff," I say, letting her into another off-limits area. I blame the drugs prescribed and the ones that I script myself.

"And he's serving life in prison?" she asks, even though she knows.

"How weird is that?" I say, and Anne looks at me strangely, not that I blame her.

"What's so weird about it?" she asks.

"Something Robert told me," I say, remembering one visit. "He said 'You can't kill a person who is already dead.'" Those words burn a groove in my brain deeper than the one in my lip.

"Do you visit him much?" Anne asks.

"No, he doesn't really want to see us, except on Breezy's birthday, and sometimes around Christmas. He's still angry about what happened to him," I say, thinking how much I hate hearing those thick steel-barred doors swing shut. "Robert just made a really bad choice."

"Joining a gang," Anne says, shaking her head slowly again and showing her contempt.

"No, killing a guy out in Grand Blanc," I tell her, as I fire up our last joint.

"What do you mean?" She's all wide-eyed and innocent. Hard times toughen you; I think that's what her dad is teaching her. Somehow they think sacrificing her nights to serve drunk rich folks will make her a better person than hanging out with the likes of me or Tommy.

"Flint cops only care when rich folks get killed," I tell her, Robert's voice in my mouth. "How many people get killed in Flint a year? The only murders that get solved are ones when somebody rich get killed. If it happens in my hood or the north end, no arrests will ever be made."

"No, you're wrong," Anne says, not that she could know or understand.

"Cops figure let's just let white trashers and black gang bangers kill each other off," I say, as the potent weed's paranoid stream swims through my bloodstream.

"What's gotten into you tonight?" Anne says, shocked at my rare emotional outburst.

"Sorry," I say, then open my palms to her. "You owe me a secret."

"Promise you won't tell anyone," she says.

"Promise," I say.

Anne pauses, then whispers, for some unknown reason, "Tommy and I are running away together after I graduate."

23

february 15, senior year

"Come on, Christy, let's see a smile."

The smile comes unnaturally, as Terrell aims the camera at me. "I'm trying!"

"This is your senior picture, so let's see some personality," he says, showing me his best smile and leading by example. He clicks off a few more pictures as I wait for the verdict. When he didn't ask me out for Valentine's Day or invite me to his birthday party, I accepted his rejection. But he still reminded me of what I'd said when we talked on my birthday: that I would let him take my senior picture. Since then, we've talked at work, gone to lunch a few more times, and even spoken on the phone, but I've resisted every time he's tried to get closer, until this morning. So today, I shined up my studs and covered up my healed wrists.

He shakes his head, so I'll try again to present my best face, but it won't be easy, since I'm cold, scared, and uncomfortable. It's ten a.m. on a Sunday, and we're standing outside, so there's no place to hide to cut the breeze. Deeply confused by Terrell's mixed intentions and feeling cold deep in my bones, I'm wishing

I would have taken up Mitchell's normal Sunday church invite. I'm bundled up, until it comes time to take the picture, when I reluctantly shed my hat, gloves, and heavy coat. We've been walking all around the area called the Cultural Center as Terrell tries to find the right backdrop for my senior picture. We've taken shots in front of the library, the Art Institute, and now I'm posing in front of Longway Planetarium. Inside this building, decades of Flint students have learned about the stars. Later, they'll learn that life on Earth isn't as spectacular a show, even if, like this morning, there are people in the world who make it pretty special.

"Come on, I know you can do this," Terrell says in his usual encouraging voice.

"I'll try to do better," I say softly.

He takes a step toward me. "Hell, you're better than most, no trying involved."

Whenever I slip into my old negativity, Terrell corrects me. His words make my face flush with heat. Terrell and I went out to lunch together at work a few mores times, but these seem nothing like a date, just our normal sorting-room conversation reshelved in a different location.

"How was your monster birthday party?" I ask, hiding the hurt of not being invited.

"Didn't go there, after all," he says as he fumbles with the camera lenses. "No big deal."

I think about asking, yet I know why I'd never have a party: I couldn't face the rejection of all the people who didn't show up. I try to force out a bright smile over these dark thoughts.

"Maybe this posed stuff isn't working because you're a

natural," Terrell says, taking time to blow on his hands, then taking a sip of coffee. He offers it to me, and this time I take it, not because I like the taste, but because I want his taste on my lips. If not now, then when?

"I'm sorry, Terrell, that—"

"Don't you be sorry," he says, then puts his hand on my shoulder, and, for once, I don't want to knock it away.

He's wearing his biker jacket, part of his cool-dude pose, but I'm learning that like the girls in the bathroom at school, there's the Terrell that he wants people to see, and the person he really is. Just like me.

"You don't need to do this," I remind him, falling deeper into debt to him.

"I want to do this, but I just don't have it yet. Gimme a minute," he says, then starts fiddling with the various lenses on the camera. I'm jogging in place to keep warm, but notice despite the morning cold, I'm starting to sweat. I wonder if it's because I'm exercising a new part of my body. My heart. Glen was always about dreaming, but Terrell's about planning.

"Can I see your senior picture?" I ask.

"I was wondering when you were going to ask," he says as he starts to dig into his overflowing backpack. "Which one do you want: mom-approved or the underground version?"

"What do you mean?" I ask him as I move closer.

"This is the mom-approved one for all the relatives," he says, handing me a full-color yet bland Hicks Studio standard-issue senior picture. He's wearing a white sweater, not his biker jacket. His arms and ears are jewelry free. His long curly hair is pulled back behind his head like it needs to be hidden. He looks like everybody and I feel like I'm looking at a stranger.

"And here's the underground version," he says, handing me a small black-and-white hand-cut photo of his long-haired self. This is the Terrell I know. But instead of one of his endless band T-shirts, in the picture he's got on a homemade-looking white T-shirt I've never seen.

"What's with the shirt?" I ask, moving closer.

"That's a RIP shirt," he says. "I'm not allowed to wear it to school or to work."

In the center of shirt, is a grainy school photo of a black kid about Mitchell's age. Over the picture are the words "Reggie Harrison, RIP." "Who was Reggie?" I ask.

"Just a guy I knew from the north end," Terrell says, his voice heavier than normal. He takes another sip of coffee, almost as if he needs the energy boost. "I went to school with him. We were friends, not best friends or anything. But after we moved and my mom decided to send me to Summit, I kind of lost touch with Reggie. I called him every now and then, but he got new friends. New habits. Bad habits. You know the rest of the story from the shirt."

I don't say anything. I know all about bad habits. I knew something was wrong with Robert, but Mama just kept saying he just had some bad habits. I didn't know Reggie Harrison, but that RIP tells me the bad habits were probably the deadly combination of drugs and gangs.

"So, my mom was working in the emergency room, and she told me," he says.

"They ever find who—" I say, but I know the answer.

"No, drive-by," Terrell says, and then there's silence. Flint was once known as the city that produced cars and trucks, but it mostly produces coffins and tears these days. A grief assembly line.

"I'm sorry," I say, edging closer yet, almost touching him. Almost.

"No, I'm sorry, Christy," he says, then takes a step away from me. "It's not about that."

"Okay," I say, trying to figure out what this is about, because I'm not sure anymore.

"So I went to the funeral, and I got this shirt, and I wore it in this picture, so people would know, know what's happening here, so we can somehow stop it," Terrell says, once again fidgeting with the lenses. "Man, I'm sorry to be such a downer. Let's take some pictures!"

"It's okay, Terrell, you don't need to do this."

"I want to, Christy, I really want to," he says, and we both seem to know he's saying a great deal in the words buried in his throat. Here's a science problem for chemistry wiz Anne to solve: how do two shy people ever kiss? Terrell has never mentioned a girlfriend, so at least he's not like Glen and making one up out of thin air. I think it's just that he's too much like me.

"Never mind," I tell him finally, filling in the silence gap with a white flag of defeat.

"It's me. I just can't find a way to capture that inner beauty. Let's try some action shots," Terrell says, as if the coffee or his confidence is finally kicking in.

My ears, head, and heart still can't understand the word *beauty*. For so long, the words *ugly bitch* have been hurled at me by Ryan. But before I can solve the problem, Terrell tosses a snowball at me. When I don't respond, he quickly makes two more and hurls them my way. I put my hands on my hips in a mock act of defiance, my mouth open but not speaking.

"Fight back!" he yells at me. Another snowball bounces off me.

I pack the snow together, turn, and fire. A perfect throw nailing him right in the stomach.

"Good thing you're not doing javelin in track. You'd kill somebody," he jokes, but then quickly fires back with glancing snowball shots to my legs. I'd told Terrell about Ms. Chapman wanting me to run track, and he's encouraging me to listen to her. *He's encouraging me:* three more words also out of place next to each other in my life up to this point.

"How about long jump?" I say, then leap toward him, snowballs in each hand.

He falls back, snapping photos and laughing all the time. He's lying in the snow, kicking his legs out, while his arms hold the camera steady. He clicks off shot after shot, each click a drumbeat of our laugh. The camera isn't stealing my soul: I'm releasing part of it.

"That's it! That's the Christy I was looking for," he says, then puts his arm out in front of him. I reach out to Terrell, and help pull him off the icy ground. He accidentally on purpose presses right up against me. We both laugh, then lock eyes: his eyes are so alive with promise and with passion. He leans into me and I allow my ugly rough lips to push against his perfect tender mouth. As we kiss, I know that the schoolchildren visiting the planetarium today are not the only ones seeing stars.

24

march 4, senior year

"Just shut up, Ryan, just shut up!"

I want to scream, but the words won't leave my throat. Mitchell, Ryan, and I are in the same room together, like dry wood waiting for a spark. We've been talking about gifts for Mama's fortieth birthday, which is next week. Birthdays, like other holidays, don't mean much at our house. I try to treat them like any other day; it lessens the disappointment, at least a little.

Mitchell sinks into the sofa, the pace of school and work killing him. "We're gonna buy her something nice, for once."

"I ain't got no money," Ryan shouts his lies at top volume, even though he's sitting in Mama's big brown chair just feet away from Mitchell. I'm sitting next to Mitchell, my arms resting on my knees, my face in my hands.

Mitchell snorts, I laugh, and Ryan kills us both with that vacant black stare.

"Screw you, Chill," Ryan shouts, then lights up a cigarette.

"Mitchell, I don't have a lot of money either," I confess. The library has cut my hours, and I've lost my Ryan-supplied supplemental income. Tommy's on his way over to pick me up to go get some pizza with him and Anne, and I don't even have money to pay for that. What little money I have is going to me, not Mama.

"Whose fault is that, little girl?" Ryan hisses like the snake in the grass he is.

"What does that mean?" Mitchell says angrily to Ryan, but he's looking at me.

"None of your business, Mr. K Fucking C," Ryan says, laughing at Mitchell.

"I asked you a question, Christy," Mitchell says.

"Loser, you ain't the boss of her," Ryan says with a sneer.

"Neither are you, Ryan," Tommy shouts as he opens the front door.

"This ain't none of your business," Ryan shouts across the room at Tommy.

"Christy, you ready?" Tommy says as he steps into the house.

"Who invited you?" Ryan says, standing up and walking toward Tommy.

Tommy's not moving. He's just standing there, looking fine, firm, and confident. "Christy did."

"What, so you're her sugar daddy now," Ryan says, but the boast is gone. I smell fear.

"Let's get going," Tommy says, but I'm not moving. Mitchell's moved toward the edge of the sofa, his eyes darting back and forth like atoms in a grade-school science book.

"Tommy, why don't you get your loser ass out of here before I cap you," Ryan says, pumping himself up and reminding us all of the Glock he tells us that he keeps in his room.

"Ryan, you're not going to do anything to me," Tommy says not as a threat, but as a fact.

"Really? Loser, you're so fucking wrong," Ryan shouts, but I notice he's not moving. Instead, he's backing down.

"And one more thing while I have your attention." Tommy's talking to Ryan, but he's staring at me. "I know about you trying to get Christy slinging shit at her school again, and—"

"I never said anything," I tell Ryan, realizing I made the mistake of telling Anne that Ryan's been on me every day to sell for him again. It's not like he couldn't find anyone else to move his product, but Ryan's got to yank back on my chain, just to prove that he always can.

"What do you have to say to him, Christy?" Tommy's staring me down, forcing my hand.

"Ryan, I don't want—" I'm looking at the hard floor, rather than at Ryan or Tommy.

"Bitch, who cares what you want!" Ryan says through a cloud of smoke.

"Tell him!" Tommy shouts.

I look at Tommy, my eyes begging him to do this for me, but he's avoiding my plea. I take a deep breath, look at Mitchell—who fears Ryan—and know that I can't chase tail lights any longer. I must become one for myself and for Mitchell. "Ryan, I'm not slinging for you ever again," I announce, and I feel the chain break.

"You'll do what I say or else," Ryan takes a step toward me; Tommy does as well.

"She said she's done," Tommy says, pointing his finger at Ryan. I notice the finger isn't shaking; he's not afraid. He then speaks to me. "Christy, you were made for better things."

"Whatever you say, Tommy," I say, thankful to finally have someone watching my back.

"Who the fuck do you think you are!" Ryan explodes.

"Somebody that gives a shit about us, not like you, Ryan," Mitchell shouts.

"You both are so fucking dead," Ryan says, but the bluster is gone. I get the feeling that I'm a kid sitting down at the library reading the book *The Emperor's New Clothes.*

"You don't scare me," Mitchell says very calmly, like a man, not a boy. "This time, Tommy, I won't let you down. I got your back."

I stood silent, soaking up the screaming conversation in front of me. Ryan is dangerous, we all know that, but living in fear of him is worse than death. If Mitchell and Tommy wake up alive in the morning, then I'll know for sure that Ryan's threats are as hollow and empty as his soul. As much as I hate Ryan, I hate myself more right now for not realizing his power was my fear.

Tommy's laughing. "Ryan, Mitchell is already more of a man than you'll ever be."

"You've made a big mistake, Tommy. A big fucking mistake," Ryan shouts.

"No, I'm the one who made the mistake," Mitchell says rising from his chair.

"What's that?" I ask as Tommy motions for me to join him by the open door.

"Ever being afraid of you!" Mitchell shouts at Ryan, who says nothing at all.

"Let's leave this sorry sack of shit behind," Tommy says, waving for Mitchell to join the two of us at the front door. Mitchell grabs his coat from the rack.

Ryan doesn't even look at Mitchell, instead his black eyes burn holes in my skin. As I get ready to leave our house, I take one last look at Ryan before closing the door and heading out into a bright winter day without the gray shadow of Ryan hanging over me. But even as Tommy opens the car door for me, I know today's just a first step. It's like running cold water over a cut: it momentarily stops the pain, but it can't heal the deeper hurt.

25

march 11, senior year

"Why don't you just tell people the truth?"

I make sure to whisper my question to Glen, even though we're alone eating lunch outside of the theater. Anne spends most lunch hours now talking on her cell phone to Tommy from her car. Since she's in love with Tommy and he has been insisting, we're not getting high anymore.

"You know how people are here," Glen states the obvious. "Southwestern is full of people like Seth who would make my life hell."

I nod, but stare into Glen's eyes, letting him know he's not off the hook yet. I can understand the comment about Seth. He's still an annoying gnat always buzzing around me, Anne, and Glen. Almost weekly, he'll throw out an insult, make a crude remark, and then just go on his way. None of it hurts, but I certainly won't miss never having to see Seth Lewis again. Glen takes a bite of his veggie sandwich stalling for time.

"It's too hard," he finally says. "Maybe when I'm in college next year, but not here, not now." Glen looks puzzled when I can't help replacing my usual serious look with a loud laugh.

"What's so funny?"

"It's just something Anne used to say to me about you," I offer.

"I'm sure it was about how immature I was, right?" he smiles when he says it.

"No, back when I had a crush on you," I start, and then I get tense thinking about the past tense. I probably still have a crush on Glen, but the fact that he can't respond no longer angers me. Still, I can't help wondering why I always want what I'll never have.

"You couldn't have known," Glen says softly.

"I just didn't know how to tell you how I felt," I say, looking outside at the melting snow. "Whenever I would come up with some excuse not to talk to you, Anne would say, 'If not now, then when?' So I just wonder why you won't come out to people right here, right now."

"You don't understand, Christy," he says. "You don't know what it's like to feel different like this, and then to let other people know it. A tattoo and couple of piercings isn't the same."

"If not now, then when?" I repeat, then the sound of chips crunching and pop swallowing fills the silence I've created.

"Maybe," he mumbles, then picks up the script for the play *The Miracle Worker*. For the first time, Glen isn't acting in the play. Mr. McDonald has Glen directing under his supervision. I open my book, *Girl, Interrupted,* and escape into it as the clock counts down the rest of lunch until Anne comes up behind me.

"Speedy, can we talk?" Anne says. I motion for her to sit down, but she's still standing, her arms wrapped around herself like she's trying to hold in her guts. She's got her new hat, a denim engineer's cap, pulled down over her eyes, but I can still see the black mascara running down her face.

"Catch you later," Glen calls out as he exits toward the stage area.

"What's wrong?" I ask. She takes off her big black frames hiding her small crying eyes.

Anne slumps down on the floor, her back against the wall. She takes a tissue out of her purse, then wipes her eyes slowly. "My dad."

"I thought you were talking to Tommy," I say stupidly.

"I was, he's so great and understanding but," Anne says and I just let her hang out. She pulls out another tissue, blows her nose, and then lifts the cap away from her eyes. "I told my dad again last night that I wanted to quit my job and then we got into this big fight."

"I'm sorry," I say, still clueless about the source of Anne's constant parental conflicts.

"He said I couldn't quit under any circumstances," she says, her words falling on top of each other. "But it gets worse. My dad thinks that I won't go to Northwestern because of Tommy."

I've got nothing to say to Anne about her parent pocketbook ride to a famous university. I've applied only to Central Michigan, but my acceptance letter never comes. "What's his issue now?"

"He won't send me to college unless I break up with Tommy." Her voice cracks in pain.

"Anne, that's terrible," I say, the shock obvious in my voice.

"I can't afford college unless he pays for it. It isn't fair him holding something over me to get what he wants," Anne says, putting her glasses back on. She may look smart, but I can tell she's never been more confused. "He's got all the power, and I have nothing. Nothing!"

"Then how can you even consider doing it?" I ask her, my heart breaking for the two of them. "How can you let him control your life like that?"

Anne doesn't say anything, but the tears in her eyes are mirrors, and my words reflect back on me: how can you let him control your life like that?

I wonder if Anne's father is like Ryan, just another school yard bully who only picks on those who won't fight back. Their power isn't real. It's something you give them, something you can take back. I'm just starting to realize this now. Ryan's a thug and a thief, but I need to take back the power I've let him steal from me.

26

morning, march 18, senior year

"**Stop crying!**"

I want to scream across the crowded bus at the small child who won't be quiet. Her mother is asleep, and the girl is upset. Her curly blond hair isn't combed, her clothes are dirty, and she's got some sort of red rash on her face. I can tell she's scared. She's sitting in the seat next to her mother, her arms reaching out across the inches, but it might as well be miles.

Scenes like this, or the bag ladies in the front of the bus talking to themselves, or the kids my age in the back playing music through headphones loud enough to shake the windows, are why I hate taking the city bus to school. I use my books as a hard pillow, then try to sleep, like the inattentive mother, but it doesn't come easy. The radios blasting out the ears of my classmates aren't as loud as the ones running through my head. While my meds turn down the volume, there's still a crash of confusion mixed with fear. Looking at, and listening to, this girl cry, burrows into my memory, even as my meds try to dull down all the pain in my past.

"Hi!" I say, then wave to her. I'm trying to remember what

I did to calm Bree when she got upset like this, but that seems like a hundred years ago. The girl continues to cry, and the mother continues to sleep as the bus makes its way over Flint's potholed main streets.

I see Anne standing by Southwestern's gray front door when I get off the bus. She shows and tells: I listen about the latest sexual remark from her boss, she tells me her dad is standing fast about college, but then she shows off a new bracelet Tommy bought her. She asks a few questions about Terrell, which I dance around, showing fancier moves than any ballerina. I'm so used to keeping my life private, it's hard to share.

Anne and I agree to meet by her locker before first period, like pre T-times: before Tommy, before Terrell. She heads off toward the library to study calculus; I head off toward the bridge to explore human chemistry. Not to get wasted, but to feel washed in Terrell's words. We've met on the bridge almost every school morning since our first kiss. I'm not chasing strange red tail lights; instead I'm looking into familiar blue gray eyes, although he closes them when we kiss. I admit sometimes I peek just to prove this is real, not a dream.

I run toward him, knowing Ms. Chapman's in her room and unable to see my acceleration. As I run, the wind blows back my short hair.

"Hey, Christy," Terrell says, then leans in to kiss me. We're still at lips only. Anne kids me that my "stud" has yet to taste my tongue stud. But Terrell's not pushing me or pushing himself on me. Anne's boss makes more suggestive comments in one night than Terrell's ever made.

"Good morning," I say after our lips part. It's a Thursday, so it's not a good morning, made worse by the screaming child of the bus and the screaming memory in my brain.

He looks like he's ready to speak, but instead he kisses me again. My body's striving to feel the right things, the normal things that everybody else must feel. But it's like when your leg falls asleep: you know it's there, but you can't feel anything but numb. Yet each morning with each kiss, each minute we spend together and with every word, smile, and laugh, the tingling grows.

As we kiss, Terrell slowly slides his hand into my back pocket. I fight the urge to knock his hand away. Instead, I allow him to pull me closer: an unnatural direction in my life. "So, how did people like your picture?" he asks once our lips separate momentarily.

"Oh, great, just great," I say, turning away, looking down at the passing cars as lies shoot out of my mouth. What am I to tell Terrell: "All two of my friends loved the picture you took." Does he really need to know that he's only one of three people who care about me?

"I'd like to take more, just for fun," Terrell says, also looking at the traffic. Cars of all colors, sizes, makes, models, and condition share the road below us. "Maybe this weekend, okay?"

"I have to sit for Breezy on Saturday, so," I mumble.

"Could I come over? We could take them at your house?" Terrell says, very softly. The time Terrell and I spend away from work and from this bridge is usually spent in his car driving too fast, sitting at Angelo's laughing too loud, or walking around downtown hand in hand. But we don't go to his house, we don't go to my house: our lips touch, but our lives remain separate.

The bridge shakes as a semitruck passes underneath; my

body quivers in response to the truck and Terrell's request. I can't keep making excuses and hiding the truth of my home, my family, and my life from him. I can't push him away, but I'm not ready or able to let him in. Confronted with the ugly truth, I finally cut through the morning silence. "I'm not ready."

"I know that," he says angrily. He's frustrated, like any normal guy would be with someone like me. I sigh in response, but he doesn't walk away.

"Thanks, Terrell."

We kiss again, holding it for the longest time. I can't breathe in all these new feelings.

"It's time," I say as the kiss breaks and I look down at my watch. "I'll see you—"

But time stops when he speaks. "Christy, I'm going away to school. I got into Oberlin." His eyes memorize the laces of his hi-tops, while mine start to fill with tears. I want to cry out, but I'm just like that child on the bus: there's no one to hold me. That one person is leaving me.

"I'm sorry," he says, rubbing his face gently against mine.

I pull it together, take a step back, wipe the forming tears away, and speak yet another lie. "It's okay, Terrell, it's what you wanted."

"I shouldn't have—" he starts to say, but stops when emotions attack his eyes as well.

The most recent book Ms. Chapman gave me a few days ago, along with her final track recruitment lecture, was *The Heart Is a Lonely Hunter*. It's a lie: the heart isn't the hunter, it is the hunted. I've run and hid, only to allow myself to be captured. And now to be killed.

"I'd applied to schools before we got together, you know that?" Terrell says softly. "I have to get out of here for a while, Christy. I can't explain it. It's something I need to do."

My eyes focus down on the cars. Next fall, I'll look for a car with Ohio plates, and imagine someone on their way to see Terrell and maybe I could catch a ride. "I know, I know."

"I'll come home weekends, over break, this doesn't mean—" he starts.

"Could I come with you?" I whisper.

He takes a deep breath, then readjusts his glasses. "You have to find your own way."

"What do you mean?"

"Whatever you want, it's not going to be where I'm going. It's probably not going to be me either." He speaks slowly, like he's practiced his speech. "Christy, your dad was wrong."

"My dad?"

"I remember you telling me how your dad said you should chase the tail lights because it will get you someplace safe when you're feeling lost. Well, that's not always true. Maybe that person will take you in the wrong direction, or maybe your life is in a different direction. I can't be that person for you, Christy. You've got to find your own way."

My hand is shaking: one half wants to slap him, the other wants to intertwine with his fingers. "So, are we breaking up?" I ask, but I want to take it back.

"No, I want every minute with you I can have." He kisses me deeply with words, not lips.

I close my eyes and realize: we're not breaking up; you're just setting me free. Maybe like my old dog Brutus, I'll be set free with tragic results. Or maybe I'll find my own safe way.

"I'll see you after school," Terrell says, the last word lost in our kiss.

I walk back to school and I merge into the massive herd filing into school as the bell rings.

Anne's waiting by her locker, but then again, so is Seth Lewis and his hangers-on.

"Anne, you look so fly!" Seth says as his pals laugh like trained seals.

"And you are so lame," Anne sighs, then snaps back as she always does whenever Seth speaks to us. Anne's always fought this battle, not me. "Nobody says 'fly' anymore."

"But you're like a fly," Seth says, then pokes one of his buds in the ribs, while pointing at me. "You just keep buzzing around trash like Christy, and now her cousin I hear."

The last word is barely out of his mouth before I let my books fall from my hand. I smack him hard in the face. All my anger at that mother on the bus, and the one in my own home; all my anger at men who control us like Ryan and Anne's dad; all my rage against the cage I've allowed myself to live in explodes. He drops his books, then shouts at me: "Shit like you."

I slap him hard again across the face, the smack of flesh against flesh booms through the hallway. He stops laughing through my blows, then advances toward me, anger filling his eyes. Anne's frozen in place, but hot blood runs in me as I ask him, "Why do you pick on me?"

"Because you let me, bitch," he hisses. There's a wall of bodies surrounding us, so I can't run. He grabs my wrist and twists it hard. I don't scream out in pain. He pushes against my chest. As I'm falling backward, I'm thinking he finally got to touch my breasts.

He's almost on top of me. Maybe it is the look in his eye, or the smell—that's it, the smell—that turns up my rage even hotter. I respond to every hurt he's inflicted upon me as I lift one of my powerful legs up straight, delivering a swift and stiff kick into his crotch. He falls down like a chopped tree, which the crowd around us hears clearly. As he's lying on the floor, doubled over, I start kicking him in the face, aiming for his ugly Ryan-like smirky mouth. He manages to get his hands up, but my feet, just as Ms. Chapman told me, are swift and I'm running laps around his greasy fat face with my dirty hi-tops.

There's a lot of noise in the hallway, but it quiets when campus security finally arrives. I don't resist and let them drag me away toward the school office.

Minutes pass like hours as I sit in the security office.

"Christy, what happened?" Ms. Chapman says, running into the room. "Are you okay?"

I just nod, acting as calm as I possibly can. "What's going to happen to me?"

She looks over her shoulder at the group gathered in the security office. "I think they'll call the police, that's the school's policy on fights. You'll probably get suspended," she says.

I reach into my jeans pocket and pull out a bent business card. "Call her then, please."

"Who is this?" she says looking at the card with Officer Kay's phone number on it.

"Just call her, please. Do this for me," I say, then take a deep breath.

"He probably had it coming, didn't he?" Ms. Chapman asks, very quietly, like a secret.

"Seth?" I ask, then she nods.

"It's good to stand up for yourself, but you can't do it this way, right?" she says, and I nod as I'm gasping for air. "You're out of shape, Christy, but we'll take care of that real soon."

"What do you mean?" I ask, but I can tell by the look on her face it's her payback time.

"Track starts April 4," she says. "You'll use those feet for running, not kicking, deal?"

27

afternoon, march 18, senior year

"Christy, tell me why you did this."

Mrs. Grayson sounds confused, and I can't say I blame her. When Office Kay picked me up at school, I gave her my usual avoidance answers. She told me she could take me to jail or to Mrs. Grayson's office. It was up to me to decide. I've decided to talk about something else instead to distract the both of us. Every time I meet with Mrs. Grayson now, I talk too much.

"I saw myself on the bus this morning," I tell her, my voice numb. I feel lousy about what I did to Seth, but enough was enough. I feel worse about Terrell but mostly feel sorry for myself.

"What do you mean by that, Christy?" Her voice is perfectly calm, like her office.

I'm sitting back on the couch, letting the pretty flowers swallow me as I tell my ugly tale. "When I was going to school this morning, I saw this woman with a crying child. The mom was sleeping, and I could see she was exhausted, but this child was just desperate to be held."

"I understand," she says. "How did that make you feel?"

"Angry, sad, and then angry again," I say, as the image of that crying child screamed into my head. It was like staring at a page of some unwritten yet forbidden emotional photo album.

"And why is that?"

"I don't know," I say, then put my head down. I realize this was a mistake to tell her, since there's no way I can take the ideas from head and get them to come out of my mouth.

"Christy, this is important," she says. "Talking to me will help in the healing process."

I slump back further on the couch. She won't let the past go. "No, it's not about that."

"You still haven't told me what happened," Mrs. Grayson says, sounding disappointed.

"I told you and the police the truth. Why can't you believe me? I don't want to talk—"

"Because your rape kit came back positive," she cuts me off and silence swallows us.

"I wasn't raped at the party," I slice the truth so thin I can see it bleed. I can see the obvious follow-up question pursed on her lips, but she takes a deep breath and holds back.

"Fine, then talk about what happened today," she says, then tortures me with silence.

"Fine," I finally say after four or five minutes, then put my arms across my chest.

"You know, Christy, Officer Kay went out on a limb for you here," she says.

"What do you mean?" I ask, my arms unmoved.

Mrs. Grayson sits with her clipboard on the table next to her, almost knocking over the vase filled with fresh flowers. Even sitting on a couch with the floral design, I still won't open up. "She called me. I agreed to see you instead of her taking you to jail," Mrs. Grayson says, hurling a stone of guilt my way.

"I'm not going to jail," I say, thinking of the kindness of Ms. Chapman's eyes and acts.

"I think in some ways you feel like you are in jail, don't you?" she asks awkwardly.

I scratch my tattooed ankle, then look for a bathroom, but say nothing.

Mrs. Grayson speaks after more silence. "Why did you get in a fight with this boy?"

"Because he picked on me," I say flatly.

"Why?" she asks, very calmly.

"Why what?" I shoot back. I guess some of the fight's adrenaline must still be pumping.

"Why did he pick on you?" Mrs. Grayson replies.

"You'll have to ask him," I say, then look at my watch. "I don't know."

"You can't do that anymore," Mrs. Grayson says, raising her voice a fraction.

"Can't do what?" I respond, then defy her again with another quick watch glance.

"Can't get away anymore with saying 'I don't know,'" she challenges me.

I look away, staring intently at the bright yellow carpet I've memorized in the months I've seen her. "How would I know why he picks on me?" I ask.

"Do you have some sort of history with this boy?" she asks as I sink further still.

"No," I say it fast, like ripping off a Band-Aid.

"Christy, you're lying and we both know it," Mrs. Grayson says as she leans toward me. That nice pleasant smile pasted on her face is missing. "Have you been intimate with this boy?"

"No." Our pathetic eighth-grade fiasco at his house wasn't about intimacy.

She leans in closer still. "Was he the one who attacked you at the party?"

I don't answer with anything other than a headshake about that always off-limits topic.

"Then why does he pick on you?" She looks ready to shake the answer from me.

"Okay, fine, we hooked up once and I wouldn't do it again. Seth's hated me ever since."

"Why not?" It's like she's a dog latching onto a bone; she won't let go.

I'm suddenly exhausted; I can't fight two battles in one day. "Why not what?" I ask.

"So, you had sex with this boy once and—"

"I didn't have sex with him!" I'm angry now.

"Then what happened? Christy, just tell me what happened," she says softly.

I finally break down and open up. I tell her about the time in eighth grade when Seth jammed his tongue in my mouth and unzipped his fly. I tell her the names he's called me since then. I tell her the only good thing about Seth was his Great Plains remark that led me to meeting Anne.

"Christy, you should be very proud," she says, breaking out a rarely seen real smile.

"Proud?" I ask. I feel dirty reliving and retelling this history of shame.

"It's hard for people to tell their stories, especially when—"

"It's their fault," I cut her off.

Mrs. Grayson looks confused. "It's not your fault, Christy. Is that what you think?"

"I let him tease me," I admit. "I let him kiss me. I let him—"

She talks over me. "Christy, you are not at fault. You were victimized."

I do something I rarely do: I make eye contact with Mrs. Grayson. "What do you mean?"

"When someone attacks you, whatever the reason, you're a victim. You're not to blame."

I get ready to respond, but instead I retreat. "What if he would have, you know, been the one?" I ask in a whisper.

"Been the one who attacked you at the party?" Mrs. Grayson sounds confused.

"What would happen?" I ask still in a whisper. "What happens to people who do that?"

"If you pressed charges, then he would probably be arrested. If there was other evidence, the police would collect it," she says, and I'm soaking it all in like a dry hard sponge.

"And he would go to prison?" I'm talking fast so she can't hear my voice quiver.

"Rape is a serious crime. I don't know for sure what will happen, but I do know that prison is certainly one very possible result if the person was found guilty," she replies.

"Would I have to testify in court in front of people like they do on TV?" I ask.

"If there was no other evidence, probably yes. It would be painful, but you're strong."

"So, in front of everyone, I would need to tell what I did." I'm back to whispering.

"Christy, you didn't do anything. Something was done to you. I don't care if it happened in eighth grade or eight days ago. If someone sexually assaults you, it is a crime." Her voice has Ms. Chapman's "you can do it" tone. "If Seth was the one, then I need to report the crime."

"I don't want to talk about this anymore," I say, rearranging myself on the couch and rubbing my eyes. If I can't see her, then she can't see me.

"Fine," she says biting back her muted anger. "Then, I want to go back to something else. Let's talk again about that child on the bus. Why do you think it bothered you so?"

I start to say "I don't know" but instead I feel almost a tingle in my body remembering how even just telling her about Seth was painful, but actually felt good. So I tell her what she wants to hear and what I so badly need to say. "When I saw that child on the bus, I guess I saw myself as I was growing up. I was always crying and reaching out, but my mama was never there," I confess, but feel more frustrated than relieved. I'm angry: angry at myself for holding all this in for so long, for denying it.

"Is that how you feel now?" Mrs. Grayson asks and then silence swallows us for almost ten minutes. She's not asking more questions; she's letting the silence confront me again.

"I don't," I reply, then return to my old habit of biting down hard on my bottom lip.

"Don't feel that way?" Mrs. Grayson leans in again; her hands almost touching mine.

"No, I don't feel," I say, as cold as a Michigan snowstorm in January.

Mrs. Grayson looks at me for a moment, sadness in her eyes. "Of course you do."

"No, no, I don't feel anything!" I shout at her. I stand my perfectly numb body up and knock the perfect vase filled with perfect flowers off her perfect table all over her perfect office.

She puts her clipboard down, then her pen. She gets up from her chair, no doubt to ask me to leave. How can you help a person who can't or won't help themselves? I don't blame her for rejecting me, but instead she sits down next to me, holds out her arms, and pulls me toward her. As she holds me tight, I stay silent, since there are no words to speak of the unspeakable.

28

april 8, senior year

"Winners never quit and quitters never win."

Sometimes I think Ms. Chapman throws out all these clichés so we'll run harder to get out of listening to them. I'm trying to pay attention to her post-practice lecture, but I'm having trouble catching my breath. It's my first week of track. Even my numb body is exhausted.

"Okay, good effort today, better effort tomorrow," she says, then waves us toward the showers, even though I usually go directly home, sometimes not even changing. Although with no one in the house tonight but Ryan and me, I'll take as long as possible to return to Stone Street.

"Christy, hold up for a second," she says. Everybody else is in great shape and they run off the field, while I'm bent over, feeling like my stomach is about to shoot up through my throat.

"What is it, Ms. Chapman?" I ask, not yet looking up.

"Out here, it's Coach," she reminds me.

"Sorry, I mean Coach Chapman," I say, almost managing to smile.

"You need to get into shape," she says, then motions me to follow her as she heads back toward the track. "Let's do a cool-down lap together. I want to talk with you about something."

"I need to get to work," I tell her, but I follow. We run at a steady pace.

"At the library, right?" she asks and I nod, not wanting to let on how out of breath I am. "Have you met my sister Ms. Coleman?"

"She's your sister?" Ms. Coleman is the library director, but I've never met her.

"Sorority sister," she says, then goes quiet as we run some more. We do another half lap before she speaks again. "So what's the story with you and Seth Lewis?"

"No story," I say, glad we're next to each other so she can't see the lies in my eyes.

"I don't believe you," she says. "If you don't want to tell me, that's one thing, but don't lie to me. I can't coach someone I can't trust, so tell me the truth."

"Sorry, Coach, but it's nothing really," I say. I'm slowing down, since we've made one full lap, but she picks up the pace.

"Okay," she replies, then lets the silence return. The only sound is my heavy breathing and the crunching of the cinder underneath our feet until she speaks again. "We have a problem."

"What do you mean?" I avoid her eyes, staring down instead at the new track shoes that Aunt Dee bought for me when I told her I'd finally joined the team, not revealing I was drafted.

"You still haven't turned in the form from your physical."

She's reminding me for at least the tenth time in two days. "You can't be on the team unless you do that. What's the holdup?"

"Maybe I can't be on the team," I say, getting ready to run home, rather than running another lap and answering twenty more questions.

"If I have to drive you myself, you'll get this done. You made a deal with me, right?" Ms. Chapman says. "After practice, why don't you call up Anne's father. He's a doctor, right?"

"I'll take care of it," I say, running faster now, faster than I ever knew I could.

"But you haven't taken care of it," she says, not even breathing heavily as she keeps up.

"I promise, next week."

"No, today, Christy. We'll set up the appointment together," she says. I don't dare fight back. After fighting it for so long, I do want to be on the team and be part of something. I didn't know, however, that taking a physical was part of the deal. I've never had one, and other than New Year's Eve, I haven't seen a doctor in years. They ask too many questions.

We start another lap. I feel my blood pumping through the veins in my legs, and my memory races to all of the mornings I pushed myself to go to school and not to run away from home. I pushed myself harder than I'm pushing myself even now. "I got into Central Michigan," I say softly, half hoping this, rather than the physical, was what she wanted to talk about in our post-practice practice. No one else knows, since I haven't heard about any necessary scholarships.

"That's fantastic news!" she says, screeching to a halt, then reaching over to hug me. I take a step back. She seems to understand instantly and pulls away. "I'm very proud of you."

"I'm not sure how I'll afford it though," I tell her.

"I have a friend who works in financial aid there," she says. "She's a sister and—"

"I thought you said she was your friend," I say as we start running again at a slow pace.

"She's one of my best friends," she says. "She's another sorority sister. You see this?"

I look over to see her pointing to a necklace that I've noticed she wears all the time.

"ASA: it stands for Alpha Sigma Alpha," she says with pride in her voice.

"What's that?"

"It was my sorority, and it's not all about parties." She's teaching, not talking now. "We believe in intellectual, physical, spiritual, and social development of young women."

"I didn't know any of this," I say, thinking how I failed in so many of those areas.

"You'll learn, because if you want, I'll do my best to get you in," she says.

I nod, then run behind her, with my head weighted down by one question, which I finally, three years too late, get up the nerve to ask. "Ms. Chapman, can I ask you something?"

"You going to get that physical from Dr. Williams?" she counters with her sealed deal.

"I promise." I know I can't break this one. I give her my word because I need to hear some important words from her. When she nods, I unload. "Why are you so nice to me?"

She laughs, but I don't think she's laughing at me. "Christy, I wondered when you were going to ask me that." We slow down the pace so we're more fast walking than running. "I guess I saw a lot of myself in you, let's just say that."

"What do you mean?" I ask, curious how this beautiful woman sees herself in ugly me.

"You don't have a daddy at home, right?" she asks. My frown answers for me. "Let me guess, your mama works really hard, but she's tired all the time and she's not there for you. You try hard to be something, but others, maybe in your own family, hold you back. If you make it out, they resent it. You dream of better things, but everybody just treats you like poor white trash, right?"

I respond with a sigh. I wonder if Ms. Chapman can see through our ripped drapes.

"That was my life, too, but I made it out. I got through high school, won a track scholarship to Central Michigan, and got a degree. At college, when times were tough, my sorority sisters saved me. But all of that, and everything I've achieved in life, is thanks to my teachers back at Beecher High educating me on two important things," she says, although it sounds like she's singing, the words are jumping so freely. "The first is learning to say no."

"Saying no?" I ask the woman who refused to take my no for an answer for three years.

"Saying no to bad choices, to people who keep you down, to people who don't want you to be anything more than they are," she says proudly. "And the other important thing I learned."

"What's that?" I ask, as I watch Ms. Chapman take off for

what my legs hope will be the final lap, although my energized ears and loosened tongue cry out for more.

"You know, Christy, you know," she replies as we sprint toward the finish line. I'm reaching deep into myself, finding speed and strength that I never knew I had.

"Winners never quit, and quitters never win," I shout, feeling my lungs about to explode and a deep truth vibrating through my skin and my soul. Coach Chapman laughs, a loud laugh, a winner's laugh, as I chase her around the track one last time without a drop of fear in my eyes.

29

Late evening, april 8, senior year

As always, it's not his words that wake me from sleep, it's the smell. My head is facing toward Bree's bed, even though I know she's not there. The room is totally dark. I never make any noise, anymore, which makes the grating sound of a zipper followed by the sound of the condom wrapper tearing open seem even louder. He's not protecting me, he's just covering his tracks. Just like some other nights, I think I hear another noise from another room. A hacking cough. Then his full weight is on me. The pain distracts me while my mind implodes on itself. He no longer needs to say "I'll kill you" because we both know I'm already dead inside. Yet, the part of me that remains looks down at the floor and realizes, finally: I can run away because my fear no longer ties me to him.

30

april 9, senior year

"Christy, get me another beer."

"Sure, Mama," I say, thinking what a bad idea it is to help her nightly habit. I go to the kitchen, get the beer and a big glass of milk for myself, then go back to the living room. My throat is dry from running track two hours after school, then talking with Terrell until bedtime.

"How come you're sleeping out here?" Mama asks. Ever since I've started track, I've been sleeping in the safe open space of the living room. I don't know why I never thought of this until the past few days. Maybe when all you see are bars, you can't imagine there's any escape. But I'm saying no, even if I'm only taking baby steps.

"It's cooler here, easier to sleep," I say, then hand Mama her oversize beer.

"Maybe we can get money for an air-conditioner," Mama says, wiping the sweat off her brow. She looks like I do at track: sweaty and breathing heavily, but for her, it's a constant state.

"Guess master thief Ryan can't slip one of those under his coat for you."

“Don’t you talk about your brother that way,” Mama snaps back.

I take my glass of milk and lie down on the floor, stretching my legs out. “Ryan’s not my brother. You can call him your son, but he’s not my brother.”

“He’s blood, so he’s your brother. He’s my one true good son.” I hate that Mama says things like this. “My one good son,” she repeats, a sign she’s drunk and ready for sleep.

“Mama, Ryan isn’t—”

“Shut your mouth, girl!” Mama says. “I don’t want to hear it.”

“It doesn’t bother you that he steals all the clothes that he gives you and—”

“I don’t care if you’re eighteen, I’ll put you over my knee,” Mama says, then lets out one of those loud hacking coughs that shakes the floor. “You hush up about your brother.”

I’m not drunk or ready for sleep, but I repeat myself. “He’s not my brother.”

“Listen, all you got in this life is family,” Mama says. “You think your friends are gonna be there for you? Think again! Everybody is in it for themselves. Watch your own, I say.”

I’m silent, as the sound of my mother’s heavy breathing and coughing fills the room.

“Like that little slutty friend of yours,” Mama continues. “Don’t you think she only cares about herself and what’s good for her? She’s just using Tommy. “

More silence from me. It feels like my skull is splitting in two as Mama slurs her speech. I’m thinking about Anne slicing open Tommy’s life.

“I know her type, I’ve seen her type before,” Mama says.

"Let me guess, she's got a real overprotective father and she's thinking what can I do to get Daddy's attention?"

I want to tell her to shut up, but I can't bring myself to stop this torrent of possible truth.

"If she's a good girl, is her daddy going to notice her?" Mama shakes her head, then slugs back the beer. "She's got to be a bad girl, and how better to do that than to date an ex-con?"

"Mama, that's enough!" I shout, even as I wonder how much truth is wrapped in her beer-infused ranting. Anne loves Tommy, I think; she loves making her dad crazy, I know.

"You can't trust anybody but your own, remember that," she says, dropping the remote in front of her while pointing her finger at me. I look at those thick calloused hands reaching out, not to comfort me, but to confront me. I sometimes wonder if her ears are calloused over as well.

"But Mama," I counter.

"No buts about it. I might have messed up with Robert, but I was a kid myself. His father was no good. Just like your daddy was no good, dying on me like that. But Ryan's father, well, that was a real man." She's slurring her mean words, and there's nothing left in the house but the two of us.

"Oh my God!" I grab the remote from the chair and mute the noise. "I finally understand it."

"Understand what?" Mama says, as she sinks deep into the chair and vainly looks for the remote so the melodramatic antics of reality TV can drown me out.

"Is that why you love Ryan so much and the rest of us so little?" I say, anger balling into my fists. "Because you think if you love Ryan more than us that his dad will come back."

She doesn't say a word because you can't fight the whole truth with half lies.

"He beat you, he left you, and you still want him back!" My words are making me sick.

"You shut up or else," she snaps back, then coughs loudly.

I shout at her, like I should have shouted years ago. "You have nothing! How can you hate yourself so much?"

Her eyes flash red-hot anger at me, but she knows that I see the truth. I don't know anyone who hates themselves as much as my own mother—except for me.

"Go to bed," Mama replies. Her lack of denial is louder and stronger than any words.

"I'm in my bed!" I shout, throwing the remote at her feet. She clicks back on the TV.

"Why do you think you can sleep out here?" she shouts at me over the blaring TV.

"Why don't you ask Ryan that?" I say, then pull a pillow over my face, shutting out the noise from the television show. She turns away from me, just like that woman on the bus, and falls asleep in front of the television. I look at my mother with a strange mixture of pity and anger. Mama's never quit, but she's never won: she just survives. She lives by believing her lies.

31

april 11, senior year

"Let's run away."

Terrell and I are sitting in a corner booth at Angelo's. Over greasy fries and weak coffee, I found more courage I never knew that I had, but his silence makes my stomach churn and my runner's legs yearn to explode. No more small steps or slow laps; it's time for a long jump.

"What do you mean?" he finally says, his voice buried in the mix of Angelo's normal late-night clatter. "Christy, come on, we're just getting started. I mean, we haven't even—"

I push my hand across the table. Our fingers intertwine, like our lives, but not our bodies. It started with an innocent kiss and there it remains. "You and me, let's run away together."

He scratches his forehead with his free hand. "Where is this coming from?" I don't blame him for his bewilderment, but he shouldn't blame me for my desperation. As school gets closer to ending and home gets harder with Ryan's caged rage, my need to escape reemerges.

"You need to save me," I say strongly, digging my fingers deeper into his hand.

"I don't know what you're talking about," he answers. The confusion evident in his voice. He sees me at work, sometimes at night, but he's never ever seen inside my home or my dark heart.

I pull my hand away, ball it up, and cover my mouth so I don't scream at what's unsaid.

"Christy, I'm sorry," Terrell says, leaning toward me, but I won't let him touch me now.

"You're sorry for even knowing me," I say to him in a shouting whisper.

"No, it's not that," he says, but I only hear what he doesn't say: Christy, I love you.

"You hate me!" I harshly tell his soft eyes as my legs spring into action.

"Wait!" he says, but I'm out the door like a robber making a clean getaway. Yet as soon as I hit the parking lot, standing on the cracked concrete under the buzzing, bright yellow neon lights and amid the rusted-out cars, empty Styrofoam cups, and discarded food, I realize there's nowhere to run. I stagger over and stand next to the pay phone, without anyone to call.

"Christy, I'm sorry," I hear Terrell yell from a distance. I know what he wants, but I can't give him what isn't mine. I should have just stayed invisible.

"Leave me alone!" I shout at him, but the roar of the busy street swallows my words.

"No, damn it, no!" he says, grabbing my heaving shoulders.

"Leave me alone!" I shout again, but he tries to hold me tighter. His arms surround me, but don't soothe me because I'm trapped in my self-made cage. If I let him fuck me, then he'll know and he'll want nothing to do with me. If I don't let him fuck me, then he'll want nothing to do with me. I'm crying, but the tears wash away nothing, instead bringing salt to my wounds.

"Talk to me!" he says, throwing his hands up in the air and stepping closer to me.

"I hate you!" I shout at him, for it is the emotion easiest to swallow and wallow in.

"Grow up!" he snaps. It's the first time I've heard ugly impatient anger in his voice.

"I have!" I shout back at him, my fingers turned to fists beating against my legs, like I was trying to kick-start them. "I hate you, Terrell, I wish I never met you! I hate you!"

"I'm sorry you feel that way, but it's not me you hate," he says pointing a finger at me.

I take off running away from Terrell, from myself. But he should be the one running away from someone as fucked up, fucked over, and unfuckable as me.

I'm ten feet down Franklin Avenue, when I hear his voice yell out, "Christy, don't do this!"

I keep my head down, not just to hide my tears, but to avoid eye contact. Sooner or later he's going to find out, sooner or later he's going to look into my eyes and know.

"Where are you going to go?" he asks, and I can't answer, because there is no place for me to go. My legs want to run, and thanks to Ms. Chapman, I'm learning to run faster than ever, but all I see is myself running in circles.

"I don't know, Terrell, I don't know," I shout at him from inches away, sounding more like a frustrated four-year-old than a soon-to-be high school graduate.

He comes closer to me, putting his hand gently on my shoulder. My instinct for so long was to shake and cringe when a hand pressed against my body, then it changed to not feeling anything at all. Every time Terrell touches me, I get the warm tingling of a human touch. "Christy, I can't run away with you," he says, pulling me closer.

"Why not?" I ask, wanting so much for him to give me some reason to believe.

"I didn't want this to happen like this," he says softly. "You know, you're the first real girlfriend I've had because I knew it would come to this. I knew I would need to decide."

"Decide what?"

"Between staying here or going away to college," he speaks a slow, simple truth. "Love's great, but it's a chain. It pulls you places you know you shouldn't go."

"Like a chain," I repeat and realize, like Brutus, I've run out into traffic only to be hit.

"So I can't stay here with you and I can't run away with you," he says softly, kissing the top of my head. "But that doesn't mean I'm going to let you run away from me now, like this."

"I can't do this. I'm so tired. I just want to quit," I say through clenched teeth, holding him tighter still. I bury my face in his broad shoulders, trying to steal his strength. I know now more than ever that I can't go on like this for even one more day or sleepless night. I need to find the courage to either live or kill myself. I can't live in between any longer.

32

april 28, senior year

"I quit."

I say the words the best I can through heavy breathing. I'm bent over, my hands on my knees, and happy that I don't have to look Ms. Chapman in the eye. Everybody else on the track team has hit the showers, but I've stayed behind, and not just because I have no desire to be surrounded by naked finely toned athletic female bodies, while I hide myself in a towel.

"Christy, are you sure you want to do this?" Ms. Chapman asks very firmly.

"Yes, I can't do this. It's too hard," I say, my lungs working overtime, no doubt in part from keeping the contents of my stomach inside. "I want to quit this team!"

"Fine!" she shouts at me, then reaches her hand toward me. "Give me your uniform."

My eyes go wide and my knees buckle. "Now?"

"Now! I don't have room on this team or in my life for quitters," she says, coming closer and not giving me an inch to breathe or squirm out of this desperate attempt for acceptance. All she needed to do was say the words that I wanted: "Christy, don't do that, the team needs you."

"But Ms. Chapman, I—" I start.

"Wear this," she takes off her warm-up jacket, taking the keys out first. She stands in front of me as I slip off the uniform, then cover myself with her jacket.

And I start to cry.

"Winners never quit, and quitters never win," she says as she jiggles her keys in front of her, like somebody teasing a dog with a bone. "Are you going to be a loser all your life, Christy, is that what you want? I know you have it in you to be a winner, but you've got to bring it out."

"I'm not a loser," I say the words, as if I almost believe them sometimes.

"You say that, but you don't act that way," she says. "Don't write a check with your mouth that you can't cash."

"What do you mean?"

"You don't think you're a loser by quitting?" she says, but never gives me a chance to answer. "You want to be on this team or not?"

I nod. "Yes."

"You want this uniform back?" She holds the dull gray track uniform in front of her.

"Please," I say, pleading for a place somewhere.

"Don't be so damn passive, get angry, Christy! Fight back, like you did with Seth!"

"I want my uniform back!"

"Catch me then!" she says, turning on her heel, then running toward the parking lot. She takes off running, her legs are a blur, almost impossible to see through my bleary and teary eyes. I take a deep breath and chase after her.

"Get in!" Ms. Chapman shouts at me as she opens the door to her dark blue Jeep Cherokee. I do as I'm told and climb in next to her.

"Where are we going?" I ask, but she doesn't answer. She takes a left out of the parking lot, merges quickly on I-69, under the bridge, then exits onto I-475, headed toward the north end.

She's not talking, and I'm taking in the scenery, or lack thereof. Some of my daddy's family still live north, but Mama doesn't want much to do with them. The north end is where Ryan likes to spend his time, and where most of his buds are from.

"You like your history class?" Ms. Chapman asks, breaking the silence as we exit the expressway and drive down Coldwater Road. It is like my neighborhood times ten: vacant houses, and on every corner a party store selling lottery tickets, liquor, and the belief in luck. The main distraction and attraction is a vacant lot, filled with empty bottles, hunks of concrete, and the memory of a huge auto factory that no longer exists.

"Sure," I say, confused and a little bit afraid as to why she's brought me here. I'm trapped in this ride through a city of ruins.

"Let me show you my history, Christy," she says, taking a sharp right turn. If the main road was run down, this neighborhood is almost zombie-movie scary. We drive down a street where every other house looks abandoned or burned out. "Here's where I grew up."

The yard is overgrown with weeds, the windows broken, and gang graffiti is painted in black on the side of the pink house. Like many of the houses on the street, it's deserted.

"One-twenty-seven Mott Avenue," she says, and it sounds like she wants to cry. We pause for just a moment, then drive down the street, if you can call it that. There are more potholes than pavement. We drive down another street filled with young children playing outside. There are fewer vacant houses; in fact, some are active with SUVs or Hemis buzzing around like vultures. We drive for a while, finally passing by a vacant school. You can barely see the name through the weeds.

"That's Beecher High School," Ms. Chapman says, sadness in her voice. "It's closed down now. Just like the Buick factory and most everything else around here."

I just nod, since no words come to mind.

"If I would have quit track, I'd be living in a house like one-twenty-seven Mott," she says.

"Just because you quit track?" I ask as she pulls away from the house.

"Because I quit," she says. "Sports gave my life a center, a reason to believe. I had a coach who showed me that vision and gave me that center. You need that center too."

We pass more pay day loans and party stores. The stores have familiar "WIC and EBT Accepted Here" signs displayed in the windows next to ads for lottery tickets, beer, and cigarettes.

"I'm not going to tell you all the stuff the school counselors do," she says. "I'm not going to kid you, tell you that you have lots of choices, because I've been there, Christy. If you're poor, you don't have a lot of choices, but that doesn't mean you have to make bad ones."

"I know," I say, wondering why I couldn't have chosen to go out for track my tenth-grade year and learned these hard lessons from Ms. Chapman then.

"Look at me, Christy," she says. I turn to face her and she

smiles. A huge happy smile a million miles away from the angry look she was wearing moments ago. “You can’t quit. If you quit, you’ll end up here before you’re twenty and be dead or wish you were by the time you’re twenty-five. This might be my past, but it could be your future. Is that what you want?”

I shake my head, vigorously.

“It is too easy to quit,” she says. “Do the hard thing.”

I rub the back of my calves, thinking how hard track is; how hard life is.

“That’s what I did,” Ms. Chapman says. “I wanted to quit track every day. But I didn’t. I stuck it out, and it was the right thing.”

“And that’s what you want me to do,” I say.

“Yes, but not because I said so,” she says, as we make our way back toward the freeway and to Southwestern, I assume. “Do it because it is the hard thing.”

“I try, I try really hard,” I say, thinking of how hard I work at practice. “My legs just—”

“You’re not listening,” she says as she pulls the car to the side of the road, then turns to face me. “Listen, Christy, running isn’t about your legs.”

She taps her fingers on my knees, but her touch doesn’t bother me for once.

“It is about this.”

She pokes me in the middle of my chest: hard enough to notice but not to hurt.

“It is about this,” she says.

She points first to her own head, then taps mine just above my left ear.

"Running is about disciplining your mind. Get your mind right, your legs will follow."

I want to tell her that for all the lessons she's been teaching, during the past eight years, I've learned some on my own, and they contradict what she's saying. I've learned the survival skill of splitting my body from my mind.

"Think about Mott Avenue. Think about this life," she says, pulling my uniform from the backseat and handing it back to me. "Run like you're escaping from there. One day, you'll have something real to run to, but for now, let me give you something to run away from. Run as if you were running for your life, because in some ways you are."

33

early evening, may 5, senior year

"I finally quit my job!"

"What did your dad say?" Anne and I are on the bridge, just taking in the twilight hours. With school almost over, and Tommy and Terrell in our lives, our time together is also in twilight.

"He's not talking to me," she says, as she pulls off her pink-polka-dot welder's cap and lets the wind blow back her hair. "And I don't even care."

"So, why did you finally quit your job?" I ask her.

She turns her back to me, and just looks down at the cars going by. "No reason."

"Anne, come on, what's going on?" I ask her again, but it's more a habit than a need.

"Look, you can't tell Tommy about this. I don't want him to get in trouble again," she says after a silent pause filled with loud traffic noise. "God, I wish we had some weed!"

"Sure, whatever," I tell her, happy that she and Tommy are still together. Anne says she's playing chicken with her father about Tommy, and she's not going to be the one to blink.

"My boss, you know I've told you about him," she says, each word very deliberate.

"Little dick." I can't help but giggle when I say it.

"It's not funny, not funny at all," she says, as she sits down. She puts her cap back on so the wire mesh doesn't press against her head. I sit down across from her, my long legs stretched out before me. "I'm going to tell you something, but you have to promise not to tell anyone."

"I promise," I say with the confidence of a school career filled with secret keeping.

"Last night, my boss and I were the last two closing out and he—" Anne says, then pauses.

"He what?" I ask, the roar of the cars below us sounding like an angry chorus.

"I'd just come back from clearing tables, and I had one of those big trays in my hands," Anne says, twirling her straight hair in between two fingers. Her voice sounds nervous, scared, and tense. "He told me that I needed to tuck in my shirt, it was hanging out in front."

"And?"

"I looked down and saw he was right. So I got ready to set the tray down, but he said—"

"Yes?"

"He said, let me do it." Anne's voice choked back tears.

"What do you mean?"

"He took his hand and tucked my shirt into my pants, then he left his hand there."

A semi rumbles underneath, shaking the bridge. "Anne, what did you do?"

"He pushed his hand deeper and harder into me, and he was smiling, asking me if I liked it, and then I screamed no really loud," Anne says, measuring each word. "And then I dropped the tray I was carrying. Plates, cups, and glasses crashed to the floor. It was so loud."

Anne puts her hands over her ears, as if she can still hear it. "What did you do?" I ask.

"I looked down at the broken dishes and I saw a big steak knife. I think he saw me look at it too," Anne continued. "I wanted to kill him for touching me like that. I still feel so filthy."

"What did he do?" I ask, but Anne takes awhile to answer, as if she's still living it.

"Nothing," she says, a tone of surprise in her voice. "He just looked at me, and suddenly he didn't look like this big, powerful friend of my father's. He didn't look like anything at all."

"Did you tell your dad about this?" I asked.

"No. I don't think he would believe me, anyway," she says. "Mr. Wallace is a friend of his, almost like a brother. I could stand up to him, but my father . . . no this is something that I can never tell him. I didn't really quit. I'm just not going back anymore, no matter what."

"But if you told him the truth?" I countered. "Wouldn't your dad—"

"He would think it was my fault, he would blame me," Anne continued. "Ever since I told him about Tommy, he's on me all the time, calling me terrible names."

"What are you going to do?" I ask.

"I'm never going back there," Anne says strongly. "I don't care if I have to dig ditches, mop up shit, or anything else, I'm not letting someone touch me like that. I don't care what happens to me, I'm not going to let anybody do something like that to me."

My insides are twisting and my feet are restless. "Aren't you afraid of what he'll do?"

"Who? My father? Mr. Wallace?" Anne's voice is dripping with disgust.

"I don't know, just afraid?" I say softly.

Anne gets up, then turns away from me. "Christy, don't you get it?"

"Get what?"

"It doesn't matter if I'm afraid. Because if I let him touch me, then there's no me: there's only him, and his power over me. I won't let anyone control my life like that, not my dad and certainly not him," Anne says.

"What if you tell your dad?" I ask.

"Maybe he'll slap me again," she says, then sighs. "Or maybe, he'll just blame you."

"Blame me?" I say over the sound of Anne's growing sobs.

"Christy, I'm sorry, forget that I said that. I'm just really upset," she replies quickly.

"What do you mean?"

"My dad's acting really strange. He's ordering me to stop hanging with you," Anne says, her words racing faster and louder than the cars below zooming into the dusky horizon.

"He's always wanted that. What's new?"

"Just the other day, he told me that he didn't want me to be friends with you anymore. He said you were a bad influence. He said you were . . . ," but again Anne won't finish her sentence.

"He said I was what?" I snap back.

"Nothing, just forget it," Anne says, then looks away from me. I grab her hands, something I've never done before. I pull her toward me, my thumbs pressing into her palms.

"He thinks you're a bad influence on me. He said his daughter wasn't going to end up like you," Anne says as she watches my face collapse.

"What does that mean?" I ask, wondering if I really want to know the answer.

"We were fighting about Tommy, about how much time I spend with him, and what he thinks we're doing. The same fight we've had over and over, but this was different. I've never seen him so angry, so out of control. He's not the only man in my life, and he hates that. Hates that."

"But what did he say about me? End up like me. What does that mean?" I ask.

"I can't say it. He shouldn't have said it. He told me not to repeat it." Anne's hurting.

"Say what?" I shout over the cars passing below.

"My dad called you a whore and a slut."

I don't know what death will feel like, but I bet it's something like I feel right now.

"He told me to stop hanging around with that 'slut,'" Anne says, avoiding my eyes.

"Why would he say that?" I ask, looking through the wires to the pavement below. I know he's never liked me, but I'm trying to figure out why he would say those words in particular.

"I don't know why," Anne says softly. "But I can tell you when he said it."

"When?" And I know before she even answers. I will hate her father forever.

"Right after he gave you your physical," Anne says. Another truck rumbles underneath, the bridge shakes, but it doesn't break and send me into the fiery furnace of hell, where I belong.

I can't breathe in a single molecule of air. "What else did he tell you about my physical?"

"Nothing, he's a doctor. But from his tone of voice and that name he called you, he knows something," she says. "You're not a slut. You're a virgin. Why would he say that?"

"I don't know," I say, knowing I'm unable to sort out all the lies in my life.

"He must have found something in your physical to make him think that you're having sex," Anne says. "Why else would he suddenly start calling you such a horrible name? What's going on?"

"It's none of your business or his." I get ready to run away, but she grabs my arm.

"Why won't you talk with me about this," she whispers. "Why won't you ever talk—"

"Shut up!" I shout at her, then cover my own ears, wishing I could cover my body.

"What's going on?" Anne's shouting. "You swore that Glen didn't touch you, right?"

"I told you that, I told everyone that!" I say nothing more, to save Glen's secret.

"Who are you having sex with? Have you and Terrell?" she asks, but I shake my head.

"None of this is your business, Anne. I don't want to talk about this!" I shout.

"Whenever I bring up sex, you never want to talk about it. Why is that?" Anne continues. "How long have we known each other? Why won't you share things with me? Christy, I'm your friend. You can trust me. There's nothing that you could say that—"

"Enough," I say, throwing my hands over my ears, and screaming over the noise below.

"Who is it?" Anne asks.

My mouth is sealed, but my body quivers with fear and rage.

"Tell me!" Anne shouts, but I'm just shaking my head like it was detached from my body.

"Christy, damn you, talk to me!" Anne shouts louder still. I turn to face her. Tears fill both our eyes, but no words emerge from my throat.

"I can't," I mumble.

She slaps me across the face, like she's trying to wake me from a nightmare. "Tell me!"

I look her in the eyes, then turn away as another truck rumbles underneath. The bridge shakes, and I feel like I'm about to vomit.

"Tell me," Anne whispers now. We're beyond exhaustion and frustration.

"I am, I am," I say, too upset to form longer words.

"I am what?" she asks, and I finally answer.

"I am eleven years old; Ryan is fourteen. I'm small and weak; he's big and strong."

first, last, and every time in between

I am eleven years old; Ryan is fourteen. I'm small and weak; he's big and strong.

You do the math.

I'm twelve years old; Ryan is fifteen. He protects himself even as he hurts me.

You taste the bitter irony.

I'm thirteen years old; Ryan is sixteen. Mitchell's too small and afraid. Robert is on the streets, and Mama is working third shift. Ryan and I are alone in the house.

You figure the schedule.

I'm fourteen; Ryan is seventeen. Robert is in prison, and so am I.

You figure the justice.

I'm fifteen years old; Ryan is eighteen. He's a man now by law; I'm a woman by force.

You guess my sentence.

I'm sixteen years old; Ryan is nineteen.

I'm old enough to drive, but I can't break free from this chain that binds me.

I'm seventeen years old; Ryan is twenty.

My past is my present and therefore it must be my future.

I'm eighteen years old; Ryan is twenty-one. I'm an adult without a childhood.

I have no dreams; I have no plans. I have only this shame and this pain.

I'm going to be nineteen; Ryan will be twenty-two.

My life will never be mine until I take it back from him.

34

evening, may 5, senior year

"Breezy, is Ryan at home?"

Bree points toward his room, then goes back to cutting out paper dolls. I got a blood promise from Anne never to tell anyone, in particular her parents or Tommy, the ugly truth of my ugly life. And then I cried, just like that little girl on the bus the other day. But Anne, unlike Mama or the mother on the bus, was there for me.

"Breezy, I need a favor from you," I say, trying to stay as calm as possible, but that's impossible; I feel like a circus tightrope walker performing outside during a tornado.

"Anything," she says, and reaches her hands out to me. I pick her up and hold her close, wrapping myself around her, trying to imagine what it would have been like to have this layer of protection in my life.

"It's such a nice spring night, why don't you go outside and play," I say.

"Okay," she says, picking up the paper doll book and scissors.

"But you need to leave those things here," I say, taking the scissors from her. I reach into the corner and hand her a jump rope. "Start without me, but I'll be right out. If I don't come out of the house in ten minutes, go to the corner store, and call Mitchell at work or call Tommy."

"Why?" she asks, but I ignore the question as I write out both phone numbers on a piece of paper, then give her a couple of quarters. "Just do this for me, okay, Breezy?"

She hugs me again and takes off running outside into a beautiful spring evening. She'll be jumping rope, feeling light and carefree, like a child should. Just like I should have.

I pace in the living room, and it feels right: I feel alive. The muscles in my legs are straining, my arms are shaking, but my eyes are clear. I walk downstairs toward the darkness of Ryan's room. Even through the closed door, I hear the bass booming through the headphones, and his singing. He's feeling light and carefree, like a child does. A feeling that he stole from me.

The door's locked: I pound on it so hard, my right hand starts to bleed. The blood trickles slowly onto the floor: a red spot in the middle of the floor, just like the one eight years ago in the middle of the sheets.

"Who the hell is it?" Ryan shouts.

"Your little girl," I say, as I choke back the acidlike vomit rumbling in my stomach.

It takes him a minute or two to open the door. He unlocks it, but doesn't open up. I wait a moment, take a deep breath, and take a giant step inside.

"Is dinner ready?" he asks, not even looking at me. Instead, he's putting his clothes on.

"Fix your own dinner!" I shout at him.

"What is your—" he says, turning around. He stops dead in his tracks when he sees the glint of the scissors.

"Ryan, I swear if you ever touch me again, I'll use these on you," I say, showing him the sharp blade. Bree's used these to cut paper dolls, enjoying her childhood; I'm going to use them to regain mine.

"You won't do shit, you ugly bitch," he says, taking a step toward me.

"Try me," I shout back at him, loud enough for the dead to hear.

He takes another step closer, smiling. He pulls down his old-school black-and-silver Oakland Raiders T-shirt, exposing his throat. "Go ahead, try it, I dare you."

He sees the scissors in my hand as I speak. "Listen to what I'm saying to you. If you ever touch me again, I promise I'll use these." It's a promise I'll keep not to him, but to myself.

"Try it," he takes another step closer. "I'll take them out of your hand before you—"

"No, you won't."

"Why's that?" he says, but he's standing still.

"Because I'll do it like you do it to me: when you're half asleep."

"No way you're cutting my throat, bitch," he says.

This time, I take a step closer and point the scissors at his neck for just a second, and then slowly, point them at his crotch. "I'll cut it off if you use it on me again."

"I'll kill you," he sneers as he backs away toward the drawer where he keeps the Glock.

"You try, Ryan, but I swear to God, I will kill you too." I'm screaming louder than I thought possible. "I will leave here right now and I'll call the police. They can haul your ass to prison and then maybe you'll get some of what you've been giving me, you fucking baby raper!"

"I don't believe you." But since he responds with words, not deeds, I know he does.

"This is over between us." I jab the scissors in his direction.

"You crazy, ugly bitch," Ryan says, never looking at me. "I should have killed you."

"You can't kill me, Ryan." I smile. "You can't kill someone who's already dead."

Another step backward for him. "You're full of shit."

"Try me," I say, my muscles almost exploding, since I've finally found my strength.

"Who the fuck do you think you are!" he shouts, even as he sits down on his bed, looking, for the first time ever, small, afraid, weak, and totally pathetic. "You'll do what I say."

"No!" I shout loud enough for Ms. Chapman to hear sitting at her desk miles away.

35

early morning, may 16, senior year

"Anne, wake up."

"What time is it?" Anne says. I imagine her confusion on the other end of the phone.

"Almost time to graduate," I say, not wanting her to know I've woken her up on a Monday before 7:00 a.m. For the past two weeks, I've slept the soundest I have in years—in the living room with my mother six feet away and a pair of scissors tucked under my pillow. Ryan's only slept at home one night, and on that night, he walked right past me.

"You're crazy!" Anne says. Obviously she's looked at the time.

"Can you pick me up a little early today?" I ask. I'm so used to not sleeping well, I don't know what to do with all this energy.

"I gotta fess up to you, Speedy," Anne says. It sounds like she's fighting off a yawn.

"What's going on?" I ask. It's strange to be talking with Anne this early in the morning over the phone. But after her father's outburst, even if I wasn't banned from Anne's house, I wouldn't want to be there. He had no right to call me those nasty names that I don't deserve.

"I can't drive us to school or anywhere for that matter," Anne says.

"Why not?" I ask.

"Because of quitting my job," Anne says.

"But you told your dad about your boss and why you quit, right?" I counter.

"I tried, but he wouldn't listen to me. I told you he wouldn't listen."

"But what does that have to do with not driving?"

"That's my punishment, that's my father's answer," she says. "He wins this battle."

"That is so unfair," I offer.

"Just like him telling me either I break up with Tommy or I kiss Northwestern good-bye."

"So, you already told me the two of you are running away after graduation, right?"

There's a long pause. If Anne were across from me now, I'd bet she'd hide her eyes.

Anne breaks the silence, and my heart at the same time. "I want to be a doctor."

"Tommy loves you," I remind her, not that Tommy has come out and told me that.

"I know, but face it, Christy, we would probably break up anyway, so . . . "

She lets it hang and I take it. "If not now, then when?"

"You don't hate me, do you?" she asks.

"No, I just think it's sad," I say. When Anne doesn't answer,

I realize sad doesn't come close to describing her mood. We hang up, and immediately I call Terrell's cell phone.

"Morning, Christy," Terrell says pushing through a yawn.

"Can you come pick me up?" I ask. I usually just meet Terrell at the bridge in the morning.

There's a pause. Any pause after I ask someone to do something for me is a long pause.

"It's okay if you can't." I break the silence.

"Don't worry. This summer we'll get in the Grand Am and drive until the wheels fall off," Terrell says, then laughs. I think about sitting next to him, speeding down the highway, and make my old sound of laughing and crying in a single noise.

"Can you believe we're almost done with school?" He sounds more excited than I do, although not as well rested. I'm catching up it seems on eight years' worth of peaceful sleep.

"Just one of a thousand steps," I whisper, connecting my present to my past without pain.

"Get off that phone and do this laundry!" Mama shouts at me as she walks into the kitchen.

"Fine," I mutter, then say good-bye to Terrell. Mama coughs. The noise cuts through me.

"I'm going to get my numbers before work," Mama says, and soon afterward disappears.

I start sorting stuff into laundry loads. I pass over the stuff from Ryan's room. He can stew in his own filth. Instead, I start on the stuff from Bree's room. I can hear Mitchell joking with Bree as they eat breakfast in the other room, but she's not laughing. I expect her clothes, towels, and sheets are going to be pretty dirty. But what I find is worse than that.

I see it.
The stain on the faded Shrek sheets from my niece's bed.
My ten-and-a-half-year-old niece's sheets.
I know exactly what it is even from a distance.
I bring my nose closer just to make sure.
The smell of it will always cling to me, and the sheet.
I remember how it began for me.
Bree's just about the right age for Ryan.
Almost the same age I was.
And I know.
And I know it has started.
And I know what comes next.
And I know I drove him there.

36

morning, may 16, senior year

"Remember when you gave me that book *Speak* to read?"

Ms. Chapman looks up from the pile of papers she's grading and motions for me to come in. I've run all the way to school, but she's gotten me in such great physical shape, my breathing's not heavy, despite the heavy stone I'm dragging with me. I close the door loudly behind me.

"You're early to school. Full circle, no?" she says.

I pause for a second to collect myself, before I unload. "What do you mean?"

"When I first met you, you slept through first period. Three years later and your last week of school no less, and you're here before first period. Full circle. Must be the track!" she says.

"I'm done running," I tell her, taking tiny steps toward her.

"No, you're not quitting on me again, not this late in the game. I—" she says testily.

But I cut her off. "That's not what I mean," I say, taking two more steps into the room.

"Then what?" she says, taking a sip of coffee.

"That book, *Speak*, remember?" I say, reaching the edge of the desk now.

"Sophomore English, you really enjoyed it. That kind of got us started," she says with a smile, then motions for me to sit down. She doesn't see the abyss I'm ready to reveal.

Instead, I kneel down next to the desk, then grab hold of her strong, athletic legs, and whisper through welling tears: "How did you know?"

"Know what?" She doesn't push me away, as a look of horror dawns on her face.

I hold on for dear life and I start: "I am eleven years old . . ."

As I speak, Ms. Chapman ignores the sounds of students banging on the door. After I finish telling her my story, not about Bree, but my story, I break into tears. She waves the students away, then makes a quick call to the school office to tell them that first-period tenth-grade Honors English will be canceled today at Flint Southwestern High School due to life.

With tears now in her eyes as well, Ms. Chapman says, "I need to report this, you know that, right?"

"I know," I tell her.

"But I want you to call first. You need to say the words, not me," she says, then reaches in the desk for her cell phone.

It takes a lot less time than I thought it would. I phone Officer Kay and take the first step in getting myself out of this prison, and starting Ryan on his way there as I start to tell her my story.

"Could we get a statement in person? Can you do that, Christy?" Officer Kay says.

I look over at Ms. Chapman, and know I can do anything. "Yes, I can."

"Good, we can send a squad car by to—"

"No, that's okay, I can get a ride in a friend's Jeep," I say, and Ms. Chapman nods.

After I hang up the phone, Ms. Chapman picks up her bag and we start out. "Ride? Are you sure you don't want to run?" she says opening the door.

"No, like I told you, I'm done running," I say as we walk from her room.

Ms. Chapman squeezes my hand as we sit in her Jeep in front of the police station, but I shake my head. She's offered to come in with me, but I'll go it alone, as I always have. "I can do this," I say.

She pulls out her cell phone. "Let me at least call for your mother to be here with you."

"No!" I say loudly.

"But she should know that—"

Then I say the words, harder in some way than any others before. "She knows."

Ms. Chapman's head snaps back so fast and hard, it looks painful. "What?"

"She knows," I repeat, telling what I swear to myself is my last lie. I can't say if my mother knows or doesn't know. That's not what matters. What matters is that either way, she doesn't care and didn't protect me.

"Oh, Christy, why didn't you tell me about any of this earlier?" Ms. Chapman says.

"I couldn't," I say after a long pause. Not "I wouldn't" because it was never about wanting to tell, because I always wanted to tell someone. I just wasn't able. It wasn't Ryan's threats that silenced me; it was my own shame and illusion of powerlessness.

"I know a therapist." She doesn't get that I'm no longer helpless or hopeless.

"I know somebody," I interrupt her, wondering where I put Mrs. Grayson's card. I could have told her, too, and I probably will now. I guess that I'll have to learn how to tell other people, too, especially Terrell. I'm graduating from high school, but my real learning is just starting.

I tell Officer Kay everything I can, and I answer almost every question she puts to me about Ryan. She explains what comes next, and I ask a lot of questions. She tells me that while this is the hardest part, more hard stuff is to come. The trial, things at home, my whole life is going to be different. I say thank God for that. The ordeal sounds horrible, but I have one last lie to tell and one life I promised to protect. When Officer Kay's finished talking with me, I finally leave the room and find Ms. Chapman still waiting for me. She's my teacher, my coach, my reading buddy, my mentor, and my friend. As I move toward her, I realize this: she didn't teach me how to run; she showed me how to walk tall.

37

Late afternoon, may 16, senior year

"Answer your phone!"

I'm standing at the parking lot pay phone outside of Angelo's diner. Ms. Chapman is inside, waiting for me to return. I told her I wanted to be alone, but she knew when I said that, I was telling my last lie. I was too exhausted to speak with her, so we sat in the noisy, chaotic restaurant that once mirrored my chaotic mind. I told the police everything about Ryan, not just his crimes against me. But now I'm screaming into the message service on Terrell's cell, as spring rain pelts down on me. Mama's working as they've come for Ryan, and I can't imagine ever going home again once she finds out. I think about all the times I considered running away, but now that I've stopped running, I know I have no place to stand or sleep. I've seen it so deep in Mama's eyes so many times that I'm a stranger in her house, while Ryan is the welcome guest. His eviction won't bring me closer to her, but instead will invite more rejection. She won't kick me out: she'll make me stay and stew in her rejection and rage.

Unable to reach Terrell, I drop two more quarters into the pay phone and dial another number.

"Summit School," some woman answers.

"I need to speak to my son, Terrell Bennett," I say, trying to sound mature. "It's an emergency."

"One moment, Ms. Bennett," the now slightly panicked voice responds to my deceit. They don't put me on hold, so instead I get to hear the muffled and muddled sounds of a school office. "We'll get him out of class. Do you want to hold or have him call you?"

"I'll hold," I say, and the answer feels right. I need Terrell to hold me.

"We'll hurry," the voice says before gentle jazz starts playing through the receiver. The soothing sounds can't calm this unleashed savage beast whose heart is fully beating. I'm thinking of everything that waits at home, and at school if and when word gets out, and what I'll tell Terrell. I've spent seven years with a shadow over me. No wonder he's never been able to find the real me. I need to tell him, to trust him, and to be prepared for his rejection.

"Mom, what's wrong?" His voice is frantic, like the tornado that awaits him.

"Terrell, I need you!" I cry out.

"Christy, what's going on—"

"Terrell, I need you!" I repeat the words, for there are no others.

"Where are you?" he asks after a short pause. I tell him, then there's more silence on the phone, but I hear voices in the background matching the sounds of the street.

"Stay there," he says, and I feel my heart stop, or has it finally really started?

I wipe the tears from my eyes, and I go inside, quickly slipping into the back corner booth. As regular customers talk over huge platters of hot dogs and fries with gravy, I sip nasty black coffee.

As Terrell is driving here, I remember the first time we kissed in the snow outside of the planetarium. I reached out to him and helped him up; I wonder if he knows he did the same for me. No, I don't need a knight in shining armor; I just need a helping hand to hold. The waitress brings me refills even though I've never been more awake as the minutes pass. I've never been happier than when I see Terrell walk in the door.

"He's here," I tell Ms. Chapman, pointing at Terrell walking toward us.

She turns, looks, and then touches my hand. My eyes tell her what my words cannot.

"I'm always here too," she says as she leaves the table, whispering something to Terrell as she passes by him. He smiles at her, then comes toward the table. He's got a puzzled look on his face, but as I rise, then hold him, the worry recedes and a smile, like a sunrise, spreads from my face to his.

"What's going on?" he asks, but I'm holding him too tight for him to say much more. Each cell in my body seems to be soaking in comfort from his returning embrace.

"Let's go," I whisper in his ear.

The waitress slowly comes toward us and hands me the bill for the coffee, but Terrell snatches it from her hand. "Do you want anything else?" she asks casually, like she says to ninety people a day, but today, the question matters to me.

I look at Terrell, as our hands intertwine, just like our lives have intersected, not forever, just for now. But if not now, then when? I take a deep breath, then answer her question. "No, I have everything I need."

38

june 11, senior year

"Christy Monique Mallory"

As I take the diploma from Principal Morgan's hand, I look into the audience. I hear a small cheer, and I spot Mitchell, Bree, Aunt Dee, and Tommy—all of them standing and clapping wildly. Mitchell's whistling, Aunt Dee is crying, and Bree is all smiles. I quickly look over and see Ms. Chapman in the faculty section applauding. I'd like to think I'm the only student she cheered for, but I know better. Even though I never won a single race, I still earned my letter, but Ms. Chapman was right about running track: it's about the mind, not the body.

There's applause from Anne and Glen, but none from Seth when our eyes meet. I spot Terrell, who stands out in the crowd of well-dressed parents with his leather jacket on his left arm, his long hair on his shoulders, and a picture of me in his wallet. He's taking pictures and teaching me something I learned too late into school: beauty supplies.

As I head back toward my seat, I realize that I won't hear any applause from Mama, since she didn't come to my graduation. Just like I won't hear any words from her at home, since she's not talking to me. I realize a high school diploma doesn't make me a genius, but I wonder what she's thinking. I imagine she doesn't hate me, but she hates herself for letting it happen. Mrs. Grayson has tried to talk with Mama, but she doesn't want any help, or need any more hurt.

Other people are going across the stage, and I'll make sure to cheer for Anne and Glen, but my thoughts are already past high school and on going to Central Michigan in the fall. I won one of the Michigan Honor Scholarships, and with some other financial aid, I'll be able to follow in Ms. Chapman's large footsteps at Central. I didn't win any of the end-of-school honors, but the last few days saw me take that first step toward getting free, even as Ryan's about to be caged.

He's still in county lockup. Mama doesn't have enough money for bail, and all of his so-called friends have suddenly disappeared. I didn't tell the police, Mrs. Grayson, or even Ms. Chapman about Bree; that information is also my power. I've learned that when they arrested Ryan, he was in his room. They probably found lots of stolen merchandise, not to mention a fair amount of unsold weed, other drugs, and a couple of stolen guns. They're threatening to charge him with raping me, although there's no way I could face a trial. Maybe he has the same fear, and will take a plea. That would mean he won't be labeled as a sex offender. It also means I won't be labeled as a victim. In return for my naming names of some of Ryan's dealers, I pleaded for the sake of our family that Ryan gets sentenced to Jackson so we can visit both of my brothers in one trip. The lawyers agreed, and it will all be worked out by the end of next month. While it will be a month late, knowing Ryan's rotting in Jackson is my graduation gift to myself.

I watch when Anne gets her diploma, and Tommy applauds louder than anyone—those big paws of his can make some noise. As he's pounding away in praise, Anne's parents and relatives are busy taping, photographing, and holding up video phones to transmit the great news across the land. They'd better get used to these graduations, since Anne has four years of college at Northwestern to get through, then med school, probably at MSU. She's ready, since she's already performed her first surgery: cutting out a little piece of Tommy's heart. But it's like Tommy told me on the way over, he's tough, he's survived worse, he'll get along.

"Christy, you looked great up there!" I hear Terrell shout. I run to him, then kiss him, gently and slowly. And tentatively: it's still the only way I know how.

"Where to?" he says, taking my hand in his.

"No place we have to drive," I say. We walk from the auditorium, out the school doors, then through the parking lot, and eventually across the pedestrian bridge over the highway. We don't talk a lot as we walk.

"What are you looking for?" he asks, as we stand on the bridge, traffic roaring under us.

"Nothing, nothing at all," I say, my finger running along his smooth face, then against the rough wire mesh. I run my smooth if studded tongue along the surface of my soft bottom lip: I've lost the groove etched in my mouth; I've found a good groove in my life for the first time. Cars pass under the bridge leaving Flint, and very soon, I'll be in one of them too.

39

august 23, before college

"Ryan Aaron Mallory"

As soon as the judge pronounces Ryan's plea-bargained sentence of a year at Jackson State Prison, I feel freer than I ever have or could imagine. Terrell, who I finally told most everything to, holds my hand as the judge speaks and Ryan scowls. When I think about Terrell in Ohio at Oberlin, and me at Central Michigan, I think about how I found the right person, but like Tommy and Anne, it's another case of wrong time and wrong place. I'll plan to see Terrell during breaks, on weekends, and over holidays, but mostly I'll dream we'll somehow stay connected forever, despite being broken apart by distance and direction.

"Just take me home," I tell Terrell. If I see Mama's car is in the driveway, I'll find someplace else to go. My mother doesn't speak to me; she doesn't see me, and still she doesn't hear me. She stomps around the house, drinking more, and slamming doors. I sleep now with my door open, and wonder when, where, and how I'll open up to her and ask, "why didn't you protect me?"

Instead, I avoid her. I spend most of my time working at the library, driving around town with Terrell, visiting with Aunt Dee, taking care of Breezy when she's at home, talking with Mrs. Grayson, or attending the support groups she's put me in touch with. You have to talk about it. And read about it, as Mrs. Grayson has taken over for Ms. Chapman, recommending books to me. The books describe the healing process. Some books say you have to forgive in order to move on, while other books say some people never forgive.

"Later, Christy," Terrell says with a kiss, then drops me in front of my house.

"Later," I reply, kissing him back, even if that's still all we've ever done.

Once inside, I call Anne and invite her to the bridge. She's headed to Chicago in a few days, so this might be our last time together before we both exit Flint. Like the cars below, we're headed in different directions. We'll stay in touch, but it won't be the same.

No one's home, not that it matters. Mitchell's working, while Bree is spending most of the summer with Aunt Dee. Bree's bed is empty, and it doesn't make me sad at all. In the welcome silence, I think about what the books say about forgiveness and healing, and then I put pen to paper. But even as I clutch the pen in my hand, I wrestle with the dark shadows of my former self and my future life.

After more crying than writing, I put the paper in an envelope, then scribble out the address. On my way walking over to the bridge, I detour by the post office on Atherton Road, buy a stamp, and drop the letter in the mailbox. I walk rather than run over to the bridge to meet Anne, enjoying the sunshine on my skin, uncovered in a tight dark brown tank top.

"Hey, Doctor!" I yell from a distance. Anne's unmistakable with her newly dyed-blond hair, uncovered by any hat. It's been almost a month since we've been up here. She's been traveling with her parents, visiting relatives in California, while I've been in Flint falling in love with Terrell.

"How'd it go in court?" she asks as I stand next to her. We're looking west, waiting for the burning orange sunset to bring out bright stars. The Flint sky doesn't seem as gray as usual.

"He got a year," I say softly, figuring I'll get it out in the open, which is new for me.

"A year?" Anne asks in shock. I briefly explain plea bargains, crowded prisons, his future years of probation, and the injustice system. Prison time Ryan got; justice the courts can't deliver.

"He deserves worse than that," she says. I nod my head, then sigh. She sounds angry, probably because I haven't talked with her about any of this or my decision not to press charges for what he did to me.

"I didn't—" and then I stop, since there's nothing left to say about Ryan. To speak of it again, even to a jury or judge makes me relive it. And I don't want to relive it anymore; I just want to live. But the books are wrong: forgiving isn't the only way to rid yourself of the anger and the hate.

"Doesn't it bother you that he'll be out again in a year?" Anne asks with shock in her voice.

"He won't," is all I say after a long pause. We're silent then, no weed to smoke or gossip to share. We just enjoy the view from the bridge, as I'm waiting for one type of vehicle for my last tail light to chase. I finally see a U.S. mail truck driving down the I-69 expressway. I imagine that this is the mail truck carrying letters from Flint to Jackson State Prison. I imagine this is the mail truck carrying the letter I wrote. A letter not to Ryan to forgive him, but the letter I wrote to Robert. I imagine this is the mail truck carrying the letter telling my brother Robert about the stains on his daughter, Bree's, sheets. I imagine this is the mail truck carrying the letter I wrote my convicted stone-cold killer brother Robert, describing what his future prison-mate Ryan did to his daughter.

I'm not dreaming; I'm planning.